Queen
of
Dragons

Queen of Dragons

Shana Abé

BANTAM BOOKS

QUEEN OF DRAGONS
A Bantam Book / January 2008

Published by
Bantam Dell
A Division of Random House, Inc.
New York, New York

Book design by R. Bull

Bantam Books is a registered trademark of Random House, Inc.,
and the colophon is a trademark of Random House, Inc.

Library of Congress Cataloging-in-Publication Data
Abé, Shana.
Queen of dragons / Shana Abé.
p. cm.
ISBN: 978-0-553-80528-4 (hardcover)
I. Title.

PS3551.B329 Q44 2008   2007041651
813/.54 22

Printed in the United States of America
Published simultaneously in Canada

www.bantamdell.com

10 9 8 7 6 5 4 3 2 1
BVG

For Shauna Summers, with heartfelt gratitude for her grace and guidance.

A zillion thanks as well to Annelise Robey and Andrea Cirillo, who always believed, and to Nita Taublib, who pushed me so wisely.

And to the family: I love you.

Queen
of
Dragons

January 12, 1774

Mother, Father,

I pen this missive knowing it will arrive a most unpleasant surprise to you. No doubt you thought me still at the Wallence School for Young Ladies in Edinburgh. It is just past Christmas, though, so perhaps you've realized by now that I'm not where I promised I would be. My heart breaks to think of the worry I might have caused you. I apologize. Never would I have done this thing had the circumstances not been so very dire. The stone you sought has been made safe.

I understand what I've done. I've broken tribal laws to a degree I've never even heard before whispered. Please know I did not do any of this lightly. I am no longer a child but a woman full grown, and one of our kind in every way. Allow me to repeat: In every way. When I return to Darkfrith, I shall accept my punishment. I bow to your will and that of the council.

I have been staying in a castle in the Carpathian Alps as a guest of a most unusual princess, who has kindly agreed to forward this letter to you. She, too, is fully one of our kind. Certainly you will be as shocked by this news as I was. There are more of us, quite a few more, than we ever imagined. They live like gypsies here, entrenched beneath the stars, in secluded villages or in this fortress. The nights descend so bright and hushed you can hear every diamond, every pebble and trickle of gold in the streams. You can fly into forever.

I am wed now. My husband is Zane. I'm sorry.

All my love,

Lia

1

PROLOGUE

There exists a world beyond your own. There exists a world of frozen savagery, of ice and snow, and needle-tipped mountains draped smoky emerald in summer, and dusky blue every autumn. In this world, your safe and pleasant life is vanished, a mere illusion revealed. Comets are born here. Stars are stirred. Glaciers steam; diamonds sparkle; silent music saturates the very air—and mighty dragons tear furrows through it all, breathing light and fire in crystalline exhalations.

All other creatures cower here. You are not welcome, so do not come. Should we see you, we might cast our pity downward to your earth, to grant you time to turn and hide.

We might not.

The sky is our realm. The mountains are our sanctuary.

We are the *drákon*.

You fear us. It is why you've stalked us for centuries, why you pursue us still in this age of reason and enlightenment. You used arrows before, crossbows, and we soared higher. You hold muskets and pistols now; you dream of stabbing our hearts clean with elegant French swords. Despite your frail bodies, over the years, you have diminished us.

So we have learned to deceive you.

All of nature celebrates our beauty, but now we look much as you do. We speak your words and wear your clothing and drink your wine. Like you, we breathe and feel and fall in love; we wed and raise our children. We bleed. We wage war.

We will not show you our true selves unless you are so unwise as to leave us no choice. That will, of course, be your final mistake, because unlike you, we have many more Gifts at our disposal: We hear the music of metal and stones. We hunt with talons, we Turn to smoke. Some of us even have the Gift of suggestion, to push you into our will.

Although there are far fewer of us, we are faster than you, stronger, more sly. All we require is that whisper of air beneath your bedroom door—through a keyhole, down a chimney—and any haven you held against us is breached.

You must understand that war against humans is distasteful to us. Our honor demands we crush you swiftly; it is shameful to toy with the lesser beings. These skirmishes usually end quickly in silence and death.

But war against other dragons...*that* is a thing of wonder. The stars themselves shudder and weep.

We began all in the same place, we *drákon*. Aeons ago we scorched into life, smashing through cosmic whirlwinds and stars, red-hot lava sizzling on our scales, living kin to fire and smoke and sooty diamonds. We were born here, at the fanged edge of sky and earth called *Carpathians*, long before you Others arrived.

We ruled and ruled well. The stones beckoned us and we heeded them. The metals sang and we unearthed them, worked them into braids for our hair, and necklaces, and chalices. We built a castle of quartzite and gems. We practiced spells without words, and listened to the sweet singing magic of the jasper and rubies and diamonds. Some stones were benign; some were not. But as a family, we mastered them.

Then *you* came, O Man. Crawling from the mud, casting your eyes upward; everything you saw you coveted. We wore gold and copper; you wore skins. We infused our glory into the mountains and woods; you ripped it away. You felled the trees, and dammed the streams, and crept in a plague up our slopes, never ceasing. We had no choice but to fight you.

Like fleas, you multiplied and spread. It is the only reason you won.

And that was when we split apart. That was the end of the dread union of the *drákon*; you managed that much, at least. Nearly all fled the castle; only two remained. From that two came seven, then fifteen, then forty-two.

We discovered we could seduce you. We could play upon your fears. In our human disguise we evolved into warriors and lords and princes. We laid our shadows across your land, and you learned to tremble and to worship us.

In time, we forgot about our original family. We forgot that once there were more of us, just as those who had left had forgotten us too.

There were better years and worse ones. There were good

stones and one of very ill fortune—I'll tell you more of that later. We survived all these things for centuries, waxing and waning, until one winter's day there came a new dragon, an Englishwoman, to our castle on the mountain. She brought with her revelations: tales of a cloudy rich shire, with heavy woods and silver mines and no Others for miles about. A land populated purely by our kind, a secret sanctuary surrounded by green English hills and meadows.

She brought with her also one of you. An Other. A thief.

Together they wrought havoc on our realm.

Perhaps such a thing was inevitable. We are dragons, after all. We do not dwell in static quiet; we crave flight and glory and can spin Change from the smallest of molecules.

It seems very strange, does it not, that there would be a tribe of us living in silence like little mice?

Letter to the Princess Maricara of the Zaharen
Of the castle Zaharen Yce
Of the D——n
Carpathian Mountains, Transylvania
[Translated from the French]

May 27, 1774

Your Royal Grace,

We find it difficult to convey in the space of this missive our great astonishment and pleasure at the news of your existence. Your letter of
January last, along with Lady Amalia's, arrived this very evening. It has
been cause of much celebration here in our shire. We are relieved to hear
of the safety of a beloved daughter of the tribe, and trust that she is now
on her way home to us. We are most pleased to discover you as well.

You must understand that, until this day, we had believed ourselves
to be the last of our kind. (Forgive our reluctance to name ourselves so
readily as you have done. Here in England, such a word is not spoken
easily.) We have been settled in Darkfrith for generations, and knowledge of our origins had long ago vanished.

We dare to presume to be related to you and your people. Indeed, we
hope to persuade you to visit our land and meet your distant kin. You
would be entirely welcome. Or, should Your Grace permit, we might come
to you. All we ask is your direction, and of course, your gracious consent.

On behalf of the Marquess and Marchioness of Langford and the
members of our tribe, we remain,

Your servants,

Kimber Ellery Darce Langford, Earl of Chasen, &
Council Members

Letter to the Earl of Chasen
Of Chasen Manor
Darkfrith, York
England

3 October 1774

Gentle Lord, Members of the Council,

We ourselves are greatly pleased to find our English cousins. Although I will not repeat the word you found so distressing, I must relay to you that here in my land, what we are is well known. It is in the history of our fortress. It is in the folklore of the serfs.

I regret to inform you that travel at this time will be impossible. Since the death of my husband last year, there has been a slight unrest within the castle. It is nothing so very serious, merely enough to warrant all of my full attentions. Naturally there is a new prince for the throne, my brother, but as I am more skilled in these matters, it is my joy to supervise the hold until he is old enough to take command as he should.

Please convey my salutations to the Lady Amalia and her husband.

Very truly,

Maricara of the Zaharen

February 23, 1775

Your Grace,

It grieves us to hear of any jeopardy or peril surrounding you. We offer our assistance in any manner you should desire. Without doubt you are a strong and capable ruler, but perhaps a widow alone, even a princess, would do well with a guard? We ourselves make use of such measures on occasion for our kind, and would be honored to offer any small skills we possess to you, and of course, your younger brother.

We may be ready in a matter of days, should you wish it. Your castle is in the northern Alps?

Chasen
Council Members

5 January 1776

Good Sirs,

I thank you for your kind and generous offer of assistance, but must firmly decline. Please do not come. Such strangers in the castle now will only invoke further unease. Although I am young in years, I assure you, I have my people well in hand. They understand who and what I am. We have only a few minor discontents, and very little bloodshed.

My gratitude for your concern.

The Princess Maricara

July 20, 1776

Your Royal Grace,

Forgive my boldness. If I might inquire: How old are you?

—Kimber

18 November 1777

Lord Chasen,

I have fifteen years.

—Maricara

⸱⸱⸱

Transcript from Special Session of the Drákon *Council,*
called This Noonday, March 9, 1778
As faithfully transcribed by Council Scribe
Sir Nicholas Beaton

In Session: Sir Rufus Booke; Calvin Acton; Theodore Henry; John Chapman; Tamlane Williams; Erik Sheehan; Adam Richards; Anton Larousse; Claude Grady; Devon Rickman; Kimber Langford, E.o.C.; Lord Rhys Langford

Without: Christoff, Marquess of Langford

[In the absence of the Marquess of Langford, eldest son Lord Chasen presides as Alpha]

The issue of the Zaharen *drákon* has been raised again. Renewed urgency at revelation of age of professed leader Her Grace the Princess Maricara. The question before the council has been raised [proposed: CG; seconded: AR] regarding the situation of HG Maricara.
Status: Widow
Status of Turn: Apparent Positive
Status of Dragon: Apparent Positive
Age: 15

[Due to continued nonappearance of Lady Amalia Langford and so-called husband Zane, all Apparents as yet unconfirmed.]

Motion made before the Council to form party to reconnaissance Zaharen *drákon.*

Motion made before the Council to appropriate Zaharen *drákon*/resources.

Motion made before the Council to wed HG Maricara to Alpha heir Kimber Langford as soon as legally viable.

All motions passed.

CHAPTER ONE

April 1782
Four Years Later

It was a night without moon or stars, the clouds boiling heavy with dark, impending snow, masking not only the ruts of the road but also anything that might be hiding above. Anything lethal.

Fortunately, he didn't truly need to see to sense an aerial threat. He felt them occasionally, or thought he did: distant tremors in the air, never too close, usually so faint he half thought he was imagining it.

The cold seemed the greater threat, actually. He'd never known a spring night this frigid, not in his life, and wondered how the bloody hell anyone managed to live here. Springtime at home meant bright green crocuses and warmed streams splashing free of their ice—not this. Not this bitter, relentless chill that sliced through his greatcoat and froze to frost inside his mouth and nose.

His horse stumbled, pitching him forward in the saddle. He righted himself and tried to calm her with a hand to her neck, but the mare only shuddered at his touch. He pulled back again.

Riding horseback was never ideal. But he'd been unable to hire a coach to take him up these mountain roads, no matter how much he offered. No one wanted to venture here.

And that was good, he knew. It meant, finally, that he was close.

The mare skipped to a halt, sending him forward again. He swore under his breath, snapping the reins, but she would not move. When he used his spurs she tossed her head and reared; he held on with both hands, but she only went into a buck, panicked, squealing, and he realized suddenly that there was something ahead of them on the road, something that spooked her.

He lost his grip. He hit the ground and then lost his breath, managing a roll to his feet, swiping the mud from his eyes. The mare pounded off and the danger-sense grew and the skin crawled along his spine—he was already Turning, but it was cold, and he was winded. And it was too late.

Her morning began the way too many of her mornings did: with the wind blowing her hair in heavy ropes across her face, her body curled in a ball atop a loose mound of hay, her fists clenched. Even her toes clenched. She wore no clothing. Beneath the hay, the terrace floor was cold, cold—nearly as cold as the ice topping the mountains, just as glimmering, milky-pale stone hewn from the hills centuries past.

Her mouth tasted of ashes. Her hair smelled of smoke.

Maricara opened her eyes, then closed them again. The sky above loomed pink and scarlet-gold, domed with soft, glamorous

clouds all rimmed in gilt. It was wildly beautiful and deeply invit-
ing, a sky fit for a princess. Or at least a serf masquerading as one.

For an instant—a brief, wistful flicker of time—she pretended
she was still asleep. In a bed. With pillows.

The wind stole her hair again, whipping it hard over her nose.
Definitely woodsmoke.

Cautiously, she began to stretch. Fingers, toes, the warm tucked
spaces of her body chilled at once as she flexed against the straw.
Nothing broken. Some pain in her left hand, bruised knuckles. A
cut along her belly . . . that could be a problem. A stomach wound
meant she had either flown too low or reared up too high.

Mari sat up and explored the wound, sucking in air to dispel
the pain. The edges were clean, razored, and not terribly deep—
but it hurt. She'd have to wash it carefully; the last thing she needed
was blood poisoning.

She climbed to her feet, brushing the loose twigs from her
torso, bending down to get her legs. She shook back her hair and
spoke to the open view before her.

"Where was it last night?"

The voice behind her was thinner, younger, and threaded with
a calm that probably was not real.

"A village several leagues away. Deda."

"Deda. That far?"

"Apparently."

She combed her fingers through her hair, looking down at the
shiny dark strands. In the past two years it had grown past her
hips; she could go the length of her arm and not reach the end
of it.

I should cut it, she thought. *Too long to powder, too heavy to curl.
I should cut it.*

"Did I kill anyone?" she asked aloud and, in the silence that followed, glanced over her shoulder at the boy who lingered against
the east tower wall.

"No," answered her brother, and shrugged a little. "Not that I know."

He was staring down at the hay, his cheeks and mouth chapped with the wind. His eyes were black-lashed, crystal-gray, exact reflections of her own, but their similarities ended there: For one thing, he was dressed, and dressed well. Sandu usually favored the plainer styles; it was a struggle to convince him to wear anything beyond breeches, boots, and a shirt. Yet this morning he was done up in one of his finest waistcoats, a wig, three layers of lace, and heels that lifted him taller than she. Mari studied him a moment, her mind turning—the barren terrace, the wind, the lanky young prince in ivory and velvet—until she remembered the day.

"Petitions," she said.

"We're almost ready to begin."

"I'll be down. One half hour."

"I'll tell them."

He turned away at once. She did not wait for him to reach the door, the footmen she knew would be stationed just inside. She couldn't walk in like this, and in any case, she didn't want to see their faces. She certainly didn't want them to see hers.

Maricara Turned to smoke.

It was a rush of sensation, an instant lightness that required neither breath nor thought. All human flesh was gone, all sense of cold or pain; all that came instead was lovely and silken. She'd had this Gift since the age of eight, the youngest of any of the *drákon* she knew—although it had taken a full year after that for her dragon form to emerge . . . claws and wings and velocity, the violence of the wind tearing at her eyes . . .

But this morning she was smoke, because smoke could roll down the side of the castle walls, smoke could skim the rough, familiar stone—like rubbing her hand over sandpaper, only without body, without weight. As smoke she could move any direction she wished, down farther, diagonal to the rampart, entangling briefly with the remains of a seated granite griffin, carved by some long-ago ancestor... down another level, and then she was at her own window, at the hairline crack in the glass she had made years ago, back when she had been imprisoned here.

It took time to sift through the break in the glass. It had been the greatest danger of discovery, the minute and seventeen seconds she needed to force herself through the fissure. But she'd never dared to make it larger, and then later, when it no longer mattered, she simply hadn't bothered. It would only be another breach in her defenses, anyway.

She became a gray well upon the sill, a plumy waterfall to the floor. When she was fully inside the room, she Turned back into woman, nude again, suppressing a shiver.

The *drákon* were unable to transform anything else in the Turn, not gemstones or weapons or food, certainly not clothing. Out of habit she remained motionless and in shadow, allowing her physical senses to surge back—her heart pumping to life, the scent of wood polish and hot coffee suddenly sharp in her nose—but her skin prickled against the fresh chill.

She heard the wind groaning through the vent of the chimney and the slow tick of the Belgian clock upon the *secrétaire.*

And breathing. And petticoats very lightly brushing stone.

Mari turned her face. From the doorway her maids took her cue, stirring and then coming forward, carrying garments and cosmetics and jewelry.

The private quarters of the princess were lavish and golden, a true reflection of the wealth of the castle. The bed was cherry and damask, the sheets were satin. She had rugs of peacock colors from exotic lands she had never seen, Turkish cabinetry and hardwood paneling from the darkest forests of black Russia. She had mother-of-pearl inlay and beeswax candles and that coffee languorously steaming in a service of solid gold by the fire. She had all these things, and always had, from the moment she'd first stepped foot here as a child, and the only aspect of this rich and blinding room that Maricara had ever troubled herself to change was the wallpaper. Or, more specifically, the wall.

Along the southern side of the room she had stripped the dyed silk from the wood, and then the wood from the stone. There were no windows there, no paintings or anything else to distract from the bare quartzite that composed the foundation of *Zaharen Yce*. It was a fine stone, solid and largely silent, which was good. Because tucked in the mortar between the ancient blocks were ancient diamonds, hundreds of them, and Maricara needed to hear them sing.

Cool and plain, colored and clear, they studded the wall in frosted bumps, every one of them uncut, every one a brilliant poem. If she ran her fingers over them, they would hum up her arm, into her heart, filling her ears and her throat and her blood with song. There had been times when their music had been her sole solace in the world.

She focused on that now, on their soft constant singing, as she bit her lip and cleansed the wound on her stomach with soap and cold water.

"No corset," she said without looking up, and one of the maids drifted back into the recesses of the room.

The blood washed off. The cut would heal. In time, she knew, everything healed.

The princess handed off the stained towel and basin to take her seat at the vanity. The looking glass showed the bed behind her tinted silver, the covers neat, no sign whatsoever that she ever once slept in it.

Like she didn't even exist.

With her hands folded in her lap, Maricara allowed her servants to begin her transformation.

No one spoke as she entered the chamber. They'd hardly been speaking before, just occasional mutters and whispers behind hands, but it seemed to Alexandru that the level of excitement seething through the serfs before him had been slightly higher than usual for this day.

Perhaps not. The room was round. Voices echoed. That could be all it was.

He'd been passing the time by putting on his spectacles and acting like he was examining the documents laid out before him, petitions written for him by his chamberlain, prepared in the order in which he would see each man. But it was all scratches and nibbles to him, tiny grievances blown into feuds: this field, that field, his hog, my acorns...

Sandu was fifteen years old. Breakfast had been hours ago. He was hungry, and he was chilled, and she was late, and he honestly didn't care about anyone's damned acorns.

The letters began to blur against the parchment. He pushed his spectacles back up his nose but it didn't help; the black ink ran to blue, the colors shifting, the words changing... they said something new now, something he could almost make out....

Pay attention, rang his sister's voice inside his head. *You are Alpha. Every man's concern here is your own.*

He blinked, and everything righted again. Sandu sighed and rubbed his nose. He wished, for what had to be the thousandth time, that the Convergence Room had a fireplace. It was mid-April but the Carpathians were still gripped with snow, and his court stockings were not woven for warmth.

The double doors opposite his table swung wide. Maricara entered the chamber, and that was when the air actually froze.

She was beautiful. No one would deny that. All their kind had a beauty, but in Mari it had grown into something beyond even them. She wore rouge and kohl, and a wig of long, heavy slate coils, and the violet of her gown lent purple to her eyes, but Sandu thought all these things really only served to distract from her true nature. It wasn't the whiteness of her skin that set her apart, or the lift of her shoulders, or the shape of her jaw. It wasn't her fashion or her figure, or her gliding walk. It wasn't anything so clear and physical. She was beautiful because she simply *was*: Of all the women of the mountains, she was the only one who could Turn.

It was why she had been chosen as princess. And it was why every person here, *drákon* and human alike, gazed at her with a seed of fear in their hearts. Sandu had realized that long ago.

It was possible they had good reason to fear her. He wasn't certain; he hoped not. This fey and otherworldly creature was his sister, and he loved her. But even Sandu had to admit he didn't fathom the depths of her.

The Convergence Room had windows filled with sky on every side, flooding the chamber with light. It was tall and vast, nearly four open floors of an entire tower, with marble pillars and tiles, and a ceiling carefully frescoed with stars and the moon and silvery, blazing beasts. For all its strength and solid luster, this was one of the few rooms in *Zaharen Yce* that was created very obviously for something other than humans. When Maricara took her first step into the morning sunlight she blazed as well, brighter and more brilliant than even the painted dragons above. Her skin and hair and colors abruptly ceased to matter; she was only planes and angles, and power simmering beneath.

Alexandru felt a brief flash of gloom. No one feared *him*. They listened to him because they had to. He could Turn, but so could a score of other men here. He was called *prince* strictly because of her, because by their nature a female could not rule, no matter how potent she was.

She moved through the rows of waiting people without glancing left or right. Her pale, cool eyes held the same faintly distracted cast it seemed she always had of late; Sandu wondered if his own looked the same. She didn't appear tired, although he knew she was. She didn't look like someone who had been missing the entire night although he was fairly certain that was true, too.

He stood, and when she was close enough, he bowed. It was a good bow, a French bow, and he knew she'd be pleased.

He rose from it just as she was completing her curtsy. He held her chair for her—to the left of his, slightly behind—and she accepted it, settling in with a gentle crinkling of skirts.

There was a tradition to this, a formality he'd had drummed into him these past eight years that was as old as the mountains, as the castle itself. This was the sole day they mingled, the *drákon* and those who served them. As a child he had once accompanied his father here to this wide, marbled cavern. He remembered just where they had sat, wrapped in their homespun: far in the back, and the prince seated in this chair had seemed as hard and cheerless as winter rime.

It had been cold then, too.

The chamberlain—human—stepped forward.

"Your Royal Graces."

Sandu turned to the first page of his documents. The petitioners were seated in strict order, from eldest to youngest. Another rule, another tradition.

He squinted at the parchment, and repressed another sigh. This was the one with the hog—

But the chamberlain at his shoulder bobbed and slipped a fresh sheet in front of him, something that had never happened before. Sandu accepted it, surprised, and dropped his gaze to the writing.

LIVEZILE:
Twelve sheep.
Two goats, one wool, one milk.

SALVA:
Twenty-four chickens, twenty laying.
Four piglets, one sow.
Shepherd hut.
DEDA:
Two sheep.
Church belfry.

Sandu kept his face blank. He looked up, not at his sister, but at the hushed mass of people in front of them. With an unpleasant sense of awakening, he realized how many Others there were here, crowded into this room. He understood their agitation now, the whispers. He smelled their excitement in dried sweat and wool.

The events of that night eight years before remained seared in his memory like a brand. The aroma of tar and burnt pine. The angry buzz of distant voices. He'd been awake because his parents had been awake, because the light from the serfs' torches had lit a patch of orange against the clouds and the castle, visible miles distant. Because the village had emptied of people, one by one, by foot or by horse, as everyone ascended the mountain to witness what had occurred: Prince Imre, the last of the pure-blooded *drákon,* was dead.

His young bride was not.

Sandu had been seven, and Maricara but eleven. His parents had latched the door to his room and refused to let him leave it. In the murk of the early morning Mari had come to him anyway, easily slipping through the shrunken slats of the roof, and materialized beside his bed.

He's gone. I've chosen you to rule.

And in his sleepy stupor, all Sandu had managed was: *What?*

I've chosen you, she'd repeated, patient. *Come up to the castle. Come up at dawn.*

And he had. It had been the last night he'd spent in the village.

He hadn't known how the prince had died. He hadn't known anything at all. But when he'd finally made it up the mountain, he saw the blood fear in the eyes of the other peasants, the fallen torches extinguished in greasy puddles around the castle courtyard. He saw Maricara, thin and brave, put out her hand and quell the uprising that wanted to come. The Alpha of the *drákon* was dead, and all that was left of his reign was a slip of a girl whose sole grasp on authority was dragon teeth and scales and little else.

She'd had that hand out ever since, he thought. And because she was who she was—what she was—she'd managed it. Barely.

Sandu stared again at the paper. He hadn't known about the belfry. Sheep and pigs could be replaced, or at least paid for. A belfry would mean a priest. A priest could bring in an outsider, a whole contingent of them.

From the corner of his eye, he saw Maricara lean forward, and adjusted the paper so she could view it better. Perfumed with powder, garbed in silk, she seemed every bit an aristocrat; her breathing remained steady as she took in the contents. She turned her head a fraction and the rubies at her throat released a knot of fiery sparks.

"Your Graces." The chamberlain bowed once more, touching the curve of his fingers to his forehead. "Your most gracious pardons. A list has been compiled of a few recent losses from the villages. Nothing so very serious, as you see, however..."

"Yes," said Sandu, finding his tongue. "Yes," he said again, and cleared his throat. "Most lamentable. Our people will not be allowed to suffer, no matter the cause. Compensation will be made."

Another bow from his servant. Mari remained taut in her chair. A farmer from the middle of the crowd climbed to his feet.

"Noble One," said the man, not quite inclining his head. "Forgive me. We wish to know how the losses will be stopped."

"Stopped?"

"It was my prize sow. Four fine piglets. Sucklings. How will this be stopped?"

23

Now, despite himself, Sandu glanced at his sister. She gazed back at him without expression. This close her eyes shone mirror clear, nearly colorless. He could see nothing at all in them.

"We do not know how, precisely, these creatures are being lost," he said at last, very slow. "We do not know the manner of their deaths, or how these structures came to be damaged. We know wolves have been sighted—"

"Destroyed," interrupted a new man, also standing. This one was paler, leaner; Sandu could sense a dim pulse of *drákon* in his blood. "The belfry was destroyed, my lord, from the inside, as if by a very great beast. Not a wolf."

"My sheep," began another serf, his voice throbbing. "My ewe, devoured—"

"None of us would do such a thing," Sandu said. "You know that. We would not."

No one contradicted him. They would not dare. Not here, and not yet. But it seemed every face before him turned to her, to the young woman seated at his side. The sunlight filling the room burned very bright.

She stood. Without touching him, without looking at him, without speaking or acknowledging anyone else in the chamber, Maricara walked carefully around the table, back down the center of the people. Her skirts trailed purple. Her footsteps struck lightly against the marble floor.

The footmen opened the double doors for her, shut them again after she had passed through.

"Compensation will be made," Prince Alexandru said once more, into the vast and hungry silence.

When she was younger, and new to this place, Maricara used to enjoy pretending she was one of the olden *drákon* who had built the fortress of diamonds and might. She would hold out her arms and pace out the massive squares of the keep—also pretending she could still find them whenever she came to a rug—and whisper secret words to herself: *Here we place the southwest stones, for our heat and security. Here we place the northern stones, to brave the worst winds. Here will go the middle stone, for heart, for completion. . . .*

And they had names, too: *Bogdan, Ilie, Lacrimioara, Rada.* Because all friends needed names.

The first time he caught her at it, Imre had asked what she was doing. She told him; she had no reason to lie—besides, lying to Prince Imre tended to lead to remarkably unpleasant consequences. So after that when he saw her counting he would only watch her with that small, condescending smile he had. Stones were no threat to him, to his dominion over her. Or so he had thought.

Maricara knew every inch of this castle. She knew precisely how many steps it would take to reach her private drawing room from the doors of the Convergence Room, and how many more past that to reach the bower window that overlooked the courtyard, and the fountain of alabaster fish.

"Breakfast," she said to the hallboy who had followed her in, and took her seat upon the cushions. She waited until he was gone to look down at her hands.

They weren't shaking. Hardly, she corrected herself. They were hardly shaking.

She fisted them together in her lap.

Sheep. Sucklings. She closed her eyes and forced down the small, strange noise that wanted to rise from the back of her throat.

As if she were naught but an animal herself, as if she were little more than some base, marauding creature that savaged belfries and squealing pigs in the dark—

She exhaled, very slowly. She stared down at the beds of her fingernails pressing white and concentrated on remembering the details of last night. The ruffles on her nightgown. The heat of the bed brick. The smooth luxury of the sheets against her bare hands and feet, the pillow cool beneath her neck. The colors of the canopy in the last of the firelight, burnished bronze and rust, the chocolate satin cords lashing it to the posts...

And after that, nothing. She had fallen asleep. She had awoken atop the tower this morning.

Just as she had nearly every night for the past six months.

When the first signs of her Gifts began to manifest, her parents had been terrified. No one knew how true the bloodlines of the *drákon* ran through the mountainfolk any longer. They were all descendants of mixed blood these days, all except Imre. Neither of her parents could Turn. Her grandfathers had been able, a few great-uncles, many years past. But for a woman to have this power, for a female child to balk at boiled cabbage for supper one night and transform into smoke rather than taking a bite—

It had not been done in generations. The Gifts were growing rarer and rarer, and no one even knew why.

She had felt so special. She had been so delighted. She had not truly realized what it meant. From that minute on her life had been mapped for her, first by her husband and then—resolutely—by herself. And Mari had thought, for a while, that she had carved her path deep enough and sure enough to thwart any new changes. That she was safe now, that her fate was secure. She had nearly twenty years behind her, and thought she knew how to bend the very mountains to her will.

Until six months ago, when her nights began to vanish.

The sky beyond the window was lifting into a sheer, bottomless azure. It was going to be a sunny day. The snowdrifts in the courtyard were already blinding, which is why she heard the crumping footsteps of the approaching party of men before she saw them. She looked out, squinting, then lifted a hand to shield her eyes.

Five men at the gate, huntsmen, carrying a dark something between them. A deer, most like. Or a wild boar. She sighed and closed her eyes, leaning her temple against the glass. She felt unwilling to witness more death, even accidentally... but when she opened them again the men were closer, and the thing they carried had one limp, pale hand trailing the air.

Maricara was not the first to reach them. The doormen had gathered in the courtyard already, along with two milkmaids, and four of the grooms. They parted at her approach, lips compressed, heads ducked. In her haste one of the maids slipped in her wooden clogs; the liquid from the bucket balanced on her head splashed into invisible drops against the snow.

The dark shape was a man. His skin was oddly gray, his hair flaxen, his eyes glazed and open. As she walked nearer the light shifted. She realized that what she had perceived as gray was actually frost, a frozen sparkle across his cheekbones and whiskers and straw-colored lashes. He was comely and somehow familiar, dressed well in a torn Parisian coat and boots that looked new. The hand that had trailed free wore a signet ring of gold. Clearly not a serf.

"Who was he?" she asked, looking up at the huntsmen.

"Noble One." The headman nodded to her, not lifting his eyes. "My deepest apologies. We don't know. We found him on the road before dawn. No horse or carriage, no papers."

"Where?"

"The woods, my lady."

"Where?" she asked again, sharper.

"Deda," muttered another man. "Near to Deda."

Mari blinked, but that was all. She gestured for the hunters to lay the man down, knelt beside the body—the ground an icy jolt against her knees—and opened the coat. It was stiff with blood, glittery and dark. No need to guess at the source: The gash that had torn the greatcoat had also pierced his coat and waistcoat, and even deeper, enough to reveal the skin beneath, his chest. What would have been his heart.

Maricara sat back on her heels. She looked down and noticed a flake of frozen blood upon her stomacher, and flicked it hard away.

"This was the work of men," she said aloud, and then glanced up at the faces surrounding her. No one met her gaze. One of the milkmaids was staring, whey-faced, at the ravaged waistcoat, her eyes wide and watering.

"Men did this," Mari insisted, and came to her feet . . . but she was forced to remain still a long moment, fighting a wave of dizziness that washed the color from her sight and sent electric barbs down into her fingertips.

Do not *faint. Do* not. *Do not surrender here.*

She set her jaw and, when she could, gestured once more at the huntsmen. They roused, blowing clouds and exchanging looks, stumping closer to the body. This time when they lifted it Mari made herself touch that cold hand, to fold it over the stranger's chest.

The band of the signet caught her eye. She worked the ring around the knuckle until its face was upright, until she could make out the design carved into the metal.

A dragon, wings out, fangs bared, entwined against the letter D.

She knew that crest. She'd seen it exactly three times before in her life, carved carefully into wax on the letters from England. From the Earl of Chasen.

This man had been an Englishman. And a dragon.

Someone, somehow, had managed to kill a *drákon.*

God help her if this was the earl himself.

"Take it to—to the granary. You, summon the prince. You five—go! Are you listening? Stay with it until His Grace arrives. Let no one else come near."

"Yes, my lady."

"The rest of you—have you not work to finish? Cows do not milk themselves, as I recall."

She watched them as they scattered, watched until she stood

alone in the courtyard beneath the sightless eyes of all the windows of *Zaharen Yce*. A long, spiraled lock from her wig blew lazily against her left forearm: gray, like the dead man's skin.

Mari could hear the pines rustling in the mountains, and birds shifting in their nests, and the small heartbeats of all the little creatures burrowed under the earth. She could certainly hear the hissed conversation of the two milkmaids as they hurried back down the walkway that led to the dairy.

"How can she *say* it was men who did it? How can we be certain it wasn't—"

"Because," answered the other, just as soft, "she wouldn't have stopped with his heart. She would have eaten all of him."

CHAPTER TWO

He'd never liked tea. It seemed somewhat ridiculous to him, to interrupt his day with miniature cakes and dry, crustless sandwiches, and fragile china that always seemed about to snap in half between his fingers. Tea, Kimber reasoned, was a feminine invention, ruled by females of a certain type: ruffled, beribboned, and iron-willed.

At least it was here at Chasen. It was the hour his sisters always paired to outflank him.

"But Kim," Joan was saying in her pretty, reasonable way, "you *do* realize how impractical it has become. We still have scarcely any idea of even how many of these other *drákon* there are. If they're as scattered as Lia's letter suggested, we'll waste a good deal of resources merely locating them."

"We have already," Audrey pointed out, taking a sip from her ridiculous, dainty cup.

"And to what results?" Joan responded, a perfectly timed counterpoint. Kim knew from experience they could go on like this for hours. "Rumors and hearsay. A smattering of frightened peasants who can barely string together a full sentence in French. No castle. No certain means of even ascertaining how the letters from the princess had managed to reach us, or ours to her. It's as if they manifested from thin air."

"Like smoke," said Rhys quietly from his corner chair, and returned Joan's glance with innocently raised brows.

Kimber regarded his siblings in silence. He supposed it did him some good to be challenged, even in such a sugar-coated, sideways manner. If nothing else, he could count on these Wednesday afternoons to sweep away the illusions of his station from his mind and remind him, quite firmly, that although he was the leader of his tribe, to these particular three people he was still family.

And that *was* good, he told himself. He eyed the tepid Ceylon in his hand. Surely it was good.

Very gently, he set the flower-painted teacup upon the table at his feet. The butter yellow of the cinquefoils was an exact match to the edging of the Westmorland rug, and the Swiss appliqué curtains that framed the parlor windows and glass garden doors. Everything in this chamber, in fact, was premeditated and coordinated, right down to the iced cakes—also yellow, with tiny pink marzipan roses swirled on top.

Chasen Manor was nothing if not vigorously well planned.

He longed for water. Or wine. Or even cider. He longed for plain bread and cheese and a decent slice of meat.

Joan, seated beside him on the settee, leaned forward to pour fresh tea into his cup, then added a wedge of cucumber sandwich beside it. Beneath her lace cap her curls glinted in the light of the candelabra; like Kimber, she had inherited their father's coloring, green eyes and dark golden hair.

Unlike Kimber, she usually cared enough about what other people thought to take the trouble to powder it.

"I am merely suggesting," she was saying, "that before we commit further to the council's scheme of finding and controlling these Zaharen, we take a breath, so to speak, and consider all the implications."

Rhys spoke again. "You act like he has a choice. You act like Kim controls the council."

"Well," countered Joan, "he *is* Alpha, since Father is gone. He could tell the council at their next meeting—"

"What," interrupted Rhys, impatient. "Tell them what? That until this princess decides she wants to trust us enough to send us her direction, we'll just have to sit on our hands and simply hope none of them decides to reveal to the world exactly what we are? Where *we* live? That we should wait for bloody Lia to show up, or Mother and Father to come home, and all our secrets will be safe? The tribe is teetering at the edge of reason as it is. You know damned well the council made the best decision possible given the—"

"Sending three of our men over to the Continent with little or no information on how to navigate to this castle—forbidding them to use their Gifts to help discover these other *drákon*—"

"We've only done what we've had to do to *survive*—"

"You say that because you're *on* the council, so it's very well for *you* to claim you know what's best for *all* of us—"

"Stop fighting," Kimber enunciated, very calm, but it silenced them both like a bullwhip cracked across the room.

The lives of every single *drákon*, male or female, young or old, were bound tight with rubric and tradition. It was necessary; with their many Gifts came also many enticements. But they had endured the centuries by learning to hide. They had endured by following their own rigid laws and by vigorously punishing anyone who defied them. Once upon a time, everyone knew, their kind had been hunted nearly to extinction. It was only by pulling order out of their chaos, by banding together here in Darkfrith, creating their own careful universe, that they had managed slowly, slowly to thrive.

They had an Alpha to lead. They had a council to govern. They had rules upon rules, the first and foremost of which were: loyalty to the tribe. Silence.

Confinement.

It was bred into their blood and into their bones. Confinement meant continuance. It meant farms and orchards, mills and smiths and schools, and black-deep mines laden with silver. It meant crops, and trade. It meant the *drákon* could mingle with the Others when necessary, that they could be simple country folk to anyone who didn't look too long or too deep at the pastoral perfection of the shire.

Some people did. Only a few. A very, very few.

And then had come that letter from Lia—runaway Lia—along with that of the princess. And on that day the tribe had realized that everything they had worked for, all the generations of struggles and sacrifices, might soon be for naught.

There were *more* of them out there, running free and uncontrolled. There were more *drákon*, foreign and wild, and no one in Darkfrith had ever known.

The news had struck a tremor of fear through the shire like nothing else in their history.

Two years ago the Marquess and Marchioness of Langford had broken their own rules and vanished into the human world in their final hunt for their youngest daughter, an act that had very nearly managed to rend the tribe into pieces. Before the Zaharen had come to light, runners were considered the most dangerous of all possible threats. A *drákon* who fled the shire without permission was desperate, unpredictable. It was nearly inconceivable that the established Alpha of the tribe and his wife would do such a thing, even in search of their child.

Kimber had been left behind, just like Audrey and Rhys and Joan. He had stepped into his father's role because it was what he'd been born to do, what he'd been trained to do, and to ignore the crisis of the tribe would have been, quite simply, unthinkable.

He'd been granted rights and privileges not given to anyone else, not even his brother and sisters, because he was the eldest son. He'd been shipped to Eton as a boy, then to Cambridge, had mingled with nobles and thieves and, five times, the king himself, all because of who he was destined to be. He was a leader and a lord, shaped for this role the entire sum of his life. And his family, his comrades and kin, had been shaped as well.

The Alpha ruled the *drákon*. Kimber was the new Alpha. When he spoke, his kind obeyed. It was their way.

Joan had lowered her gaze to the teapot, a sullen slant to her lips. Rhys had subsided back into his chair, his hair a brown tangle against the damask, his arms crossed, and was staring up at the painted cornices along the ceiling. Only Audrey, Kimber's twin, fixed her dark gaze to his and then pursed her lips to speak.

"I saw Zoe Lane in the village the other day," she said, matter-of-fact.

Zoe Lane. Kimber didn't need to scan his memory to place her: She was the fiancée of Hayden James, young, striking. Blond, like most of their kind. Pale, like all of their kind. He remembered her stoic face as she'd bid Hayden farewell a year past, on the manor drive that unspooled to the outer world. He remembered seeing her later that evening at her sister's tavern, where sometimes she worked, and how red her eyes had been, even by candlelight.

Like Jeffrey Bochard, the man sent out two years before him— and Luke Rowland before *him*—Hayden James had simply disappeared.

Just like Lia. Just like Kim's mother and father.

"No one blames you," Audrey said softly. "It isn't your fault, of course."

And as soon as she said that, Kimber knew she thought it was. She was right.

He rose from the settee and walked to the beveled-glass doors, gazing out into the garden, the woods spreading thickly beyond.

If his home was as tranquil and studied as a great deal of money could ensure—and it was—at least the weather was yet beyond the control of the *drákon*. It was a stormy day, not miserably so, but with a cool, steady spring shower that drenched the earth to black and jeweled the trees and plants that were only waiting for sunlight to bloom. A soft blue fog crept through the vales, winding in fingers and curls along the low-slung hills that surrounded the shire.

He imagined himself out there in that wet. He imagined breathing it, and then becoming it, smoke misted with rain.

He heard Joan straighten on the settee, the firm scrape of her pumps against the floor. "I must be off. Erik can't control the twins for long, and Cook always feeds them too much pudding before bed."

"Yes," said Audrey, also rising. "It's time for me to go as well. I promised the boys a game of backgammon. Rhys?"

"No, thank you. I live here, if you'll recall."

"I meant, dear, will you see us out?"

"No. That's what the footmen are for."

"*Such* a brute."

"Aye, but at least I'll be dry."

Both his sisters approached and Kim turned around, accepting their brief, rouged kisses upon his cheek. They had houses to return to, families, husbands. They had their fine and ordered lives.

"Next time," he said suddenly, as they were crossing to the door. "Next Wednesday, let's take tea outside, in the pavilion."

Everyone looked surprised, even Rhys, but it was Joan who

could switch from tears to smiles in a trice. She gave a bubbling laugh. "Why, Kimber—it's April! It's been raining practically every day. What a mad suggestion."

He looked back at them without speaking, then lowered his lashes and offered half a smile, to let them know he was in on the jest. From behind their sisters, Rhys gave a soft snort.

Then they retreated into the shadows, Joan and Audrey arm in arm, their footsteps measured, striped skirts and fans and cashmere shawls, venturing out into the main hall, and then the graylit storm.

The footmen would only walk them as far as the end of the drive. After that, his sisters would find their own way to their homes. They didn't truly require an escort at all. The thought that someone—anyone—would dare harm them was far-fetched enough to be laughable.

He'd seen them fly, both of them. He'd seen their claws and their deadly stealth. Individually they were remarkable enough, the only two females still in the shire who could Turn. As a pair, they were formidable.

Rhys waited until they were gone, until they both heard the massive wooden doors of the mansion close with their particularly well-oiled *click*.

"They're getting worse," his brother said.

"I know it."

"Soon they'll be demanding seats on the council."

"*That*," said Kimber, "would be worth seeing."

They shared a look. The council was governed by men—in Kimber's mind, a majority of ancient, surly men—and always had been. Females weren't even allowed to attend the meetings, something Kim's mother had found particularly galling. But like every other aspect of life here, the rule was ironclad.

He wondered if anyone else knew what he did: that Rue Langford had taken to knitting during the council sessions, her chair positioned close to the hearth in the Blue Parlor, which shared a common wall with the council's private chamber. Kim had received more than one lopsided scarf in his packages from home while at Eton, and a great deal of understated irony in his mother's letters.

They should have let her join, he thought suddenly. *Perhaps she might have stayed if they had.*

The rain began to intensify. It speckled the glass and slid downward in silvery tears, smearing the fog and the trees and the grass into plots of muted colors. The light from the candles lent a warm soft circle to their little corner of the room.

Rhys flopped back into his chair. He was two years and a lifetime younger than Kim's thirty-one, handsome, poetic in the way only a second son could be; a single, flawless emerald dangling from one ear; a pirate's heart beating beneath white lawn and a waistcoat of Italian silk.

"Tell them I'm going," he said. "You can do that. Tell the council."

"No."

"Kim—"

"I am not having this conversation again with you."

"Actually, you are. Look here, I speak French, Italian, and German; I fence; I'm a deuced fine shot, as you know. I've pored over the maps and I think I have a fair idea of where this castle might actually be. There are only a certain number of roads that lead to—"

Kimber's patience snapped. "Pray do not be an idiot. Mother and Father are gone—the marquess and his mate missing without word, their youngest daughter allegedly wed to a human and nowhere to be found—three tribesmen have vanished—even if I *wanted* to let you go, the council would never permit it. Too many of our family have disappeared already. We've effectively lost six members of the tribe due to our charming little princess. I don't fancy the headache of convincing the council that *you'll* be the one to miraculously return."

Silence took the room; the patter of the rain grew louder and then softer. From somewhere deep inside the labyrinth of the manor, someone started to cough.

"Sorry." Kim closed his eyes and rubbed his forehead with stiff fingers. "I think perhaps I'm delirious with hunger."

His brother's response was carefully light. "It *would* be pleasant to dine on something larger than my thumb."

Kimber dropped his hand. "Let's try the kitchens. I'd gnaw on boiled leather at this point to get the taste of sugar out of my mouth."

He waited until nightfall to fly. It was difficult, because the need to shed his skin had become a persistent itch, growing stronger and stronger as the day wound on. They could Turn at any time, of course, but they were supposed to wait for dark. The night was their best domain, full of secrets and shadows that tricked the human eye.

Darkfrith was deceptively ordinary by day. By night, her skies glistened with scales.

Tonight was especially ideal; the clouds were still low and heavy like tufts of wet fleece, easy to pierce. It would be just like shooting an arrow through a blanket.

From the balcony of his unlit quarters, Kimber watched the skies. He watched as the men of his tribe dissolved, one by one, into gusts of smoke that drifted upward from houses and farmsteads, up to that billowing mass, churning and fading. He felt them Turning again above the haze, becoming more than smoke. He cocked his head, and he could hear the very air above the earth sliced into rivers by wings and tails.

His blood began to pulse in harmony. His heart in his chest began to hammer, a gilded beast poised to break free.

He removed his garments. He stepped forward, closing his eyes in appreciation, expanding his lungs until they hurt. The rain perfumed him, it cleansed him, sent anticipation along his bare body in slick beaded welcome.

He opened his eyes and at last became smoke.

The first time he'd Turned, pain had flamed through his being like the molten core of the sun. The initial Turn was always the most treacherous—too many young *drákon* perished in that first instant of disintegration—but the subsequent joy of breaking free of his human form had been akin to nothing he had ever known. And after all these years, there was nothing still to compare to it: not food or drink, not power or money, not women. Nothing.

He let the rain pour through him, effortless. He willed himself to rise and he did, another plume of gray, another drifting coil, until he grazed the edge of the clouds, learning their cold sapphire weight, pushing through, merging.

He did not wait to Turn again. Kimber became a dragon right there, still cloaked in rainclouds, and did a spinning loop that swirled the mists. He stretched his neck and his wings and charged higher, breaking free all at once, an arrow indeed of scarlet and blue, and talons of bright hard gold.

His tribe was about, hunting and diving. Sinuous, lustrous as polished steel, the other dragons instinctively swerved away, letting him soar where he wished.

The moon was an ivory pearl encircled with stars, ever tempting. The land below the clouds was soft and living, and his.

His people, his home; every aspect, every atom of the air, every heart that beat.

He could not imagine wanting to leave. He could not imagine a more perfect place.

Kim bared his teeth and pumped his wings to climb higher, until his memories of the day had blown clear, until there was nothing of him left but the harsh, animal ache of straining muscle and breath.

The second body was found in a mine. A mine that the princess—and every other dragon of the mountains—knew well, in fact. It hadn't been dragged very far inside, but the winter had been long and even more frigid than usual. It had snowed nearly every week from November into February, and the winds had pushed great mounds of leaves and powder into every cranny of the world. By May, the snows were beginning to let loose their grasp to rain, and a peasant boy, a sheepherder, had ventured into the tunnel entrance by chance to escape the hammering downpour.

Once it had been a great and prosperous mine, as all the mines stabbed through the Carpathians were. Once, it had yielded cartloads of ore riddled with copper, and dragon-men and human men had worked together to empty it of its wealth. But that was centuries ago. On this day it offered only one fresh discovery to the drenched shepherd: the remains of a man with a hole in his chest, and fair hair that had frozen into icicles, slowly thawing beneath a blanket of snow.

And a ring made of gold. A signet ring.

The news reached the castle that afternoon. By four o'clock Sandu had tracked Maricara not to the mine—he wasn't surprised she wouldn't go there—but to the high and bleak peaks of the most remote of the mountains, higher than any of the Others would go. Higher than trees, higher than hamlets or monasteries, higher even than *Zaharen Yce.*

She stood alone with her feet planted in the snow, her arms folded over her chest, gazing out at the cloudy tors of stone and ice that stretched as far as he could see. He knew she sensed him, although she really didn't move. Only her eyes cut to him, that pale and penetrating stare finding the curve of smoke he took to funnel down to her side.

She did not stir as he coalesced. He became human with his back to hers, not touching. Neither of them turned around.

It was *damned* cold up here, and blustery. She was always doing outlandish things like this, going off to stand naked in the snow atop a mountain. Sometimes he wondered if she did it just to test him, to see how far he truly would push to follow her.

"The situation is poor," Alexandru said.

"Yes. I imagine so."

"No, Mari, I mean *poor.* The worst I've ever seen. The Others are frightened, and they're angry. They're no longer complaining about their sheep or pigs. They're hiding their children. Great God, Maricara. Even the serfs have heard whispers of what's been happening in France."

Her hair whipped his back with the wind, a brown so deep it was nearly black; loosened grains of snow whipped with it, embedding in his skin.

"I don't know what to do," Sandu confessed, hearing the frustration in his voice. "Tell me, Princess. What should I do?"

She was silent a long while, and just when he was beginning to suspect she wouldn't answer him at all, she did.

"You must go back to them and tell them the truth. Tell them that men have decided to hunt us again. They should take all precautions."

"Men?" he echoed, and in his astonishment turned his head to see her. "What are you talking about?"

She glanced back at him, sober, her cheeks pink with cold. "I didn't kill anyone—at least not those two. They were *drákon,* and English. If they'd wished to, they might have killed *me* in a fight.

No doubt they would have been bigger and stronger. But they died in human form, which means they were taken by surprise. There were no claw marks on the body, just that one wound to the chest."

"You saw the new body?"

"I did." His lips pressed tight, and she sighed, looking away. "This afternoon, first thing. I flew there as soon as I heard."

"Oh."

Sandu faced away too, his eyes tearing. His feet were numb to the ankles. He crossed his arms and clenched his fingers into his elbows to control the shivers, but Maricara only stood there like a rock, like a statue, unmoving. Her hair curved around him once more, a cloak of dark wind.

"I don't think they'll believe me," he said softly, and blinked to rid the salt from his vision. "I don't know. I don't know."

"Then they are going to die," she answered. "The proof will come to you soon enough. I'm leaving. If the killings continue, you'll know it wasn't me."

Deep in his heart, Sandu had braced for this moment. He might have even been searching for her to tell her so himself. But it was a relief that she said it aloud instead of him. He felt lighter at once, guilty and thankful in a rush of warm confusion. The snow, the jagged peaks, the relentless blue and white of his world all came together, all crystallized into a new and clarifying sense. She was leaving, and all would be right again.

When the air cleared from his exhalation, he spoke to the ice on the ground.

"Where will you go?"

She reached up to tuck her hair behind one ear, a girlish gesture, one that made her seem both younger and more ordinary than she really was.

"To the west, I think," Maricara said. "I have a message to deliver."

"Mari—"

"You'll do fine. Keep your head up. Keep your eyes open. You're the prince now, and the people will want you to be ruthless. Never forget it."

How could he? Because of her, the gilded wires of *Alpha* caged every second of his life.

CHAPTER THREE

It is no small task of will to veil ourselves from Others. Temptation tantalizes from all around—the tang of delicious sky upon our tongues; the fierce, burning stretch of our wingbones as we clasp a channel of wind. The pleasure of rolling through clouds, or of becoming one; of stealing into locked inns and cafés in thin, smoky tendrils, to do as we like.

Food tastes better as dragons. Colors that appear to you as dark and bland are as vibrant as the sunrise to our eyes. Scents can overwhelm us; from miles away we can smell mice or apple blossoms or that small teardrop of fear that winks from your eye as you gaze up at us lancing the heavens.

Cold, heat, water, wind: Everything slides off our scales.

We are more beautiful than you, and infinitely clever. We can glide so high above your common little towns, you'll convince yourself we're just the expression of your wildest imagination. Too much ale. Too little sleep.

So if a *drákon* of such extraordinary Gifts was forced to travel, would she choose the ordinary human way, with horses, and reeking carriages, and ships that crawled at a slug's pace across the open seas?

Or would she merely open her wings and fly?

You know what *you* would do, if only you could.

CHAPTER FOUR

Years later, when his life had resolved once again into reasoned lucidity, Kimber would remember the night that his sensible and fortified existence shattered with one particular, acute sensation: sweat.

It was hot in Darkfrith, the hottest June anyone could recall. Summer had come early in a wave of heat that shimmered across the land, that dried the tender tips of anemones and meadow grasses, and burned the sky into a deep, humid cobalt. The fresh green shoots of wheat and rye slowed their spectacular growth; the many streams that fed into the River Fier grew sluggish and shallow. Only the forest remained unaffected, dense and fragrant with wildflowers and bracken, elm and oak and birch.

The village elders convened for gossip over whist and lukewarm lemonade, wearing muslin and lace in shadowed parlors with the casements opened wide.

The young retreated into the woods.

At night those who could would still take to the air, finding relief in the thinnest upper curve of the atmosphere; there were no clouds to hide behind. Even the moon seemed to withdraw, her light wan and blued. Excepting the new mosquitoes darting above the ponds, nothing flourished.

That afternoon a letter had arrived from the marquess and marchioness. It was postmarked from Flanders, addressed to Kimber, and consisted of just two lines:

Others come. Guard the shire.

Kim pondered that, sprawled atop the duvet of his ebony bed, as he followed the moonlight creeping along the ceiling, and then gradually down the walls. He'd left the balcony doors open to the garden of flowers and gravel pathways two stories below, but the only aroma that lifted was of wilted petals and baked stone; there was no breeze. It was too hot for coverings, too hot for riddles. He'd already crossed the shire and back, had set his guards in constant flight at the perimeters, and still had no idea what his parents might have actually meant.

Others come? Would it have been too bloody much trouble for them to be more specific? It was unlike them to be so cryptic— well, unlike his father, at least. Kimber rolled to his side and pushed away his pillows, irritated. Except for the initials scrawled across the bottom of the page, there wasn't even a hint of who had sent it.

He fell asleep as the moonlight shortened into a slit along the raw silk curtains, dreaming of fire and boiling water, of the sun reflecting off the sea.

And when he woke a few hours later, something had changed.

The air felt different, charged somehow, a heaviness eating

down through his bones, crackling the hair on his arms and legs. He lay very still a moment, breathing slowly, the sheets at his waist, smelling and tasting and measuring that subtle, smoking sting like gunpowder lingering at the back of his throat.

The doors were still open, the night was still sweltering, but that wasn't it.

Someone was here in the mansion. Someone new, someone with power. Someone he had never felt before.

A *drákon.*

He rose, folding back the sheets, his toes pressing the warm maple floor. He wouldn't Turn—too obvious—but he could hunt without Turning. In the quiet, in the heat, in storm or total blindness, Kimber knew he could hunt.

In his drawers and bare feet, his hair a heated weight down his neck, he padded to the door of his chamber, pushed it ajar. A breath of more temperate air washed along the length of his body, cooling the moisture on his skin. The beast within him stretched into sinew and blood, eager to surface.

Downstairs, it whispered.

Chasen Manor had been built with an eye for grace and updated for luxury, another cunning ruse in his family's presentation of itself to the world. The main hallway of the upper level yawned wide and open, floored with checkered stone tiles; skylights of clean, polished glass illumed the corridor and allowed in the night. Kim avoided the brighter patches. He stole through shadows to the grand staircase, pausing to listen, but heard nothing beyond the usual background of distant snores, and the creaks and groans of timber beams cooling with the dark.

But he was not mistaken. Despite his guards, despite his vigilance, Chasen had been breached.

Yes, murmured the dragon, flexing, growing. *Danger. Destroy it.*

He moved utterly without noise. His foot found the first step down the white marble stairs, and then the next. He reached the base swiftly and fell again into shadow.

The scent, the rippling of fresh power, was coming from the music room.

He wondered briefly where Rhys was, why he hadn't sensed the threat as well, but there was no time to wake him. The stinging charge was nearly electric at this point, the friction of thunderheads against ether, remarkably strong. He approached the open doors and, his back to the wood, glanced in.

Faint moonlight still rinsed through these windows, tracing black and blue and charcoal across the furnishings. Frozen elegance, the drapes and rug and cream agate mantel framing the hearth, the pianoforte—the chamber appeared empty. The fire was feathered ash; there weren't even any dust motes to settle with a draft. The only sound to be heard was the bracket clock ticking, very loudly, atop the cabinet in the corner, its grinning cherubs just visible in a gleam of dull metallic blue.

The air was oppressive. The heat, the living friction, the sting against his skin. He was burning inside, expanding: The dragon writhed to be free, to taste blood.

Kimber stood motionless. He waited.

And in the blackest of the corners he saw at last the something he had sensed, a slight, languorous movement that seemed almost joined with the night, just as sultry and silky slow. It resolved to become a shoulder, a bare pale arm. The curve of a neck and cheekbones and lips; a wash of moonlit hair; dark-lashed, amazing clear eyes—eyes like water, like the light—watching him without blinking.

A woman.

And now the dragon became an exhalation, hissed hard between his teeth.

Great *God*, what the hell—

"I know who you are," said the woman in French. Her voice

was soft, melodious; it sent fresh shivers across his skin. She hesitated, then walked closer. Against the rigidly polished lines of the pianoforte, he realized she wore no clothing at all. "Do you know me, Lord Kimber of Chasen?"

He took an involuntary step forward. A thousand stories raced through his mind, explanations, excuses. There could be only one answer here, only one female in the world who could steal into his home undetected—

She lifted one hand, her fist closed. Without looking away from him, her fingers opened, and she inverted her palm. Twin flashes of metal fell to the rug, bounced against the woven flowers with a muffled tattoo before rolling flat.

She'd dropped rings, a pair of them. Signet rings.

Tribal rings. Exactly like the ones worn by Jeffrey and Luke and Hayden.

Kim raked his eyes back to hers.

"I've brought you a gift, as you can see." The Princess Maricara gave a small, chilly smile. "But perhaps we might make this an exchange instead. Is there something you wish to tell me?"

Mari's experience with Others was limited. She knew the peasants of her land—knew them well, in fact, as she had once been among them, although the manifestation of her dragon Gifts had set her undeniably apart.

She knew the visiting clerics who would on occasion attempt to ascend her mountain and preach to her people; after a few weeks of the feral alpine nights these men would nearly always retreat back into their safely walled chapels.

And she knew Zane, the thief, the husband of the *drákon* Lady Amalia.

She had not known him well, granted. Nearly all of their time together had been spent with Lia there too, the pair of them thick with secret looks and a language Mari hadn't mastered. But she had liked Lia well enough and was disposed to like Zane, who—for an Other—was handsome and quick-witted, and had eyes of golden amber.

It was possible that Mari had developed the very slightest infatuation for Zane during his months of stay at her castle.

But he was in love, and Lia was in love, and eleven-year-old Maricara had seen for herself what their love meant: blood and sacrifice and a great deal of noble, unspoken suffering. It had all been a little tedious.

Yet she remembered the man Zane for something more significant than his looks, or even his devotion to one of her kind. Maricara remembered Zane most for the very last words he spoke to her, just before climbing into his carriage and disappearing from her life.

He had turned to scan the small crowd in the castle courtyard waiting to see them both off, then limped slowly back to Maricara. She'd been standing farther away than most. The horses spooked when she ventured too near.

He'd taken her hand. He'd swept her a bow, even though he'd already bid her *adieu*.

"They're going to come for you," he'd murmured in French, very low.

Mari tipped her head, puzzled. There had been some discontent in the hold since the death of Imre, but surely even this human understood she could manage it.

"The serfs?" she'd inquired.

"No, Princess." Zane lifted his eyes and sent her that clever, crooked smile that had, just perhaps, made her heart beat somewhat faster. "The *drákon*. The English ones. They know about you now, and you'll be far more dear to them than any mere diamond. They *will* come." He released her hand with a final squeeze of her fingers. "A bit of unsolicited advice, my pet: They'll court you and flatter you and offer any sweet vow they'll think you want to hear. But you'd be a fool to trust them."

And he had walked back to the carriage and was gone.

So when she'd finally found her way to the outskirts of Darkfrith—a land as lush and distant as Lady Amalia had once dreamily described—Maricara was already on her guard, flying low, her senses prickling. Yet she was still taken by surprise at the sheer number of *drákon* patrolling the skies of this dark English place.

From miles away she had first begun to perceive them, initially just one, then three more, and then, suddenly—as the half-moon glowed across her back and she caught the fresh, warm scent of a river below—over two dozen. And they were a patrol, she could see that. They followed a set pattern, not deviating. Some were smoke; some were dragons.

Mari had banked instantly, wheeling back a few miles to conceal her trail, darting through a cover of hills and trees. It seemed to work; no one followed. Perhaps she had escaped before any of them felt her.

She landed beneath a shadowed outcropping of granite crumbling with lichen and remained there a good while, considering, observing.

She could not Turn to smoke to slip past them, not carrying her valise. It held all her garments and bread and cheese and some of her most favorite gemstones. Damned if she was going to leave it behind just to avoid a troop of sentries, and she suspected it was still much too far to Darkfrith to walk. Everything around here was either forest or field; she hadn't seen anything like a village in nearly an hour.

And if they were patrolling the skies, they were likely patrolling the ground as well, so she needed to be closer, already hidden in their center, if she was successfully going to avoid them.

She had crossed a sparkling channel of ocean that very morning. Mari didn't know what these English dragons were looking for, and at the moment, she didn't care. Her body ached, every joint and tendon. As a species the *drákon* were exceptionally strong, but she'd been approaching her limits for weeks now just to reach this place. It didn't seem fair that she'd have to surrender so near to her goal.

Maricara did not consider herself a fool. The English had sent envoys to her home despite her repeated directives they stay away. They'd been pushing to enter her realm for years and had apparently decided to no longer wait for an invitation. She would not simply promenade into their midst and request an audience with their Alpha, this Kimber earl. She needed surprise on her side. She needed every advantage.

Mari dug a single talon into the granite, thoughtful, pressing deep enough to crack the stone as she weighed her options.

She would have to be fleet. She would have to be silent. And she would have to fly very, very high above them, high enough so she would blend with the infinity of heaven should anyone glance up. At least there she had an advantage: By fate or chance Maricara was the only dragon she had ever seen without color. Even the creatures scoring the sky ahead of her shone bright like May ribbons in the light.

But *she*...she was formed of space and stars, her scales gleaming jet, her eyes and mane and the bare tips of her wings burning silver.

From the safety of her rock she Turned human to devour the last of the bread, the final, thin slices of the Camembert melting against her fingers. She licked her fingertips clean and settled back naked against the lichen, examining the patrol's distant flight.

After a full hour of surveillance she was able to predict their patterns, where they would loop and dip, how the wind would steer them. They were organized and tightly knit, but there was no real sense of urgency threading through the group. If they were hunting, they had not yet spotted their prey, and by all appearances the search was focused below them. Very well. With any luck at all, they'd keep their heads down and their sights fixed to the earth.

At least her valise was dark—not an accident.

Mari stood and brushed the bread crumbs from her stomach. She sent the English *drákon* one last glance, then Turned, picking up her valise—the leather handle like a familiar bit in her mouth—and launched herself high into the night.

The atmosphere was thicker here in England than in the alps, far more moist. Her wings beat against it. The air sucked hard between her teeth. It was never comfortable to attempt a straight rising vault, but she had to do it. She climbed and climbed, until her lungs labored and her claws opened and closed convulsively at nothing, scratching at the wind.

At the pinnacle of her ascent the ground was a remote, alluring span of ruffled darkness, the dragons below small toys and cottony flecks. Mari drew in a final enormous breath, took aim, then tucked her wings close and began her dive.

She had a single chance. There was only a single spot, a narrow rectangle of air left unguarded between the left-banking of a yellow dragon and the right return of a bottle-green one. It would be left exposed for twelve short seconds. If she hadn't made it by then, they'd discover her.

She dropped nearly without sound. The English weaved their paths, hushed and rhythmic, yellow dragon, bottle-green. The valise pressed like an iron weight into her throat; her stomach rose to meet it. A half league above the patrol, Maricara closed her eyes. She would make it or she wouldn't. She could feel the night with fiercely honed clarity, the *drákon* energies, their humming vigilance, the empty patch of air; she didn't care to see.

She shot through in a blur, the wind around her parting with the barest siss. The yellow dragon veered up at the last moment, then twisted right—the wrong way, but by then Mari was gone, Turning to smoke mere inches from the deadly tips of a grove of trees, losing the valise after all. It went smashing into the branches, striking the earth with a loud *thump.*

She sank into mist. She held close to the base of the trees, inert, willing herself into nothingness, only steam, only nature, nothing new or strange or wrong...

A host of dragons convened in the sky, circling. Two of them dropped into smoke and then became men, less than thirty feet distant.

Atom by atom, inch by inch, Maricara began to slink upward, following the knotty crevices of the pine tree she hugged, thin as a thread. She lurked in the first fork of the trunk as the men began to stalk the forest floor.

Her valise had not crashed all the way to the ground after all. It lay snared between two thick, high branches of a yew several yards away. A sprinkling of bark and small broken leaves dappled the ferns spreading beneath it.

The dragon-men hadn't yet drawn closer. They spoke to each other in low, English words, and paused at something Mari couldn't see. One of them squatted down and ran his fingers over the dirt.

She smelled it then, what he had found—deer scat, fresh. Blood on the thorns of a patch of briar. A hart had braved these woods tonight, perhaps more than one. Perhaps even as she had fallen.

Multumesc. Run faster, hart.

A hot breeze stirred and tried to pry her from the bark of her tree. She clung to it as the leaves on the ground flickered, releasing an aroma that covered the scat, thick and rich and earthy.

The dragon-men conferred a while longer, glancing around them. But eventually they Turned and left, rising up again to the stars.

Mari waited anyway, in case it was a trap, but when she opened her senses she found no trace of them nearby. They seemed actually gone.

She slithered back down to the roots of the pine. She Turned, crouching, lifting her face to that breeze, searching for a scent beyond that of trees and humus and whispering wheat.

No luck. England might be formed entirely of forest and heated air, for all she could tell. She rubbed her palms against her cheeks and tried again, fighting the exhaustion creeping black into her mind, and then, when she was ready to give up, to find a safe place to curl up in the leaves—she discovered it. A whiff of gold metal with saffron and hours-gone partridge, roasted with wine.

Surely the bouquet of a prince . . . or an earl, at the very least.

She Turned to smoke to reach her valise, to free it and tuck it deep within a hollow beneath its chosen yew. The case was very large, and it didn't fit easily, but she managed. When it was done she shook her hair over her shoulders and began, barefoot, to walk.

It took almost another hour to slip through the woods, to come upon the manor house in all its moonlit magnificence.

It *was* imposing. She'd truly seen nothing like it before, not in Hungary or Austria or Amsterdam. It was dun and massively sprawling, with three full wings and more glossy windows on a single side than all the walls of *Zaharen Yce* combined. There was a colossal dome of glass topping the main segment, an upside-down chalice of ice. Chimneys and cupolas studded the peaked slate roofs; limestone tracery scrolled across balconies and down every corner, ending in shaped shrubbery and waterfalls of flowers, and gargoyles that leaned and stared across silvery-blue gardens.

It was a place designed for humans, she thought, and then realized: to enthrall them. To ensure they would have no desire to glance in any other direction, especially upward.

So Maricara did, seeing nothing but the stars and the setting moon. Quickly, before she could change her mind, she darted across an expanse of cool, thick grass that cushioned the soles of her feet, ending in a coppice of willows. The main doors weren't far now. She could see them clearly even through the dark, planked wood and solid steel bracings. Another quick glance up; another sprint across the grass. She reached the doors and threw herself into the shelter of the carved stone archway surrounding them, panting.

When she could, she pressed her cheek to a panel and then one spread hand, seeking the presence of a hallboy or footman in the vestibule beyond.

Nothing. Her fingers slipped down to the latch.

The doors were locked, of course. More than locked. There were no keyholes, no slits of any kind piercing the heavy panels. The entire entrance was sealed tight against both men and smoke. Even the handles were soldered solid into the wood.

Well. At least she knew she was in the right place.

Mari turned around to face the lawn again, flexing her hand to get rid of the steel chill. That left just the windows. If the doors were that secure, no doubt the chimneys would be as well. At least glass could be broken.

She had to steal along the base of the manor to an entirely different wing before she found one open. And it wasn't even open, just cracked, as if someone had meant to shut it all the way but had gotten distracted before finishing the job.

Good enough. She Turned to smoke beneath it, squeezing past the sash.

It was a music room, very much like her own back home, with a pianoforte and a gilded lyre propped in a corner, pretty openwork chairs and cool, soothing colors on the walls. She became a woman in its darkest place, by the curtains, a sliver of a breeze from her passage bringing the scent of crushed flowers, stirring her hair against her hips.

There was no one else here. She was quite certain of that. There were smells and vibrations of the *drákon* everywhere, almost over-whelming—noises of them deeper in the halls, snoring; muttering; the sound of blankets rubbing, wool on wool—but this room was well deserted, and felt like it had been for some while. Even the pi-anoforte looked sleek and abandoned.

Such a place. She closed her eyes once more and inhaled deeply, taking in everything that she could, but nothing changed. The floors were beech over limestone, the ceiling was plastered, she was alone. So she moved back to the window, opened it wider and Turned again, siphoning outside to stand softly amid the bed of pansies below.

It was proving somewhat inconvenient to travel with things that would not Turn.

She tossed the rings she had left atop the dirt inside, followed them at once as smoke, and caught them in the palm of her hand before they even hit the rug.

Then she merely stood in place in the dark, savoring her victory.

Another girl, in another life, had once submitted to lessons on the pianoforte, but it was the harp that had captured her interest. The harp, with its taut strings and secret songs, with delicate har-monies only waiting to be revealed, had proven to be the favorite of a young princess. It was the only instrument that ever came close to echoing the music of diamonds.

With the rings in her hand Maricara found herself standing be-fore the lyre, a smaller thing, less majestic, but still shining with strings and a promise of the same sweet, sad songs. She wondered if any of the English ever really played it.

Her hand reached out. She touched a finger to the wood, and then to a string, long and tight, feeling the coiled note that wanted to come.

And it was in that exact moment, with her arm outstretched and her back to the door, that she realized she was no longer alone.

Nothing visible had changed. No new shadows, no new breath. She couldn't even hear a heartbeat, which was the most startling fact of all, because Maricara had never met anyone, not human or dragon, whose heart did not betray them, even by the slightest murmur of sound.

But no—all she felt was the difference. The change around her, intangible, a subtle, mounting shock against her unclad skin, vibration that did not cease but expanded, enveloping her body and her blood and nerves, piercing down into the corners of her marrow:

Animal.

Virile.

Male.

She moved her head, only that, and saw what she had not before: the outline of him against the doorway, more stealth than man, and the pulse of *drákon* pounding between them, so powerful she felt herself rocking with it.

He eased forward. She remained where she was, breath caught, and when he shifted again she saw him fully.

The *drákon* were comely. Every one of them, from newborn child to wizened old man, was comely, because that was one of their Gifts. As dragons they were lithe and elegant; as humans they were nearly the same, with skin pure as alabaster and colors reflecting all the best of nature, gold and copper and oak, sky-blue, deep mahogany. Even a faded hint of dragon blood could be obvious in otherwise ordinary serfs: an unmarked complexion, slender bones, lips that smiled cold red.

But this man...this man was different. There was nothing faded about him.

He had the golden hair, the fair skin she had seen grace a few others of her kind. But he was muscular where Imre had been slim, tall and substantial where her husband had been like vapor in the night, never stable.

He was motionless as well, staring at her, his eyes pale green and hostile, and she realized that also unlike Imre—who seldom desired direct confrontation—this creature was poised to attack. *Would* attack if he thought her a threat—without pause, without regret.

She caught his scent now too, night and wine and musky perspiration. A faint tinge of saffron.

Ah. Of course the earl would find her. Of course he would.

He let out a breath, and with it—everything changed. His expression turned sharper, more wolfish; he shifted instantly from one kind of predator to another.

With the sudden impression of sinking into a hot, murky lake, Maricara began to understand the depth of her folly. They stared at each other with the heat and the tension aching between them, his musk and her surprise and the moonlight burning white fire across her shoulders.

The earl's gaze flicked up and down her body, just once, but it was beast bright, enough to sear her to the bone.

Zane's warning of so long ago had been in vain after all.

Too late. Only a fool would have ventured here.

CHAPTER FIVE

It was interesting to note that in all his years of superior education and well-financed travel, in his time spent at Eton and Cambridge and London, all those carefully shaped lessons in society and etiquette both human and *drákon,* not once had anyone ever mentioned to Kimber what to do when confronted with a nude, unexpected princess in his music chamber.

Nude... and gorgeous. Undeniably gorgeous.

"I beg your pardon," Kim said, also in French. "Would you care to sit down?"

Her eyes narrowed. "I would *care* to have you explain these."

He did not glance again at the rings she'd tossed between them; he didn't even follow the flash of her arm as she gestured at them. He didn't quite dare lower his gaze below her chin. Not again. Instead, he studied her face.

He knew her age, but she appeared younger than that; it might have been the moonlight smoothing her skin, or the long, shining fall of her hair that—thank heavens—managed to conceal most of her body. She looked familiar and yet not; a *drákon* and not; he was accustomed to females of flaxen locks, or ginger, or gilt. Only a very few of the tribe had such dark hair, and no one at all had eyes like that, strange and clear and haunting.

Alpha, whispered the dragon in him, still rising. Every nerve ending in his body felt it, the strength of her Gifts, her subtle, feminine perfume. She *was* Alpha, just like him. She'd been naught but smoke minutes past, and he could feel that as well, the force of her Turn—that smoldering, pleasurable sting of gunpowder. It flooded his senses; he felt nearly dizzy with it.

Even his sisters weren't so Gifted. Perhaps not even Rue.

Mother of God, once the council realized she was here—

"Your men are dead," the princess said, when he only stood there staring.

"Yes," Kimber said slowly. "I see."

"I did not kill them."

"I didn't say you did. Excuse me, please, I think perhaps I'll take a seat, if you won't."

He found the peach-blossom Hepplewhite chair, the one he always sat in because it was closest to the door. The stuffed satin felt cool against his back, stiff and uncomfortably real. He made a conscious effort to keep his hands on his thighs, his posture relaxed. Princess Maricara watched him without moving.

"You seem quite at ease with my news." Her head tilted; she studied him without expression. "You sent two men to me, Lord Kimber. I've come to tell you they died brutal deaths, deaths I would not tolerate for even the lowest of creatures."

"Three," Kim said.

"What?"

"I sent three men to find you," he answered softly.

"Oh." That reached her, at least a little. Her brows knit; she lowered her chin and returned to the pianoforte, slipping easily back into shadow. "Why?"

"Why did I send them to you?"

"Yes."

He felt his lips curve, nothing close to humor. "We're family. Families should be intimate. It generates . . . trust."

"Dispatching spies to my home against my expressed wishes is hardly an act of trust, Lord Chasen."

"Ah, but we *drákon* are an altogether different sort of family. Don't you agree?"

She laid her hand flat atop the pianoforte, not answering. His vision was better adjusted now; he could see her very well even in the gloom, the line of her back beneath her hair, the slope of her buttocks. The rise and fall of her chest.

"The strong devour the weak," she murmured, and lifted her head. "That's what my husband used to tell me. Is that the sort of family you are, as well?"

"No. We're not wolves. We protect the weak."

"I am not weak. And I don't require your protection."

Now his smile came more wry. "Clearly not. You've evaded an entire contingent of my best guards. I rather think I might need protection from *you*."

She stared at her spread fingers against the wood, then shook her head. "You've no idea."

He let that settle between them, trying not to betray himself: not to breathe too deeply, or move too quickly. Not to follow his instincts and act to bind her here and now. Instead, Kimber said, "Tell me who was killed."

"I didn't discover their names. There were no documents on the bodies. They had nothing but the clothing on their backs, and those." She motioned again to the rings. "It was enough to lead me here."

"And where is your escort?" he asked, very mild. "Do they wait in the woods?"

She let out a sound, a small huff of air that could have been either amusement or offense. "Do you truly imagine I would tell you?"

"I'm not your enemy, Your Grace."

"No?"

"Nor were my men."

"I told you—"

"You didn't kill them. I know. But as of this moment, I have only your word that they're even dead. Summon your escort here. Have them enter my home in peace, no weapons, and we'll discuss the matter further. No one need get hurt."

Her face turned to his. Against the pianoforte she was a sylph, a frozen ghost. She gave him a long, measuring look with eyes of frost that seemed to strip every secret from his soul.

"I've made a mistake," the princess said at last. "I see that."

Kimber gripped his hands to the arms of the chair. "Let me get you a room. And—perhaps some clothing—"

"No, thank you."

He could have stopped her. He was reasonably sure he could have. She was smaller than he, by nature less strong, even if she was a leader among her kind. But instead he remained as he was, holding her gaze, silently willing her to show him the proof of what he already knew, what the dragon in him recognized and roared through his blood.

She smelled of youth, and power, and heated woman. It was all he could do to remain in the chair.

"Maricara," he said. "If you go now, you know I'll simply have to fetch you back. Surely we could spend our time together in more productive ways than that."

It was a provocation, a deliberate one, and she rose to it with merely a disdainful lift of one finely arched brow.

"I didn't grant you leave to call me by my given name," she said, and Turned, flowing like water out the open window, dissolving at once into the night.

His fingers cracked the wood of both arms.

It was true. Lia's letter, the *drákon* of the Carpathians, all of it. *True.*

Kimber released the ruined chair, one finger at a time, then glanced back at the pair of rings on the floor, small gleams in the weakening light. He scooped them both into a palm.

Two of his men were dead, two at least. There was simply no other way they would have surrendered the rings. The signets were given to young men of the shire upon their completion of their first Turn, a mark of pride and maturity, of union with the tribe. In their own way they were considered sacred. Some men even used them as wedding rings; widows would wear them on chains.

The three *drákon* he had sent in search of *Zaharen Yce,* in search of the princess, were more than just trusted comrades, more than just friends. They were his kin. And they would have died with these rings still on their hands.

The irony of it was not lost upon him: that in their deaths, they had delivered him his bride.

A dim flare of gold encircled his finger, his own signet, masculine and heavy but exactly the same as the other two in his palm.

Kimber shut his eyes. He felt the warm weight of the metal in his hand, its muted song, and closed his fingers hard around it.

It was time to rouse the manor house.

That morning, in the short, shadowed hours that lingered just before sunrise, in the darkest depths of the sky—a nexus so deep even the stars had abandoned it—a black dragon flew, twisting, writhing, a streamer of frenzied grace.

And when the members of the tribe saw her, when they

launched in pursuit, she vanished, black on black. They were left chasing only the dawn.

The windows to the council's quarters were normally kept sealed. The room faced north and was darker than most within the mansion; the candles in the chandelier burning above them managed to banish the shadows from the corners. But council meetings were formal affairs, with wigs, and cravats, and full coats. It was cursed hot.

The tradition of secrecy weighed heavy against Kim's craving for unstifled air. After forty interminable minutes of suffering, he abandoned his chair and opened every casement. None of the others protested. They were all tired of sweating.

Besides, very little of what would happen next would remain secret for long. The council knew of the princess, the village knew of her. Half the population of the shire had witnessed her flight early this morning. Everyone expected action.

It was difficult in the harsh light of noon to recall her in the night, to summon the image of her face and form. He remembered that she was beautiful; he remembered being unable to breathe with her beauty. But caught first in his memory were brighter, less typical impressions: how her skin glowed in the moonlight. How her hair divided around her shoulders. The smoky-sweet timbre of her voice. Her scent, a perfume of flowers and gunpowder and summer heat.

Kim slouched back in his chair, tapping his fingers idly against one thigh. He listened with half an ear to the meeting as he stared out the nearest window, immersed in his memories. The colors of the day were sun-washed, bleached pale . . . but what he saw was a slender dragon dyed midnight, with silver eyes and delicate wings, reaching for the infinity of the cosmos with a high and reckless abandon.

His people were so contained in flight. Even hunting, even soaring for joy, there was discipline in every motion, bridled deliberation. Watching Maricara fly had been like watching a kite cut loose from its tether. He'd never truly realized how controlled they all were, until he'd caught sight of her.

She flew utterly without fear. She flew with something almost like—desperation. He'd never seen anything so fascinating in his life.

Perhaps it had only been a taunt. He couldn't imagine why else she'd take to the skies after their meeting. She had to have known he'd have every man in the shire combing heaven and earth for her.

"...could not be more than twenty, thirty men," one of the council was saying. "Because where would they be? Obviously they're nowhere near Darkfrith. We would have felt so many. We would have felt even one if they were hiding so close to the shire."

"We didn't feel *her,*" challenged Rhys, setting off a swell of muttering. Kim dragged his attention back to the chamber. Accompanying the sweltering thick air were distinctly rising tempers.

The room was set up with four rectangular tables placed as a square in the center of the room. The scribe and all twelve members of the council sat facing each other, with Kim's chair—larger, slightly more ornate—placed off the side of the empty west corner, where he could view them all. His father's father, the first Marquess of Langford, had devised the arrangement to convey a very calculated message: This was not Arthur and his round table. The council members passed laws for the good of the tribe, and the Alpha would conform to those laws as long as it suited him to do so—but in the end, he remained sovereign, alone and apart.

Always apart.

As the second son of the marquess, Rhys had been born to his position on the council, and Kim was usually glad of it. Behind his brother's nonchalant veneer was an astute, practical man who more often than not could be counted on to rein in some of the more extreme suggestions of the others. But today that veneer was beginning to fray. His hair showed disheveled beneath his iron-gray wig, his cheeks dark with new beard. Like everyone else here, he'd been up since the middle of last night. Also like everyone else, he'd glimpsed the princess in flight.

It had been only moments; just a few short minutes of her silhouetted against the hollow sky, her remarkable eyes, her cunning flips and tight rolls. It was one thing to read in a letter that there existed another female who could Turn. It was quite another to see her in real life, to *feel* her: sensuality and black glittering splendor, a dragon unlike any other, supple and absolutely feminine.

Feminine.

Aye. And every male had noticed *that,* Kim knew.

What he'd said to Maricara last night was true. They were *not* wolves. They were not like any of the lower beasts, and not even like humans. They had their pack of sorts; the tribe was an intricately knit society of families who wed and bred and seldom looked beyond the boundaries of the shire for mates. It did happen on occasion—Kim's own maternal grandfather had been a Welshman, his legacy still visible in Rhys's dark hair, Audrey's chocolate eyes. But there were punishments for such transgressions, not the least of which was social banishment. His grandmother had died a widow, and alone. It was better to keep to their own.

The *drákon* chose mates for life. It was a plain fact among them. One male, one female, and from them new generations to sustain the shire. Courting and wooing followed a more human path, it was true, with a fair amount of leniency allowed to young sweethearts. There were lovers' games and tears and heartbreaks aplenty across the village—maidens who liked boys, boys who liked other maidens, an endless cycle of flirtation and investigation. God knew he'd spent enough time himself as a youth exploring all the best pockets of the woods.

Wedding vows put an end to all that. Once man and wife

brushed lips in the cool marble sanctity of Darkfrith's chapel, their lives were bound. Fidelity was etched across their hearts, as bright and undeniable as gold upon the sun.

Young as she was, Maricara was a widow as well. There wasn't the slightest chance in hell she was going to remain that way long, no matter where she flew.

She'd been engaged to him since she was practically a child. It didn't matter that she had no idea; all that mattered was that Kimber knew, and the council, and all the members of the tribe. Alpha mated to Alpha. The fact that the princess possessed the Gifts she did catapulted her into that status, no matter her background.

Once, every single *drákon* grew into their abilities. Once, males and females alike would reach puberty and take flight. But the Gifts were inexplicably thinning from generation to generation. There hadn't been a female born who could Turn since—well, years.

And just like Kimber, Rhys Langford was directly related to the only other four who could.

Kim lowered his lashes and considered his brother. Rhys noticed; his gaze shot to Kimber, then back to the man opposite him. He leaned forward in his chair to clasp his hands loosely upon the table. There was a subtle edge to his voice Kim had not heard before.

"She managed to slip past *you*, Rufus, even on full patrol. She rendered moot all your impressive defenses and infiltrated Chasen Manor as easily as if it were a public coffeehouse. And for all that, the only person who even felt her intrusion was the Alpha."

"No," said another man at once. Anton Larousse. Good-looking. Unwed. He also sat forward, a scant indication of belligerence in the set of his jaw. "I felt her. But I was at the mill, miles away. I didn't know where she went."

"I felt her too," declared Claude Grady, also unwed. "I was on the patrol, and I knew something was wrong—"

Rhys snorted. "Bullocks. She got past all of you. I'd wager she and her men are holed up somewhere right under our noses."

"That's not possible," said Grady flatly.

"No," agreed a third man, John Chapman. Unlike the others, he was in his sixties, stout, very married. He dug a finger against the creased collar of his jabot, his neck flushed and moist. "Even in the woods, such a contingent of *drákon* would be noticeable. It's possible they're disguised as humans. They could be in one of the towns, Durham or Ripon, somewhere like that. Someplace fairly large, where they could more easily establish a base without a fuss. She's far more likely to slip by in a city than anywhere rural. Country folk notice strangers."

"Especially those who don't speak English," said Kim. "I think John's got the right idea. We need to expand the search."

Rhys unclasped his hands. His voice kept its strange, hard note. "I'll take Durham. I'll need four others who don't mind..."

But Kimber was no longer listening. Between one breath and the next, he felt the change. It was that sudden, that complete. He was looking at his men, the pewter shadows of the room, the waxed reflection of the tables and the chandelier above them throwing crystal blades of light, and then he turned his head and saw the gentle, betraying billow of the pale blue velvet curtains of the far window. The almost invisible swathe of smoke that condensed into something more substantial: a woman's leg. A woman's hand, her fingers fanned against the blue, holding the material high against her chest.

Her face. Her eyes, lifting straight to his.

Kim held immobile, wondering if he was more tired than he even thought, if after hours without sleep he was finally imagining her standing there behind the drapery. But Maricara looked away from him to the rest of the room and released a little breath. A beat of suspended silence followed; small as it was, everyone had heard it.

"*Princesse,*" he greeted her, and surged to his feet before anyone could wrench from their surprise to do something stupid. He sketched a short bow, continuing in French. "Welcome back."

"Lord Chasen." She offered him a nod, her cheek and chin cupped with blue velvet. "I thought I'd spare you the fetching, as you put it. But I see you're busy."

He had to think without thought; he had to convey what he wanted of his men without a single glance in their direction.

Don't move. Nobody bloody move a bloody damned muscle—

Kim gave an easy smile. "You've had us a bit tangled in knots, I fear. There was some concern for your welfare."

"How sorry I am to have worried you. But I've been quite safe, I assure you."

"Excellent. Happy to hear it." He risked a glimpse at the council then, their ominous faces, their shoulders taut with restraint; he smiled again at the princess. "And your guard?"

"Most content."

"We didn't spot them with you this morning. They allow you to fly without accompaniment?"

He hadn't really expected much of a response; she seemed as polished as porcelain. But at his words emotion flashed behind those clear gray eyes, alarm or consternation, swiftly erased.

Perhaps she'd thought she'd been unseen. It seemed unlikely— she had crisscrossed the sky nearly just above Chasen. But she'd been so quick, and disappeared so effectively. It was conceivable she'd thought she fooled them all.

"It was a lovely dawn," he said placidly.

"I fly as I please," Maricara said at last. "The guard allows me nothing. *I* am the princess."

From the corner of his eye Kim saw Larousse, damn him, begin to push back his chair, rise to his feet. Maricara switched her focus instantly to him.

"Your Grace," he said, also bowing. "You honor us. Please, won't you—"

But he obviously couldn't offer her a seat, not as she was. Kimber watched him comprehend it, that not only had she managed to show up without warning, that she was nude, that she had to be, and the lines of her figure were clearly visible even beneath the curtain's folds. The councilman's face slowly began to flush.

"I won't trouble you long," said Maricara. "No doubt you have all manner of pressing plans to consider. Spies to engage. Betrayals to enact. That sort of thing."

"Only on Sundays," Kim replied. "It's Tuesday. We're discussing stealing sweetmeats from small children today."

She didn't return his smile. The fingers of her right hand remained pressed lightly against the velvet.

She had to realize the danger surrounding her: that she was alone, and female, come to a room full of silent, eager beasts who certainly all felt her as strongly as he did in such close quarters. She had to have realized everything she chanced, and still she only stood there with an air of bored civility, as if she had arrived to take tea instead of facing down the living dark congress of the tribe.

Kim began to shrug out of his coat. He was glad to do it, glad to have an excuse to walk toward her, to put himself between her and the tables of other *drákon* men. With his back to the council he held out the coat, lapels open. Maricara gave him another long, assessing look with her mirror eyes—he felt exposed with it, like she was plucking the thoughts from his head—he hoped to God not— and Turned to smoke.

Damn.

Silently he willed all the men to calm; he still didn't dare to shift his gaze to warn them. He'd seen her do it before and yet again the sensation lit through him, as blatantly alluring as that bare leg had been or the image of her body beneath velvet. She could *Turn*. There was scarcely anything more desirable in a female. But she had gotten in twice; she had escaped twice. How difficult could it be for her to manage it a third time—

Yet all that happened was someone's chair tapped against the table, and the blue drapery sighed back into place.

The princess became a pillar of smoke before him, rising, filling the shell of his coral brocade coat all the way to the sleeves. Then she was woman, scent and power, just like last night, the back of her head nearly bumping his nose.

He released the heavy coat as if it burned. It fell to her shoulders, pinning her hair. She bent her neck and reached up to run a wrist beneath the trapped strands—in the daylight he could see the color wasn't black but the deepest brown he could imagine—before taking a step away.

He was taller than she, much larger. He'd never thought to be glad the council held to court dress, but the coat was old-fashioned, long-skirted. It reached almost to her knees.

"My thanks," Maricara said.

"My pleasure," he answered, and put another step between them. "Do join us." He motioned to his empty chair.

She traversed the chamber on silent feet. The skirted coat rose to her thighs when she sat down. Kim looked away, drew in a slow, silent breath, letting it burn before he released it.

Beneath the scattered prisms of the chandelier, Rhys was staring at her, his eyes masked and brooding. Everyone was staring at her, but Rhys...

Something cold began to uncoil through Kimber's gut. Something painful and unpleasant.

"I thought you'd wish to know the manner in which your men died," said Maricara, crossing her ankles beneath the chair. "I realized only this afternoon that we didn't discuss it."

"No. We didn't."

"They were ambushed. That's what I believe. Others found them and took out their hearts."

No one gasped; no one stirred. Only Kimber said, "Pardon?"

"Others. Human men. They stole their hearts."

He'd informed the council of what she'd told him the night before. He'd shown them the rings and let the speculation unwind.
There was no proof of anything—until she'd shown up hours later,
flying through the dark, there was no proof even that she had ever
come—except for those rings. And the fact that three good men
had dropped from the face of the earth.

"Don't you have hunters in this land?" the princess asked.

Rhys leaned forward again, intent. "What do you mean?"

"At home we call them *sanf inimicus*. I don't know a term for
them in French. Hunters. Humans who hunt the *drákon*."

"No," Kim said. "Not for generations."

"We do," she said simply.

He stared at her blankly, for the first time seeing not her beauty
or her potential, but only a woman in a chair, calmly informing
him of the unthinkable.

"If your men confessed before they died," continued Maricara
in her attractive, melodic voice, "if they traveled with papers that
mentioned you, or carried any hint of this place, the *sanf* now
know of you too."

It wasn't possible. It should not be possible. These were not the
Dark Ages. This was today, and England, and it had taken them
centuries to get here, to embed themselves in Darkfrith's safety. No
one would truly dare breach it.

They were *normal* here. They *fit*. This was their home.

Others come.

Kimber thought of the sprawling village unprotected, of the
women who could not fly, and the dragon-children who played
openly in the fields and dells. He thought of the thick woods and
the manor house and all the careful, careful lies that had been created to sustain their lives in this idyllic place.

He thought of Hayden, and Jeffrey, and Luke. Of Zoe Lane's
stark, pinched face.

A great, static rage began within him, a storm of blinding white.

Maricara uncrossed her ankles and stood, forcing all the council to hastily scrape back their chairs. She smoothed a hand down the front of Kimber's coat. "By the by, is there anything to eat? I'm famished."

CHAPTER SIX

I should not have to speak to you of your own history. No doubt you know it far better than I, who was merely able to glean chunks and tidbits from terrible conversations under the worst of circumstances.

For nearly as long as there have been dragons, there have been humans come to hunt them. You are lesser and jealous and brimming with false conceit: Centuries ago, when we first realized you were more than a few misguided knights or villagers—that you were organized, that you were brutal—we devised a name for you. *Sanf inimicus*, the enemy of soft skin. And you snatched it from our lips and wore it like a badge, with all apparent pride.

You have your own traditions, I know that. You have your secret order, nearly as secret as ours, with a leader of not inconsiderable skills. We are born to our magnificence, family after family; you recruit from the lowest of your own kind and of ours to fill your ranks. I imagine it's not entirely effortless to persuade any human of reasonable intelligence that they ought to begin hunting dragons. Yet you do persevere.

I understand your rage, your envy, your blood-cold fear of us.

I even understand your desire to do us harm. I will admit that once, a very long time past, there were those among us who enjoyed the taste of your flesh—although frankly I myself can scarcely stand the stench of you. Devouring you would be repulsive at best.

But it took me a very long while to understand why, after you killed us, you desired to tear out our hearts. Was it to prove the illusion of your strength? To extend your short, hollow victory over a creature greater than yourselves?

This is what I believe, and really, it could hardly be a surprise: You wish you were us. In the black sticky chambers of what you call a soul, you think to compensate for your weakness by consuming our cores. Our hearts, the throbbing muscle of our power.

Well, eat away. You're still going to lose.

CHAPTER SEVEN

It was a vast and mysterious place. Chasen Manor held all the en-
trapments of an opulent palace, with rock crystal and precious
metals lavished about, and oil paintings of villas and masted ships
and unsmiling people. There were busts carved from jasper and alabaster and shiny black onyx. There were statues of goddesses with
arrows in their hands, and a pair of bronze lions prowling around
the corner of the main staircase.

And there were *drákon* everywhere.

In *Zaharen Yce* dragon blood flowed through the veins of nearly
every person who walked the halls, freeman or noble or serf. There
were a few like her, with the Gifts readily apparent, but time had
diminished the population of the keep. Most of those left were
more human than not. They lived there and they served there, and

the echo of a shared, glorious past kept them all bound to the land and the principality. Yet every single being Maricara sensed here— in the corridors; in the elaborate, elegant rooms; above and even below, far below, in what felt like the basements—every one of them gave off the distinct, sparkling sensation of *drákon*.

They were not serfs. When she glanced at them they stared boldly back at her, men and women both. They wore their hair powdered into curls, or wigs of human hair, not horse. They twinkled with stickpins and necklaces and earbobs that chimed with melodies, louder and softer as she came closer and then moved away.

There were no diamonds hidden in the walls here. She supposed there didn't need to be; Mari had never been around so many people who dripped with gemstones. Even the earl's tailored coat had bands of seed pearls stitched along the lapels and cuffs. She'd kept her fingers cupped to touch them, to feel their small, pleasant humming as she walked the halls.

Her night had been oblivion. She'd returned to the woods without being followed—it appeared the earl hadn't even bothered to try, actually—and found again her secret tree, her valise. Mari had slept in all manner of accommodations en route to this place, from dank caves to empty attics, and once an amazing bedchamber of silver looking glasses and ormolu wood, with a feather mattress that sank beneath her weight like a cloud. The sunset that evening had struck the glasses and suffused the room with blinding, amber-pink radiance, picking out the pattern of crossed lavender stems painted up and down the wallpaper.

That had been in Beaumont-sur-Vesle. France had been littered with deserted estates.

Last night she'd slept on leaves, burrowed up against the ancient gnarled roots of the yew. She'd awoken hours later right where she was supposed to be, even still wrapped in the blanket she'd packed.

No one seemed to have discovered her. Nothing seemed to have happened, except she'd gained a bruise on her hip from an inconvenient shard of granite embedded in the ground.

But she'd flown. The earl had said it and Maricara believed it. Even here, even so wrenched with exhaustion she hadn't minded the grit of dirt beneath her cheek, as long as she could lie down and close her eyes... she had flown.

Little wonder she had roused so late, and still felt so drained.

She'd only discovered the bruise when left alone in someone's private quarters, changing into the same someone's day gown stored in a cedar chest. Lord Chasen had suggested it, and this time Mari had accepted. It seemed prudent to continue her day in something more than just a layer of brocade over her uncovered skin.

She chose the simplest gown; she'd already refused an offer to send for maids. With panniers instead of a polonaise it was slightly *démodé*, but it fit her very well, ivory muslin embroidered with sprigs of lavender, a scalloped petticoat of translucent plum gauze. It reminded her greatly of that sad, empty chateau in France.

Still, it was better than Lord Chasen's coat. If the men of this place still stared at her now, at least she knew it wasn't at her legs.

Silk stockings, satin slippers. Hoops. A corset that squeezed her breath. A white ribbon for her hair. It felt odd to garb herself as a real woman again. She'd spent so much time in scales, or beneath her blanket. Mari lifted a wrist and took note of the lace that fell from her forearm to almost the overskirt; the English did naught by halves.

There were no listening holes in the walls here. She'd tapped her knuckles against the rose-colored plaster and heard nothing hollow. The windows were tall and offered a panorama of china-blue sky and sloping green hills. The door had a brass polished key lodged in its socket.

There were people speaking; there were footsteps, and wood creaking in the joints of the floors. She heard her name whispered over and over, like ripples on the surface of the ocean, surging and fading, doomed to repeat.

Mari stood a long while before the window and gazed out at the hot, empty sky. Slowly her arms rose to press her palms over her ears.

That was how the earl found her.

This time she felt his approach. He was near, the door opened. When she didn't turn around he walked closer, the minute vibrations of his stride traveling up her legs, settling in her center. He came to stand beside her, avoiding her elbow, his hands clasped behind his back. His coral-and-pearl coat lay where she'd tossed it on the bed. He wore a waistcoat of matching brocade, a shirt with lace much shorter than her own.

Kimber sent her a sidelong look. His eyes were very green.

"Does that work?" he inquired.

She lowered her arms. "No."

"Pity. One might imagine the joy of absolute silence."

"I don't believe there's such a thing."

"Perhaps not. Not for us."

Then he was quiet, apparently examining the view. He smelled now of coriander and freshly baked bread; she willed her stomach not to growl. She wasn't going to ask again for food.

"You have a bird out there," she said, "due east. It's singing."

He frowned slightly at the woods. Now that she was more attuned to him she could sense his concentration shifting, beyond the forest of heavy trees, to space and distance and those pure, perfect notes that broke the air. Between this moment and the last time she'd seen him he'd removed his wig, tied back his hair; the light from the window revealed layers of tawny brown beneath the burnished gold.

"It's a thrush."

She repeated the English word, liking the feel of it on her tongue. "A thrush. It's very far away."

"Yes." His tone grew drier. "They don't come near."

"It's the same at my home."

Mountain or woods, valley or windswept canyon: Every animal that could stayed away from *Zaharen Yce* and all its surroundings. Until she'd reached her fourteenth year, she'd never even glimpsed a living deer. How much worse it would be here, with all these shining, human-faced dragons milling about.

"She sings a beautiful song," Mari said.

"Yes," the earl said again. And then: "This chamber was—is my sister's. Amalia."

"Oh."

"Clearly she's not using it. It's yours if you like. I don't think she'd mind."

"Thank you, but no."

"There's room for your men, as well. It's a deuced big place."

"I see that. But we'll do better apart."

"Maricara—"

"No," she said, firmer than before. "I will not lodge here with you, Lord Chasen."

He opened his mouth, then closed it again. He looked away from her with an air of complete tranquility. She didn't imagine he was accustomed to refusal; he didn't seem a man who would take resistance lightly under any circumstance, Alpha or no. But he only subsided back into himself, as if he had nothing more pressing to do than appreciate the perfectly framed vista before them.

She felt the contradiction in him, though. She felt the raw power boiling beneath his elegant restraint.

"Dinner," announced a voice behind them, "is well served."

They turned together. The man leaning his shoulder casually against the doorjamb was not a footman or servant but clearly another nobleman. His cravat was bleached and fine; there was a large rounded emerald strung from a wire hoop in one ear, just a few hues darker than the color of his eyes.

"Your Grace," murmured Kimber. "My brother, Lord Rhys Langford."

She lifted a hand, and the brother pushed off the door. He bowed low over her fingers but did not kiss her; she felt the faintest prickling across her skin where his mouth would have brushed her knuckles.

She remembered him from the meeting of all those red-cheeked men. She remembered the particular touch of his stare.

The earl shifted a fraction on his feet. Lord Rhys dropped her hand at once.

"I hope you like trout," he said cheerfully, and looked at Kimber. "Mac and his boys went to the lake this morning and caught a cartful. We'll be lucky if we finish it tonight. I don't fancy fish for breakfast."

Mari loathed fish. She loathed it almost as much as she loathed cabbage.

"That will be lovely," she said, and accepted the earl's arm as escort from the room.

Kimber smelled of bread because he'd been near the kitchens, he must have been. Not only was there bread and herbed butter, there was potato custard, and baked apples with Cheddar, and a salad of tossed greens and oil. The dining hall was even more elaborate than any of the rooms she'd seen yet, entire walls composed of sheets of malachite and amber, a ceiling adorned in painted animals and sunset clouds, bleeding down into the stone yellow and green. It was cooler in here than the rest of the mansion. Great black iron braziers in the corners held dozens of candles, unlit, teardrops of honey-scented wax falling frozen in twists and turns.

White wine had been poured; the china was edged in a chorus of bright silver. Mari took the seat offered her, to the earl's left. The brother sat opposite her. There were footmen and livery boys lined along the far wall. None of the council were present.

The wine held the aroma of pears and crisp autumn. She missed her castle suddenly, the mountains and the vineyards cut like stair steps into the vertical hills; missed it all with a ferocity that clenched like a band around her chest.

"Pray forgive the informality," the earl was saying in his flawless French. His accent wasn't quite Parisian. Marseille, she thought, or Monaco-Ville. Somewhere south. "With such short notice for a meal, I thought you'd like it better if we kept the company small."

"There are more of us," agreed Rhys, flicking open his napkin. "Two more, our sisters. Well, there's three of them, actually. But there—you knew that."

Mari took her eyes off the platter of boned fish softly steaming atop the sideboard. "Yes. Lady Amalia spoke well of you all."

"Did she indeed?" Lord Rhys glanced at his brother. "That's a goddamned shock."

Kimber's mouth thinned, just slightly. "Rhys."

"Oh, sorry." Rhys picked up his wine. "How was she, the last you saw her?"

"In good health. Pensive. Happy. At least with her husband, she was happy."

"Oh, yes. Her *husband* Zane."

"You don't approve of him," Mari said, unsurprised.

In the shadows of the room, Rhys gave a shrug. "What's to approve or not? He's a thief. He's human. She's made her choice clear, wherever she is."

"She's in Brussels," said Mari. Both men stared at her; she looked from one to the other. "At least, she was about a fortnight ago. Didn't you realize?"

"No," said the earl at last. "We've not heard from her, not for years. Not since that initial letter she sent with yours."

"Ah." Mari lowered her gaze to her hands on her lap.

"What's she doing in Brussels?" demanded Rhys.

"I don't know. I didn't see her. I only felt her as I went by."

"You *felt* her." The corners of Kimber's lips now took on a peculiar slant, the barest hint of doubt. "In a city that large?"

"I didn't actually go through the city. I went through Schaerbeek. It was more direct."

Rhys shook his head. "You weren't even in the same vicinity, and you felt her. Just...going by."

"Yes. Lady Amalia's Gifts are most distinct."

Rhys let out a laugh. "That's splendid. I expect she's using them well in *Brussels,* with Mother and Father gone searching high and low for her. God forbid she return home with that bastard in tow—"

"Rhys," said the earl once more, silky soft, and his brother gave another shrug, subsiding back.

"He's a fine man," said Maricara. "Human or not."

Kimber nodded to the footmen to begin serving. "I'm sure that's so."

"Attractive. Intelligent. Devoted."

"So's a good dog," said Rhys.

Maricara flattened her hands upon her skirts. "I'm not going to marry you, Lord Chasen."

Rhys choked a little; the head footman fumbled and recovered his serving spoon. Kimber only paused with his water goblet raised to his lips, then lowered the glass gently back to the table.

"Excuse me?"

"I will not marry you. I want that to be plain between us right now."

"Your Grace, I assure you—"

"I know how we are, Kimber." Her use of his name startled

him; she'd meant it to. "I know how we think. You're the Alpha, and you're not wearing a wedding band, and no one has come forward to me as your wife. You perceive that I'm also Alpha, and this is true. But I'm not one of your people. I rule a land, even though it's far away. I control my fate, not you. I won't wed you."

Kimber lowered his lashes. He kept his fingers loosely cupped around the stem of his goblet.

"You're not remarried?"

"No."

"I thought your brother ruled *Zaharen Yce*."

"Nominally. In my absence."

His eyes lifted to hers, bright piercing green. "Your people allow a female to lead them?"

It was a trap, she realized. If she said yes, he'd think the Zaharen weak, the castle open for the taking. If she said no, he'd think she was lying before.

She wasn't willing to be bartered. Not ever again.

Maricara motioned to the footman, who hurried over with the fish. She allowed herself to be served one thick, blanched fillet, the flesh oozing butter across her plate. Without waiting for the others, she lifted her fork and took a bite, chewed, and swallowed.

"We're not so very alike," she said at last, to the fish. "Whatever kinship we once shared has been stretched thin with time. No doubt there are many of our ways you would find foreign, as I do yours."

"No doubt," Kimber replied, unmoving. "But I look forward to celebrating our differences, Your Grace."

"As long as that's all you wish to celebrate."

"It's a promising start."

"Or a natural conclusion," said Mari, and took another odious bite.

She used the lemon fork for the fish, and the fish fork for the salad. She ate in small, tentative mouthfuls, as if the flavors were all new to her, as if she had to explore each and every texture and spice before moving on to the next bite. Her expression remained aloof as she dined, her dark hair tied back with a simple ribbon like a girl's, like a *drákon* maiden off for schooling in the village.

She kept her gaze focused downward most of the meal, her eyelashes long and sooty. Kimber did the same, Rhys noticed, and so felt free to let his own gaze roam.

She drew him in. Brash and brittle on the outside, looking out with eyes of endless gray, an oddly wounded depth to her every glance... she seemed a princess trapped in a shell of ice; a strange magic indeed in this heat.

Rhys glanced at his brother and wished, for the first time in his life, to be more than what he was.

To be eldest.

She desired to walk outside after the meal. His instinct was to refuse her—hell, his instinct was to lock her up, to keep her bound to Chasen, let the dragon in him take rein. It'd been done before. There were dire instances of *drákon* run feral, there were precautions already in place. For all her cool composure, Kimber had witnessed Maricara's other face, and he'd felt her other heart. She would Turn in a flash if she felt the need.

The council had convened a new, whispered meeting while she'd dressed. Within moments they'd abandoned the whispering—no one knew how well she could hear, and in light of what he knew now, Kim thought it a good thing they'd switched to scratching out messages with what quills and ink they could gather from the scattered corners of the mansion. That thrush had been miles away. She might not understand English, but she would damn sure know her own name.

It'd taken three sheets of paper and all his authority to convince them that entrapping her was not the solution, not now. If she went missing, who knew what her guardsmen would do. Far better now to adhere to diplomacy; there was too much at stake to risk losing her, or provoking an unnecessary fight. They needed her.

He needed her, it seemed, in more ways than a scribbled block of sentences on parchment could convey.

In the end—ten long minutes later—he'd achieved unanimous agreement. For all that she had their senses spinning, no one had forgotten her news, or the rings.

So Kim only nodded when Maricara commented over her sliced strawberries and cream that she'd like to see the sky, and suggested the garden in the back of the mansion, where there were trees and a fountain, and a chance for water-cooled shade.

They strolled out into the blistering sunlight. He removed his coat once again and left it dangling from the arm of a stone cupid that marked the beginning of the herb maze. At least his waistcoat had no sleeves.

Rhys remained inside. He hadn't even needed Kim's pointed glance before declining to join them on the walk.

The princess had no fan. He hadn't thought of it when he'd offered her the use of Lia's room, and Lia's gown. Ladies used fans. Ladies wore hats. Gloves. Yet Maricara moved forward into the day without these things, wearing only an expression of supreme indifference. The sunlight rippled down her hair, shifting between walnut and bronze. It fell in a tail down her back; the ribbon was slipping loose, its jaunty bow wilting somewhat in the humidity.

Her throat, her arms, the soft contours of her chest. Her skin appeared nearly as snowy as the ribbon, dewy, untouched by the heat. With the sun high above them the shadows drew sharp and deep; he found himself watching her hands as they walked, how her fingers curved and her wrists bent; no bracelets or rings, no adornment of any kind. But she shone like a flame by his side.

The fountain was in the center of the maze, easily spotted. Few of the herbs grew higher than his hips, but the fountain was as tall as two men together. It was Botticino marble with carvings of palm fronds and lilies; a single nymph at the top held a shell that bubbled with clear water, splashing down to the layers below. His parents, he recalled, had it imported before his birth. His mother had enjoyed the sound of it as she clipped roses nearby.

Rising warmth from the graveled path bent the air into shimmers. Maricara raised a hand to her brow and lifted her face.

"You've made me your prisoner, I see," she said calmly.

Dotting what had been a previously cerulean clear sky were now a dozen small, drifting clouds, following the lofty path of an invisible zephyr.

There were more of them in the woods. There were *drákon* all about, Kim knew, honed to their every move.

He could stop them from detaining her. He could not stop their curiosity, the profound, primordial instinct to see her, to bear witness to her presence. Every man in the shire would have sensed her by now.

"Honored guest," Kimber replied, smooth.

"Lord Chasen, I have been wed. I know full well what imprisonment is." She halted at a turn in the path and studied him, speculative. Beds of nodding anise surrounded them with hot licorice perfume.

"Do you think I could escape?"

He sighed.

"Shall we wager on it?" she persisted.

"No."

"The English never gamble?"

"Not in matters of the heart."

"How very suave. A Frenchman could not have said it better."

His voice roughened. "You must understand, Maricara, what you mean to us." He spread his hands, palms up. "There's never been anyone like you here before, never a single *drákon* beyond our own blood. You're—of immense interest to every member of the tribe."

"I wager I can evade you and your men up there. I wager I can do it for at least one full day. Should I win—"

"Your Grace—"

"We take our walks," she gestured to the clouds, "without accompaniment."

He paused, curious in spite of himself.

"And if you lose? If I'm able to find you?"

She tipped her head, and the shadows from her lashes threw dusk across her eyes. "What is it you want?"

He couldn't help it; he smiled.

"Oh," she said flatly.

His smiled vanished. "If I win, I want you to reconsider the possibility of . . . of a union between us. I want you to stay here at Chasen at the very least."

"Well, which shall it be?"

Marriage, he almost said, but saved himself in time. "You'll promise to stay here."

"Oh," she said again, this time breaking into a wide, glorious smile. "I'll promise it now if that's all you require."

"No." Kim reached for her hand and lifted it to his lips. She wasn't immune to the day after all; she was warm, very warm, and just as soft as he'd imagined. He realized he'd not touched her bare skin before this moment, not even in passing. Her fingers kept a faint, questing pressure against his.

"No," he said again, huskier. "I want you to mean it."

She gazed up at him. Without warning, without even a blink, she Turned and was gone, leaving smoke in his palm and her empty gown to the path. The hair ribbon floated sideways in a flourish, last to fall.

The Morcambre Courant
Friday, June 28, 1782
Wilde Beasts Devour Cattle

Master John Wilcox of Hetton-le-Hole reported the Loss of Two of his Finest Charolais White cows to a Vicious pack of Angry Beasts at an Unknown Hour in the Dark Night of Wednesday last.

Mistress Edith Shelby of Hought-le-Spring reported the Same on Thursday regarding her Ribbon-Winning Spotted Hog, awarded Best Pig at the Sunderland Spring Faire two years past.

Each of the Animals was grazing afield. Little was left of Any but bones and a single horn. Heavy Claw marks upon the Remains revealed the Monstrous Strength of the Creatures.

Wolves have not been Sighted near Our Fair Province for nigh a full Century. It is Assumed the pack has Arrived from the uncivilized Wilds of Scotland and is Moste Fleet to have Traveled so swiftly between the two Townes.

Huntsmen have been Dispatched with Great Haste to Eliminate the pack.

Gentle Readers of all Regions are urged to spend their evenings Indoors with their young Children and Pets until the Beasts have been Destroyed. Shepherds are urged to Bear Arms.

CHAPTER EIGHT

"Explain to me again," Kimber said, in his most aggravatedly patient voice, "how a woman weighing no more than nine stone, and reaching no higher than my forehead—a *foreign* woman— has been able to elude an entire population of the finest hunters on this earth. For eight days."

"Did you actually think," responded Audrey politely, "that she would be easy to find because she is a woman?"

"No." Kim placed a careful hand upon the crinkled newspaper spread open before him on his desk. "I thought she'd be easy to find because *she is a dragon.*"

The Marquess of Langford had made a point of subscribing to every periodical available that might contain news of Darkfrith, in addition to several of the London weeklies. Preventive measures, he would tell his son. Don't drown in the comforts of the shire. Pay heed to the outside world before it pays heed to you.

The *Morcambre Courant.* The *Durham Chronicle,* the *York Afternoon Advertiser.* Three papers carrying stories about a pack of savage, mysterious beasts that carried off cows and pigs—and according to one, an entire gaggle of fat geese—in the black of night, leaving behind only feathers and ravaged bones.

But the worst one, the worst one by far, was a small article that had appeared in the *Whitby Daily News.* It detailed the account of a tinker and his kin who all declared they saw a giant, winged "Serpent Fiend" in the sky Friday evening as they'd camped in the North York Moors.

Not wolves, not feral dogs. None such creatures could travel from town to town at the speed of flight. Trust a bloody tinker to get it right.

It was the princess, or her guard: another taunt. Kim couldn't imagine why she'd hazard exposure in such a blatant manner, but as she'd said, their ways were different. No doubt in the ruddy Carpathians dragons flocked the skies as common as blackbirds, but out here, in this rural and sleepy land...

She was putting his people in danger. She was jeopardizing all of Darkfrith, all for a ludicrous wager.

None of the papers were less than four days old. He was fortunate they'd reached the shire in that amount of time, actually. It usually took almost a week for even the *Courant* to wind its way through the gates of Chasen Manor.

It was the late afternoon of the eighth day of the hunt. He'd been out with the others, searching day and night, following scents and trails, doubling back, guessing at routes that seemed to evaporate midflight. It was as if Maricara had managed to erase every trace of herself, magically, utterly. He was still sensitized to her, he knew he was; all he had to do was close his eyes and imagine her face, her voice, the shape of her hand—and the elements of her rushed back to him, sent goose bumps along his skin.

But except for a fleeting hint of her by an old yew in Blackstone Woods, there was nothing of the Princess Maricara left in Darkfrith. And there had never been even the slightest indication of a guard. It was baffling. Beyond that. It was infuriating.

He'd come home that afternoon to see if there was anything new; every day brought a fresh batch of periodicals. Cows, sheep, that prized pig. Men with guns.

Kim pressed a hand over his eyes, rubbing against the gritty ache until his lids flashed red. Slanted light from the Tudor windows behind him felt far too good at the moment, soothing warm across his taut shoulders. He needed to shave. He needed to eat, and to sleep. He needed to shake the worry that gripped him, that itched across his skin and sent evil whispers into his brain: Something was wrong. Something she'd not anticipated had caught up with her, a farmer with a pistol and excellent aim. Human men who wanted to pluck out her heart.

He imagined her wounded. He imagined her shot, plummeting to the ground, her wings torn apart, her body broken.

Kimber was developing a healthy abhorrence of the press.

"You'll find her," said Joan. She perched on a corner of the mahogany desk, covering his free hand with her own. "You will, or Rhys will. Or one of the council. I'm sure she *wants* to be found. It's just a game to her right now. It will play out."

Both of his sisters had, naturally, been anticipating his return. They'd found him in the marquess's study—Kimber's study—staring blankly at an untidy stack of newspapers and old mail, with his elbows on his desk and his fingers clenched in his hair.

"I can't wait for that." He rubbed his eyes one last time—it only made them hurt worse—then sat back in his chair, frustrated. "I can't wait for her to decide she's won." He waved a hand at the papers. "For God's sake, have you read any of this?"

"Yes," said Joan. "All of it. She's gone far beyond the pale. So we've decided to join the hunt."

That got his attention; Kim looked up. "You have? What does Erik have to say about that?"

"Erik," she answered stiffly, "gave me a peck on the cheek this morning and wished me the blooming best of luck. Did you think he wouldn't?"

"No." Almost against his will, Kim felt his lips curve. Joan was fire and passion, as surely as Audrey was calm, cool water. Together they made a frighteningly crafty duo. He glanced at his twin. "And you?"

"Of course. I won't be left behind. It seems you need everyone you can get. Perhaps, as the other two females who can fly, we may offer some insight into her patterns."

"A few feminine suppositions," added Joan, with a slight, steely smile.

Audrey matched it. "Quite."

"All I need," said Kimber, "is one damned good guess."

Audrey nodded. "Fair enough. I daresay we're up for it." She stood and locked her fingers together, stretched her arms out before her and then up over her head. She was wearing her chestnut hair loose, he realized, long and uncurled, a style that would be shockingly inappropriate just about anywhere else in the world.

Joan stood and began to work free her rings.

"Oh," said Kim evenly. "Did you mean right now?"

"Have you a better time?"

"I suppose not." But the truth was, he was done in, and it made him uncomfortable to see them like this, preparing to Turn; he couldn't get the image of Maricara's empty dress, her chemise and stays, from his mind.

Kim dropped his head back to his hands and stared instead at the postmark of a letter peeking out from under the corner of the *Chronicle,* just as Joan kicked off her shoes.

Seaham. Who the hell did he know in Seaham? He reached for the letter with one hand, broke open the seal with the edge of his thumb, and began to read.

"Kimber?" Audrey dropped her arms to her skirts. "What is it?"

"You're going to want to put your hair up," he said slowly. "She's staying in the Crown Suites at The Bell & Star. In Seaham."

"What? How on earth can you be certain? Did she actually *write* you to say so?"

He glanced up with a hand still propped to his head and held out the letter so that the script showed clear in the bright July light.

"Not exactly. But she was kind enough to have them bill it to me."

Like every other people on the planet, the *drákon* had legends.

There were legends of diamonds, of course. Diamonds had been linked to them since the birth of time, and the tribe had its share of mythic stones. *Herte, Dramada, Eloquise*—each with its own dark glimmering story, each kept in the mansion's most secret places, treasured and adored.

And there were legends of dragons. The ragged, long-ago leaders who had brought the tribe to the shire from a place since forgotten, who had struggled and forged a home for them all. The Alpha who had first touched claw to the land that would become Darkfrith was named Nadus, red-haired, mighty; by force of will alone he'd pulled his kind from the Continent to this rough and untested isle.

Illan, who'd captured and loved a Celtic princess, and claimed her as his own.

Clarimonde, whose Gifts were said to include Fire and Water, and who once charmed an entire legion of human soldiers who had set out to kill her.

Theodus the Mystic.

Kieran the Unfortunate.

William the Blessed.

But of all those great dragons who had come before, perhaps the most famous of the *drákon* were two who still lived.

Christoff, Marquess of Langford. And the Smoke Thief, his wife, Clarissa Rue.

The king and queen of England could hardly command more esteem from their subjects; Kim had grown up in their shadows, and he'd never even realized it—how tall and strong they had both stood for the tribe, trouble after trouble, year after year, putting out every little fire, containing every new threat—until they had left.

Until they had abandoned him and everyone else.

There were times he sat behind his father's desk and wondered if he could ever manage half what Christoff had done. He did have the respect of his people, he knew that. He had his title, and his place in the order of things. But the *drákon* were splintering along their edges, every day a little more, and it seemed no matter what Kim tried, he could not stop it completely.

It was as if when his parents had fled, they had left behind an open door to the outside, and more and more of Kimber's tribe looked back out at the human world and wondered: *What if?*

Maricara, young and lawless and born of that outside place, was like a windstorm blowing past the opening, and everyone had gathered around.

He had to close that door, lock it, before it was too late.

The English were a people who embraced everything pastel. That's what Mari noticed most about this country, aside from the sticky air: the colors. Walls, furniture, gowns and breeches, even jewelry, everything pale and pallid, as inoffensive as boiled oatmeal in the morning. In Transylvania—even Hungary, Austria—no one was afraid of scarlet or turquoise or black. Fashion meant enjoyment; saturation of color meant life. In her gown of sleek cocoa satin, in sapphire bracelets and clips of yellow diamonds in her unpowdered curls, Maricara lazed like a panther in a garden full of placid doves in the stylish seaside resort she'd chosen for her retreat.

The other guests here had no idea she was a panther, naturally. But the man walking through the glass-and-gilt doors leading to the patio did.

He lingered a moment there as one of the waiters stationed nearby intercepted him with a bow. A breeze swept in from the beach below, heavy with salt and sand. It lifted the tails of his sage-gray coat, stirred loose strands of gold against his cravat; like her, he hadn't bothered with a wig.

The Earl of Chasen handed over his gloves and cocked hat without glancing at the waiter. His gaze went past the palm fronds and twisting vines of the artfully arranged potted plants to Mari at her table, relaxed on a chaise longue set beneath a wheat-and-white-striped umbrella. Its large, square shadow protected her—and the tableful of delicacies she'd ordered—from the rays of the noonish sun.

She smiled at him, lifting a hand. The sapphires at her wrist winked in band over band of faceted blue radiance.

He began to weave past the other patrons toward her. Eyes cut to him as he walked, men and women both, a flurry of whispers in his wake. Even the fiddler in the string trio sawing at a sonata in the corner missed a beat when the earl passed by. He was clearly aristocracy, clearly gorgeous and well moneyed, even for this plump and pretty crowd. Ladies snapped their fans to their heated faces. Gentlemen began to stretch a leg beneath their wrought-iron tables, their chests puffing, peacocks trying to seem bigger than what they were.

No use, she thought. Kimber Langford outshone them all, and he wasn't even trying.

"*Bonjour,*" she greeted him, holding her smile. "A lovely afternoon, isn't it? I've discovered I very much enjoy the ocean."

"Your Grace," he said, and presented her with his own elegantly turned leg, a bow that would have done credit to a real princess. "A pleasure indeed to discover you once more."

"You're very kind. Please, do sit down. Will you take tea?"

He settled into the chair she indicated, his handsome face neutral—his eyes sharp, frozen green. "No."

"No? Oh, dear. I've ordered a great deal of food for you, and it wasn't easy to do so in French, let me tell you. It's a shockingly provincial place. I fear the caviar alone is going to cost you at least four pounds. It would be a pity to let it go to waste."

He sent her a smile that didn't thaw his eyes. "You ordered for me? How very thoughtful, if somewhat implausible. Especially since you had no idea when I'd come."

"Lord Chasen," she said cordially, "I felt your approach more than three hours past. Are you sure you won't have any tea? I'm really rather proud of my timing. It's still hot, you see."

She reached for the Maricoline teapot, her fingers closing around the handle of ceramic fruit and leaves with all the supple skill she'd learned from Imre's most polished Russian mistress. The earl said nothing as she poured. The tea was mint, sugared and fragrant; she didn't spill a drop as she leaned from her Cleopatra pose to pass the cup and saucer to him.

Their fingers brushed. Mari was glad she was already seated. The jolt of power she'd received from just that short, swift touch felt like lightning to her toes.

"Thank you."

"Of course."

He did not drink. The sonata ended on a long, resonating note; the trio launched at once into a minuet.

Mari poured her own cup and held it close, letting the steam rise up to sting her senses.

"I think I begin to understand why you English enjoy this beverage so much. At first I found it quite bland. But really, once you learn not to expect good coffee or a decent pot of hot chocolate, tea can be nearly as fine." She took a sip, placed the cup back by her flowered plate. "I like it very much with this particular pastry, as it turns out. What do you call it?"

"A scone."

"Yes. Scones. Delicious. I must take the recipe back to *Zaharen Yce* when I return."

"Why are you out here, Princess?" Kimber asked, abrupt. "Why not inside, a private parlor? We'll have a much better conversation alone, I assure you."

Mari made a small gesture to the sweeping wide terrace, palm trees and a pink-granite balustrade, the rushing ocean a deep navy strip beyond. "But this is *so* much more entertaining. Do you see that good sir over there, for example? The one in the pea-colored coat and the wig that's slipping askew? He's been thinking for the last half hour about how much he'd like to abandon his poor plain wife and join me over here."

"You can read thoughts," said the earl, still so neutral.

She laughed, startled. "No. That would be quite a Gift, wouldn't it? But no. It's more that he can't take his eyes off my jewelry." She paused to break off a piece of scone. "Or perhaps it's my décolletage."

Kimber gave a very slight smile. "Both, I would say."

Maricara inclined her head. She wasn't so unwise as to think that this smile was any more genuine than the last. There was a coiled rigidity about him, a suggestion of aggressive action just barely held in check. There wasn't a chance in Hades she was going to leave this very open, very public patio to go anyplace more private with the Earl of Chasen right now. God knows what he'd try.

She'd worked too hard for this moment to let it go quickly. He had no idea what measures she'd taken just to be able to recline on her chaise and look like a panther.

"Well, if you're certain you won't eat any of this," she said with a sigh, "I suppose we can leave it to the birds. The *maître d'hôtel* warned me of the gulls. But really, they seem to be hovering at a very civil distance."

"Please. Begin without me."

"Hmm. I'm not actually hungry. For some reason, I find myself particularly satiated these past few days."

That arrow struck home, she saw that it did. His beautiful eyes narrowed; she rushed on before he could speak.

"Perhaps you'd like to invite your friends to join us, then. The ones waiting in the lobby. There are . . . three of them there. One is your brother. And, let me see . . . five—no—six more *drákon* outside on the street with the carriage. Poor fellows. They must be very hot."

The earl drew in a deliberate breath, still staring at her. The salt breeze returned and sent the corner of the umbrella flapping; he was highlighted with light and dark—brows and cheekbones, unshaven skin, the pleasing arc of his lips. Then he pulled his chair closer to her, back into the shade, and sat forward with his forearms braced to his knees. His hair swept gold again by the line of his jaw.

"Who else can you feel?" he asked quietly.

"Everyone. Nearly everyone. A few more easily than others."

"And me?"

"Yes." She looked at him from beneath her lashes. "Definitely you."

He drew back, his face impassive. After a moment, he picked up a croissant stuffed with cheese and began to tear it apart with his fingers.

"It's interesting that *I* don't feel *your* guardsmen anywhere, though."

"Perhaps you're not as skilled as I, my lord."

His slight smile returned. He didn't glance up at her. "Perhaps not. But you've put me in something of a bind. We had a wager. Obviously you've won. Yet I can't leave you here."

Mari pushed a plate beneath his hands, catching a barrage of flaky crumbs. "No?"

"No. The council's adamant about that. Too much press, my love."

"The press knows nothing."

"Too much danger," he emphasized, and lifted his eyes, pinning her with that sharp green look. "They've assembled a throng of human men to kill the 'beasts' running wild. You'd be surprised how fond people are of their livestock."

"A few cows gone—"

"My dear princess," he interrupted, his voice lowered to whispered steel, "you have deliberately broken a host of our most sacred laws. *Drákon* in the past have been put to death for a fraction of what you've done. You've appeared as a dragon in public—repeatedly—you've flown openly in the skies, and it's pure fool's luck that the only people who've sighted you so far happen to be gypsies, so no one will believe them anyway. I can't imagine what you were thinking. If you wanted my attention, you've certainly gained it, but there were better ways, my lady. We don't... we do not expose ourselves like that here. This is not *Zaharen Yce*. This is not your home."

Mari turned her face to the blinding luster of the ocean, staring out until her vision blurred. "No," she said. "I know that."

"Every time you break our laws, every time you plunge into the human world as dragon, or as smoke, you put my entire tribe at risk. I'm sorry. The council demands your return, and I concur with them."

"I'm not of your tribe, Lord Chasen."

"Yes, love," he said, more gently. "I'm afraid you are."

She glanced back at him. There could be little mistaking what he meant, or more significantly, how he was looking at her.

Like she was his already. Like he had her already locked up, with chains and a new title and the weight of all those unknown English formalities. Her gaze fell to his left hand, his empty ring finger there, and then down to her own, where she would swear the small indent from her own wedding band still lingered, a scar that would never pass.

"You're stubborn," she said, dispassionate. "I understand that. But so am I. You won't persuade me."

"It's not about persuasion, Your Grace. It's about primal nature. It's about who we are. You cannot change that."

"Did I say stubborn? I meant, actually, pigheaded."

Kimber shifted forward in his seat. "Maricara," he began—but broke off at the approach of someone new to the table.

"Hallo, there you are." Rhys had apparently decided no longer to wait in the lobby. He pulled out the nearest chair and collapsed into it with a luxuriant sigh; two fashionably dressed women trailed behind—dragon-women, Mari sensed. The other sisters, no doubt. One wore a gown of silver, the other wore gold, like they were baubles from a vault, iridescent and rare.

Mari ignored them all, lifting her eyes to center upon the earl. She kept her words very soft.

"There is nothing you can do to me here. There is nothing

you can say that will compel me to rise from this seat and leave with you. So you truly *are* in a bind, my lord. I summoned you here with an innocent heart. But I will not be at your command, and I will not be subject to your laws. No lasting harm has resulted from my actions or those of my men. We may be friends yet. I suppose it's up to you. You may have my goodwill or not. I suggest, very sincerely, that you consider your next move with the utmost care. I won't be trifled with. And whatever happens next, I won't forget."

At the end of Mari's speech one of the women hesitated, then sank into the next nearest chair. The other followed. They were lovely, with complexions of alabaster and rose, both older than Mari by several years. They wore elaborate wigs and cosmetics and strong, singing gems. The one in the silver gown had dark brown eyes and a tiny patch for beauty by the corner of her lips; she smiled at Maricara, taking charge of the teapot, beginning to pour.

"I regret we've not yet been introduced. I'm Audrey. This is Joan. It is a singular honor to meet you at last, Princess." She refilled Mari's cup, still smiling, and switched smoothly into English. "It wouldn't take much, Kim. We've both blindfolds and hoods, and a hat large enough to conceal her face. Just a small instant alone, that's all we need."

"There is no way to get her alone," replied the earl, in the same relaxed tone.

"There's always a way," murmured the other woman, green-eyed, like both her brothers.

"Certainly," agreed Maricara, also in English. "For instance, you might shout the word 'fire' to the crowd. Humans do tend to panic over that. You'd have me to yourselves nearly at once. Of course, that would be a waste of this rather marvelous luncheon. I was looking forward to the raspberry tart."

No one said anything. The faint cries of the gulls over the surf sounded very distant.

"And," Mari continued, "you should know that I have no qualms about Turning right here and now, in front of all these cow-witted people, if any of you make the slightest move toward me. How will your council like that?"

The earl recovered first. "You speak English."

Maricara tapped a nail against her teacup, exasperated. "Naturally I do. I've had years to study it. Wouldn't you have?"

Rhys began to chortle, and then to laugh. It lit his face with a dark, wicked charm; when he tipped back his head his throat worked and the emerald at his ear flashed like the eye of a cat. He held a hand to his brow, and when he could draw enough air, he spoke.

"None of you thought of that?"

"Apparently not," said Maricara. She took a final sip of tea, set it back in its saucer, then slid from the chaise longue. Both the men automatically stood. The sisters remained as they were.

"Well, let's have it packed up, then," she said, surveying the platters of food. "There's something I'd like to show you all anyway."

Kimber had gone frozen again, staring at her. He was hardly alone; half the men on the terrace had lapsed into silence as soon as she'd taken a step from the table.

He cleared his throat. "What in God's name are you wearing?"

"Oh—do you like it?" She lifted her arms, turned a small, neat pirouette; the cocoa satin made a closed bell at her feet. "It's called a chemise dress. No hoops. Very freeing. It's all the rage in Paris."

"I like it," said Rhys.

"Shut up," snapped the brown-eyed sister, and came to her feet with a lithe, contained movement, standing face-to-face with

Maricara. Both wore heels; both stood tall with their shoulders back; it was complete chance that they happened to be exactly the same height. "Please, Princess," the sister said, without a trace of inflection. "Won't you lead the way?"

"Yes," answered Maricara. "I will."

CHAPTER NINE

All creatures born are burdened with a fatal flaw. The nimble rabbit, with its bobbing white tail. The clever fox, with its conspicuous red coat. Fat fish in shallow streams. Tiny birds in slow flight. Clams that can never bury themselves too deep in the sand lest they suffocate.

The *drákon* must see to Turn. Take away our sight, and we're trapped in our human shapes. Hoods, blindfolds, searing pokers to the eyes—these are all weapons we have good reason to fear. Even old age can defeat us; when our vision clouds over, our days of soaring under the sun are done.

We cannot speak as dragons. We cannot communicate but by the language of our bodies. In war, we fall into battle silent as snowfall, only the sound of the air around us revealing our fury.

And you, with your cocked pistols and your knives, and your hoods in waiting. You're learning, aren't you?

CHAPTER TEN

She took them up to her rooms. She made certain she did *not* go first, but instead instructed them down the airy, sea-scented corridors to the proper set of doors as she trailed behind. Beneath the glass canopy capping the lobby she'd turned to give the key to Lord Chasen. He'd taken it from her hand with just a hidden, sideways look from beneath lashes lit the color of warmed ale.

The lobby was open and quite crowded, teeming with Others, everyone jostling around a real pond set in the middle of the chamber filled with lily pads and restless orange carp.

"After you," Maricara had said, and the earl smiled—that slight, unnerving smile—his fingers barely grazing the center of her palm as they curled around the metal.

And it was there again, that fleet shock of sensation, that undeniable, sensual pull. It was getting stronger.

It made her think of inappropriate things. It made her think of what his hair must feel like, freed from its queue. How the muscles of his jaw would flex under the stroke of her finger. How her lips would fit against his.

His lashes lifted; he held her in a gaze of ice-pale green. Maricara took a step back.

"Princess," he'd acknowledged in English, and only moved away, shouldering through a clutch of dandies waving their handkerchiefs against the heat.

The Crown Suites took up the entire third story of the hotel, plush and expensive, the best the place had to offer. She let the others file in first so they could take in her precautions: the curtains tied back with their jade-colored sashes, the windows all open, that current of ocean air lifting and pulling at the tasseled corners of the duvet on the bed in the next room. She lingered in the doorway as they gathered in the front parlor, four watchful, sophisticated dragons surrounded by pongee silks and marble-topped furnishings. A large cloisonné urn stuffed with lilacs and tea roses lent a soft, thick spice to the wafting breeze.

It would be easy to Turn here, to be gone in an instant. Mari knew it to be true, because she'd done so every single night.

Every night. She'd walk to the old-fashioned windows, running her hands over the ripples in the glass. She'd close her eyes and inhale the sweeter aroma of ocean and the night-blooming jasmine growing wild in the dunes below, thinking of what it would be like in the mountains now. How the peaks would look with the wind blowing moonlight across their faces. How the stars would beckon with fierce shining brilliance.

She would not glance back at the rosewood bed. She would not be tempted by crisp sheets and that pillowy duvet of woven birds and periwinkles.

Maricara had all her worldly goods here in these rooms. But every night, as late as she could stand it, she would leave.

There was an abandoned priory not very far inland. A princess by day; a darker creature by night. She had blankets and a pillow in what used to be a monk's cell. She would stare at the decayed bricks of the walls until she was dragged into sleep with their rough, rectangular lines imprinted on the backs of her lids, all the while praying that *this* night, this *one* night, would be the one she finally slept through.

Then she'd wake up . . . she'd wake up in such terrible places. . . .

"Adequate, wouldn't you say?" She faced her guests. "I'm especially fond of all the windows."

"What was it you wanted to show us?" asked the earl, slapping his gloves lightly against one thigh. He radiated that tight, coiled aggression once more. She could nearly see the caged animal gleaming behind his gaze.

"Oh, it's not here. You're going to have to Turn and follow me to see."

Kimber gave a short laugh, mirthless. "That's not going to happen."

"Only to smoke. We'll be floating mist to all the people out there."

"It's a hot day," pointed out Rhys.

"Clouds, then. Dragons. Whatever you like. You may follow me or not, but I'm going to Turn no matter what you say. And I think you need to see this." Mari lifted her chin and looked straight at Kimber. "For the sake of your tribe, Alpha lord."

The other three were silent, also looking to Kimber. He stood with his weight on one well-muscled leg, his hat under his arm, the gloves striking a muffled, repetitive *crack* against his breeches. With the light behind him picking out the satin piping on his coat and the buckles on his shoes, he might have been any man—any fine-looking, human man . . . but for the waves of *drákon* power he emitted. And that flat, dangerous light to his eyes.

"Very well, Your Grace," he said at last, with a small bow of his head. "But pray allow me to be exceedingly clear: We travel as smoke only. Under no circumstances will *any* of us Turn to any-. thing else in front of humans."

"*Naturellement.*" Maricara looked to the others. "My safe is beside the armoire. You may put your gemstones in there if you like."

It was big, nearly as tall as the escritoire in the corner, painted steel with the key hidden behind a loose tile in the water closet.

The earl turned his head to survey it, still standing in place.

"You traveled all the way from Transylvania with that?"

"Hardly," she said. "You'll receive an account for it soon, I expect. The locksmith in town assured me your credit was perfectly good."

She'd warned them not to touch the ground once they reached where they were going. She'd judged the airstreams and the angle of the sun and agreed with the earl it was best if they stayed as thin as possible, sparkling thin against the blue atmosphere, a haze of sea-sprayed moisture to anyone who might happen to be looking up. They would go slowly. It wasn't far, she told them, but it would take time.

She guided them inland. She avoided by miles her collapsing old priory, moving instead southwest, nearly in harmony with the winds. They only had to shove against it a little. The most difficult part, Maricara thought, was not giving in to the urge to leap forward at full speed.

Smoke was one of their more wily deceits. Smoke was the Gift most designed to fool the human eye. It allowed them to mist into places no person or dragon could fit, through mouseholes or the slats of a shutter, a tendril through the eye of a slender needle. Too many Others of ancient days thought the smoke around dragons meant fire, when in fact it meant resolution: stealth, stalking, death. At least for their enemies.

The ground below them became pretty and remote, as perfect and broad-stroked as a painting. Woods, downs, roads and hedges. Brick-and-slate villages pressed up against rivers. Churches. Mills. A group of red-coated men hunting quail.

The baying of their dogs as Mari and the rest passed overhead.

The earl remained close beside her, so close that at times their edges brushed. She'd never experienced such a thing with another before; the men of the Zaharen always avoided her when she took flight. Even her brother kept his distance.

But Kimber...Kimber was a sheet of whisper-thin gray, an echo of herself. He tilted as she tilted; he rose as she rose. The other three trailed behind but he remained exactly where she was, how she was, even when a jet of heated air swept up in a curl between them.

They spun with it. She rolled and flattened and found he'd done the same, and that was when he first touched her, and it felt like the most beautiful, intangible silk rushing along her senses. Like living wind, or the zinging pleasure of metal or stone. She was overcome with it—just for a moment—and lost her path. He touched her again, slower this time, more deliberate, and she was shaken enough to shrink away, to increase her speed so that the treetops and meadows became a blur of sun and shadows.

He kept pace.

By then they were nearly there. The farm was set apart from any hamlet or village. It consisted of a thatched house and two barns, a pen of wide-eyed sheep, and field after field of yellow-green wheat.

She took them past all that. She took them to the muddy clearing by a windmill, the blades creaking slowly with a sultry weak breeze. Water from the mill kept up a steady trickle that leaked from a crack in the tin holding pool. It had been the perfect wading place for a flock of tame geese.

She'd awoken here in the heart of night. She had come back to her-

self in this alien place, a naked, shivering woman with sludge oozing between her toes, standing upright by the pool, bewildered. The odor of goose blood mingled with that of the peaty muck, a dark slick of color reflecting the moonlight at her feet. Feathers gleamed angelic white all about her, a few still spinning in slow whorls to the ground.

And she could hear—she'd swear she could hear the final, garbled scream of the last goose as she doubled over and vomited up what she had just killed and consumed in her sleep, her hands and knees and hair plunged into the filth, tears hot down her cheeks, dripping from her chin—

One corner of the clearing was still speckled with feathers. Maricara floated over to it, not too close, and waited for the others to follow. She gave them a few minutes there, letting them take it all in. Her scent lingered still, and that of the dead geese, the rusted pool. The earl left her; she watched as he drifted closer to the mud—clearly nothing now of nature, no cloud would move like that—but at least there were no Others nearby here. Maricara was certain of that.

He glimmered in the sunlight. He shifted, thickening and then thinning once more, ascending back to where she waited, a flag of vapor caught at the tip of the windmill. As soon as he was level to her, she took off again.

The second place was not much farther, more north. More farms, more fields, more Roman-straight turnpikes and trees that kept the woodland's secrets beneath their leafy cover. She felt deer down there, and hedgehogs, and finches and squirrels and drowsing owls. And then, as she neared the second farm, she felt something more.

An ox, for one thing, tethered to an oak tree in one of the farthest pastures. Less than a week ago there had been cows in that pasture along with the ox, but that was before Mari had come.

Two cows. She remembered nothing of that night but impressions: grassy pasture; pools of blood; massive bones. And the ox, pressed hard against a canted wood fence, staring at her through the darkness, too terrified even to tremble.

It lay now with its front legs tucked under it in a patch of dirt worn barren of grass, listless upon the ground. When she was near enough to see its eyes it lifted its head, abruptly alert, and then lurched to its feet.

The men who had tied it there were back at the farmhouse. One would remain behind—they would not leave their bait without a watch—but he had wandered into the woods that bordered the pasture, reeking of ale and urine: a human who had no qualms about doing murder in the open air yet still required privacy to relieve himself.

She did not understand the Others. Perhaps she never would.

Still, Mari went no closer; the watch would return soon. Kimber remained beside her this time, and the other three flowed near.

She wished she could tell them what was down there, the menace that lurked and polluted the pasture. She wished she could speak to them, or at least point, but all she could do was wait and let them feel it for themselves.

When Kimber began to descend she followed promptly, shooting under him, using her velocity to twine around him, pulling him back up. She felt silk again, the velvet sensation of his essence as smoke, but he was also force and determination; he moved past her, still descending.

She tried again and this time he twirled with her, looping about her so that for a split second they were both rising—but then he was gone, a narrow siphon to the ground, and he was smoke by the ox, and then man.

The ox rolled its eyes until the whites showed like half-moons. It let out a bawl, towing hard at its rope.

Mari dropped to the earth. She Turned human, her heart taking life as a sick throb in her chest. She grabbed the earl by his arm, her voice a fierce whisper.

"Are you mad? Don't you sense him? Get out of here!"

"Yes," he answered, very calm. His hand lifted to cover her own. "I sense him. But he's not here right now."

"I told you not to touch the ground! I merely wanted you to see!"

"Sorry, Princess," he said. "Some might call me pigheaded, but I really do enjoy getting my own way."

He wasn't looking at her. He was frowning from the ox to the woods, thoughtful, as the beast began to quaver, yanking harder at its tether. Its tongue worked pink as it tried to scrape the rope halter from its face.

She realized abruptly that Kimber was naked. Of course he was, and so was she, but—the sun was hot, and his skin was bright, and there were golden hairs on his chest, and his arm was hard like iron beneath hers. Only his fingers cupped over hers remained gentle; he pressed her hand to him like he held a flower, delicate and firm.

"Ah, pardon me," said Rhys, suddenly behind them. "But what are we doing here?"

Kimber glanced back at his brother. His fingers tightened.

"We're taking care of a brief bit of business," he replied, and turned his face to the sky. One of the hovering clouds cascaded down, became Audrey close beside Maricara.

"For heaven's sake, Rhys, look away," she said, and threw her arm around Mari's shoulder, drawing her near. Her hair was long, nearly as long as Mari's own. When she moved it skimmed both their waists.

Mari broke away. "We need to go," she insisted, as the earl walked to the ox. "They could have muskets. Or arrows."

"All right." He circled in front of the frantic beast, reached out and secured the rope. The ox let out another wild bellow, trying to buck free, but Kimber only gripped the rope with two fists, his face set, pulling until the hemp ripped apart in a burst of fiber and grit.

He dropped the ends. He backed up a step and the ox bucked again and then bolted, charging past them all with a thunder that actually shook the earth.

"Maricara is correct," said a new voice, Joan, to her left. "We need to go. The second story of the farmhouse is in view, and there are men headed this way."

Without another word, Kimber Turned, and so did the other three. Mari was last to leave, still sickened with her heart and the jolting of the ground as the ox fled for its life into the sun-baked fields.

They dined this time. He was too hungry not to dine, and at least if they retreated into the human convenience of the princess's hotel, he'd know exactly where she was. And that was of the utmost importance.

"Now they know," she was saying, her lips slanted down, her lucent pale eyes accusing and extravagantly long-lashed. "If you had not broken the rope, if you hadn't freed the ox, the hunters might not ever have known we were there—"

"They know anyway," Kimber said, and took another bite of his roast. "The ox was a blatant trap. Breaking its rope changed nothing."

"*You* were the one who said *not* to Turn—"

"With humans nearby. And we didn't."

Maricara muttered something foreign under her breath; he didn't bother to ask for clarification. She began sawing at the beef-steak upon her plate, her gaze cast down, as if the rare meat and grilled asparagus offended her nearly as much as Kim had.

He'd reserved the hotel's sole private parlor for their supper. He'd had to impress the resort supervisor with the weight of his title in addition to laying out a preposterous sum for the teal-and-smoked-glass room—which the supervisor assured him was quite booked for months in advance—but it was worth it, because they all had to eat, and the things the five of them had to say now could not be for any ears but their own.

He had no idea where Maricara's guard might be; his own were in the public room adjacent to this, eating a meal no doubt just the same as his own...and a good deal cheaper. They were strong men, solid. The fact that more than half the house of their Alpha was currently confined to this chamber would keep them extra-vigilant.

Every now and again a lace-capped maid and two footmen would enter through the white swinging door that led to the hall, bearing food, taking away food. Out of habit Kim and his siblings would fall silent whenever the chamber was breached. The princess was hardly speaking in any case.

Candles had been placed in front of nearly every sheet of glass striping the walls; the hearth was unlit. The candlelight reflected as if from the bottom of a cave, or a distant firestorm, yellow-gold flames stripped to sepia, shadows the color of tarnished copper twitching back and forth across them all.

Maricara sliced at the stems of her asparagus. She'd donned again the bare sheath of satin she dared to call a frock; the diamonds in her hair caught the smoky light in dim, scintillating glimmers. She'd taken the chair at the end of the table, close to an open window and far from the four of them. He supposed she still thought they might rush her, or trick her, even amid a semipublic evening supper. And she had a point, he had to admit. He was at the head; she was at the foot; silver salvers of steaming roast and potatoes and boiled carrots dotted the bleached holland between them. It put him in mind of what they might look like together in the formal dining hall of Chasen Manor.

As husband and wife.

She took a bite, chewing carefully. She seemed tired. Even with her beauty, even with her diamonds and obvious displeasure, her movements had noticeably slowed. There were faint circles under her eyes he hadn't noted before.

Perhaps it was just the lighting. It was gloomy as a tomb in here.

She glanced up at him without lifting her head, catching him staring. Kim was held in a gaze darkened to stone and felt something in his chest begin to squeeze.

Yes, whispered the cold, cold dragon, turning over in his heart. *She's Alpha, and she's untamed, and still she belongs to you.*

He knew, logically, that it was true. He knew what had to come. But when she looked like this, smaller and more fragile than before, her perfect poise beginning to fracture, just a little...

He didn't want to hurt her. He didn't want to force her. He didn't want her to be thinking about the window behind her, of men and guns, and how soon she might be rid of him. He damned sure didn't want her anywhere near livestock again.

The world offered a rich and intoxicating mélange of aromas to their kind, at times so many it could confound even the most acute of warriors. But Kimber had spent years learning how to separate the nuances; he could smell the difference between river water and pond; between an owl on the wing or a hawk; between a butterfly quaking over flowers and a moth over leaves.

Everything around the windmill today had reeked of blood and days-old animal panic—and of Maricara. There could be no question she had been there before. The combined scent of mud and animal and her had been so strong it had very nearly drowned out something more important, something he had not at first even recognized was significant: the more pervasive odor of men. Many men. And something else with it, something mild and elusive... not unpleasant, not unfamiliar. But he'd never encountered anything like it before; Kimber didn't know what it was.

The smell rippling around the ox had been primarily of dust

and hay and more sweating fear. The princess once again. The oak tree had the correct bouquet, as did the grass, and the pile of manure not far off. But this time he'd noticed at once the stench of man. The same men, in fact, as the ones from the windmill, which seemed bloody unlikely indeed. The trail there had been fresher, much fresher. Someone had scraped his hand on the rough knot of the rope not more than two hours before; perhaps the man in the woods. Kim had smelled the human skin on the hemp. The barest thin whiff of human blood.

Emanations of hammered steel, when there had been nothing of metal about. Cotton drenched in dye. Leather and perspiration. A great deal of saltpeter and flint.

And once more, it had all been accompanied by that elusively familiar scent of the Unknown.

He rubbed a finger over his lower lip, considering it.

"It was a stupid thing to do," his bride-to-be said now.

"Pigheaded," Kim reminded her.

"That too. I took you there only so you could see what the hunters had done. If they'd been any closer—"

"But they weren't. There was just the one fellow, and he was taking his time in the woods. It's not as if they could follow us, after all. It was a clean getaway."

"For their lure, as well!" Her cheeks began to flush. "They were waiting for a *drákon*. You might as well have left a calling card."

"You don't know it was a trap for a *drákon*," said Joan.

"Of course I do."

"The papers said wolves."

"The papers," commented Rhys, who was on his third glass of wine, "are run by gin-guzzling fatheads. They're hardly going to print the word 'dragon,' are they?"

Audrey intervened before Joan formed her retort. "Why *did* you free the ox, Kimber?"

He shrugged, uncomfortable. He wished the deuce his twin

had stayed out of it; she alone probably guessed that he'd no good reason.

The ox had been afraid. That was really all there was to it. Perhaps he shouldn't have Turned, but he did, and once he had, he'd had no cause not to set it free.

It had been afraid. Through no fault of its own, through an accident of birth and circumstances, it had been tethered to its death.

"What's this?" Rhys sounded amused. "Tenderness for a mere beast?"

His brother had found the one spot in the chamber that held no light. Shadows crossed back and forth around him in layer over layer; even from here Kim could hardly make out his face. But there was that note to his voice, that particular hard tone that sent a dull warning across Kimber's skin.

"In the end," Kimber said, "we're all beasts."

Silence fell. It took nearly a minute before the clinking of silver sounded again against the china. When Kimber raised his eyes it was to find Maricara now staring at him, unblinking.

"Speaking of beasts." Rhys lifted his drink; the ruffles at his cuff fell back in ghostly folds. "What was it you called these men before, Princess, in the council meeting? You had a name for them, these human hunters."

She looked away, the spell broken. "*Sanf inimicus.*"

"What does it mean?"

Maricara sighed, examining an asparagus tip at the end of her fork. "Something like... 'soft enemy.'" She returned the asparagus to her plate without eating it. "Or, some of our kind prefer to call them *delis inimicus,* instead."

"Delicate?" guessed Joan.

"More like 'delicious.'" The princess looked up at the sudden hush around the table. "Oh. Not I, of course."

"You have no guard here," said Kim, laying down his utensils. "Do you?"

She lifted a brow. "How very perceptive, my lord. It only took you all this while to riddle it out."

Audrey made a sound of disbelief. "You came to England unaccompanied?"

"Why not?"

"Why not? You're a princess, to begin with, or so we've been told."

Kimber murmured his twin's name; her voice only rose in response.

"No, Kim, honestly, I want to know—she arrives unannounced, she's placed us all in danger—how did you book passage? Who acted as your maids? Who handled your meals, and your lodging, and your clothing and jewels? I doubt very much indeed you managed all that by yourself. You're what—nineteen? Twenty? Was there not *one* reasonable soul among all your retinue who perhaps mentioned it was *not* a fine idea to ravage the countryside?"

"No passage," said the princess. "No maid, no retinue. I flew here alone."

Joan set her wineglass upon the table with a *thump;* the Riesling inside sloshed like liquid amber. "You . . . flew?"

"Yes."

"Brilliant," said Rhys, from his dark place.

"Or just bloody *insane.*" Joan forgot herself so much as to lean forward with her elbows on the holland. A pair of side curls from her wig skimmed right above her plate. "You flew as a *dragon* across entire *countries?* What if you'd been seen? What if you'd been shot? I cannot conceive your people allowed you to leave your land without escort."

"Well, that's the difference between us, isn't it? You English have rules to confine yourselves. My rule is only to be free."

"*Brava,*" said Rhys.

"Free to kill cattle," retorted Audrey, with a flick of her fingers. "Free to consume hapless geese."

"*Stop this*," hissed Kim, and his family lapsed back into silence.

Maricara placed her napkin upon the table. Kimber tensed, prepared to push free of his chair. But she didn't rise, and she didn't Turn. She only took a heavy breath, the bodice of her gown straining, gleaming satin.

"Maricara," he said softly. "We've all had a long day."

"No," she said, first to him, then to the rest. "No, she's quite right. It wasn't well-done of me." She offered a shrug and then a small, tight smile, her gaze angled downward. "I don't even like goose."

The swinging door creaked open; the maid reentered, carrying a tureen of what smelled like curried lamb. As if on cue, everyone resumed eating, even Maricara, although Kim did see her throw a subtle glance to the night beyond the window.

The maid served them in silence, the sound of the ladle tapping against the plates painfully sharp in Kim's ears. Only after the girl had curtsied and backed out of the room did Maricara break the silence, speaking very, very quietly.

"Because of the kills, because of the publicity, the *sanf* were able to find my last-known location. They were able to secure bait, and set the trap, and no doubt right now they're still out there waiting with another ox, or a cow or a pig. And also because of all of that, we now know they're in England, searching for our kind."

He'd been watching the princess, her downward look, the shaded contours that defined her face. But an instinct he couldn't name turned his gaze to Joan: All the blood seemed to drain from her cheeks. He didn't need to read thoughts to know what she was thinking: She had a crippled husband who could not fly, two little daughters. And Audrey—with three boys and a girl, all of them audacious and merry—looked even paler.

He'd told them. He'd told everyone. But it hadn't been real until this afternoon. Until the specter of knives and blood and the black, terrified eyes of the ox—it hadn't been real.

"Did the *drákon* you sent to me carry anything of you on their persons?" Maricara asked Kimber. "Bank notes, letters of introduction?"

"No." Kim took a swallow of cold, tart wine. "We didn't know what your circumstances might be, who knew of you, who would not. We don't even openly say the word for what we are here. I wasn't going to risk writing anything down. The only introduction I assumed you needed would be in realizing who—and what—these men were."

"So, these hunters, they're not there yet," said Audrey, still stricken. "Not in Darkfrith."

Kimber wanted to answer her. He drew breath for it, felt his lips shape again the solid and reassuring word *no*—he could speak that word with all the firm resonance of any absolute leader; he could make it sound like truth without even trying. But instead, Kim cut himself short. Like his brother and sisters, he looked back at Maricara, who once more dropped her eyes. She picked up her soup spoon, examining the curve of the bowl as it caught the dark yellow light.

"What is it? What now?" Audrey demanded.

"It's commonly known that years ago . . . not quite a decade ago, a stranger came to us, a new sort of dragon, who upset the balance of my people. It's known that she was English, from the northern aspect of your country. Your sister Lia was a guest in my castle for eight months. Her true name was openly spoken. It would be no great ordeal to discover her birthplace, I would think. All one would need is a rudimentary knowledge of English, and a map." She tapped the spoon lightly against her plate, her lips pursed. "I did come to warn you."

"Oh, God," said Audrey, even whiter than before.

"Aye," said the princess.

"Why didn't you warn us before? Why wait until *now* to—"

"I didn't wait. By and large they've left us alone until now. It's been almost a century since they've last hunted us, my grandparents' time. I don't even know why they've started again."

"We can return home tonight," said Joan, resolute. "We can take care of this."

"They're not there tonight." Maricara lifted her gaze to Kimber's. "They're here. The *sanf* have set the trap here."

Joan pressed a fist against her chest. "You can't be sure—"

"I *am* sure. *This* is the place. This is where they believe we are. At least, where they think *I* am. It is a most excellent distraction from Darkfrith."

"But—"

"We have a rotating contingent of our finest warriors patrolling our territory," Kim said under his breath, tensed in his chair, leaning forward to be heard over all the noises of the people dining in the next room. "We have traps of our own in place, and an entire shire of the most fearsome creatures ever to live ready to defend our home. At any given time, there are over thirty *drákon* in the air, and another two dozen on the ground, in the village, all of them willing, all of them eager, to safeguard our tribe. And as for all of you— remember what we are. Remember *how* we are. I don't give a damn what these so-called *sanf* think they can do to us. If they come to our shire, I very nearly pity the bastards. We're going to slit them end from end."

A new hush took the chamber. The draft from the open window sent a spiral of black smoke from the nearest candle coiling in a long, snakelike arm across the table.

Rhys stirred in his chair. "I have another question. What was it today in those places? What was that thing lurking behind the human smell?"

Maricara cocked her head. "That thing?"

"That scent. Not human, not animal. Never smelled it before."

"Yes." Joan straightened. "I caught it too, almost like perfume, but not. What was that?"

"I don't understand," Maricara said.

"Didn't you sense it, Your Grace?" Audrey's voice was still not quite back to normal, a shade too brittle and bright. "Or are your Gifts not as keen as you've portrayed?"

"It was *drákon*," Kimber realized, when Maricara only continued to stare at his sister. He had been watching her, the changing light over her face, the shadows hollowing her cheeks, the uncharted depths of her eyes. When she blinked and angled them back to his, he felt the truth of his words strike like a punch to his gut: *drákon*.

So Kimber held very still. He kept his features composed, as if he'd known all along, as if the new and awful comprehension rising through him didn't exist; he was the Alpha; he was his father's son; so of course he had known. But the wine burned sour in the back of his throat.

He swallowed the sour. "It was the scent of *drákon*, wasn't it?"

"Yes." She lifted a shoulder, almost helpless. "Of course it was. That's how I knew it was the *sanf*, and not merely people. You've never encountered such a scent before?"

"Not like that."

"How can that be?" said Audrey. "It wasn't anything like us!"

"It was *something* like you. A small something, not a full-blooded dragon, but someone lesser. Didn't you know? It's how they find us. They're only Others. So they use someone of dragon blood, not too powerful, just enough to track us. Just enough for the kill. It's how they've always done it."

"A victim," Kimber asked. "Or a collaborator?"

"Both. Either. The *sanf inimicus* don't care."

Joan had her hand back at her throat. "But—who has blood like that? There's no one of the shire so diluted that we couldn't tell what they were."

"*None* of you are like that?"

"No," said Kim. "Some of us are stronger than others, but

everyone has Gifts of varying degrees. It's—it's how we breed. Our lines are carefully kept."

"Ah." The princess picked up her spoon again, rolling the edge back and forth against her plate. She spoke with that small, tight smile that sharpened the curves of her face. "Yet where I come from, I assure you, there are bastards aplenty."

CHAPTER ELEVEN

It was going to rain. She could feel it in her bones, most particularly the smallest finger of her right hand. It had been broken when she was ten, and had healed before the human physician could even make the trip up to the castle from his hamlet three days away. It had healed straight, of course. There was hardly a bump at all from the fracture. But it still ached occasionally, a phantom pain to remind her of what it had once been like to be ten, a newlywed alone in an echoing palace, in a chamber leafed with gold and studded with diamonds, and a husband who chided her for trying to lock the door to her room against him.

The dark English clouds were seething over the dark English sea. The moisture saturating the air was enough to feel like slime clinging to her hair and skin. Maricara was a creature of the cool, arid alps. Rain was not her element.

"You should stay here tonight," she said to the earl. He had followed her nearly into the hotel bedchamber, was standing silently near the doorway with his arms folded across his chest. Sconces of candles behind cut glass adorned the walls, their flames burning dim but steady.

Kimber's position kept him from the light. She wondered if he did it deliberately, if he had begun to realize how much she could fathom from his eyes.

She crossed to the nightstand, holding on to a corner as she removed her heels. She could hear Rhys and the sisters in the parlor beyond, the three of them caught in an unspeaking circle, everyone waiting, it seemed, for the rainclouds to rupture, for the weight of the water to fall.

"You're most generous," said Kimber. He spoke his native language exactly the same way he had spoken French: with effortless elegance, as if the words themselves were made just to be shaped by his lips, to resonate with his low, agreeable voice.

"The roads will be too muddy tonight to return, in any case." Mari stripped off the right pump, balancing a moment with her arm out, then the left. "The bed is large and comfortable. If you try, the four of you might fit."

His brows lifted. "That's not quite how I envisioned it."

"Well, I suppose a gentleman would offer it first to his sisters, but they seem hardy enough." The looking glass on the nightstand caught her face in a square of pewter; she began to remove the diamonds from her hair. "Frankly, were it a matter between me and the brown-eyed one—"

"Audrey."

"Yes. *She'd* be on the floor."

The glass was small. She couldn't see his face in it, so she couldn't see if he smiled. She felt him though, felt him as clearly as ever, even through the stifling humidity.

He was anticipating a thousand outcomes to this moment. The

rainstorm boiling off the sea only heightened his awareness; he would be like her in that way. They could not help but feed off the energy of the air.

The sconcelight, the shape of the room, the downy bed. The bright, heavy stones she'd used for adornment: all factors into this instant, into what she might do next.

Without her heels, the hem of the cocoa gown rumpled against her feet, an accidental train bunched at her ankles. She turned around and walked carefully back to Kimber, holding out her hand. He accepted the diamond clips she poured into his palm without comment, a baron's fortune singing and sparkling against his cupped fingers.

Thunder began a long, distant rumble. She removed her bracelets, one by one, never looking away from his face.

"And where," asked the earl, "are you planning to sleep, Your Grace?"

She smiled. She tilted her head and dropped the bracelets into his other palm. "You feel where I hid the key to the safe, don't you? It's a fairly simple lock. I have faith you'll manage it."

"Pray do not delude yourself," he said courteously, "into thinking that you're leaving this hotel alone."

"Try sleeping head to foot. That's how we did it in the mountains when I was a girl. You can fit more people on the mattress that way."

"Charming. I'll bear it in mind the next time I actually cannot afford to acquire my own hotel room. My dear child, you do realize the second you Turn, I'll be after you."

"But I rather think you won't catch me, Lord Chasen. You haven't yet."

Now he smiled, a half smile, a predator's smile, cold and gleaming; it turned his gaze to flint. "Maricara. You don't want to goad me into action tonight."

"Yes, that's true. What I want is for you to take my belongings back with you to Darkfrith tomorrow. I'll join you there. Really," she added, when his smile never changed. "Do you think I'd let you abscond with all my best jewelry?"

"It's not actually *absconding* if you *give* it to me."

"And I'm not. I'm merely handing it to you with the conviction that I'll get it back soon."

Without another word, the earl spread his fingers. Sapphires and diamonds tumbled in a shower of light to his feet.

"There are monsters out there," he said quietly. "And I don't want to have to fight them yet. Stay here, Princess. Stay here, where it's safe."

"I wish I could," she said, and Turned before he could add anything else, before he could finish reaching for her waist with his hands, and she wouldn't have to feel the urge to close her eyes and lean into him, to believe in words like *stay* and *safe,* no matter how beautifully he said them.

He did follow, of course. As far as she could tell, he didn't even take the time to alert his siblings; he just Turned to smoke, exactly as she had. But she knew the town in a way that he didn't; she knew the crooks and crannies of the rooftops; where the wind held a constant upsweep; which alleys were longest and darkest; which garrets would be empty.

She also knew that he'd be able to feel her—but she was willing to take risks he wouldn't. So she raced to the town square, where cobblestones echoed with horses' hooves, and carriages could be found at nearly any hour, jingling as they struck the bumps and holes. A foursome of oil lamps stuck atop poles threw light upon a statue of Poseidon in the center. She wound around his trident and then his beard, and all the horses trotting nearby began to shudder— then to veer. Coachmen, hauling at their reins, started to shout.

The earl remained a sheet of gray above. She'd been right; he would not descend.

So she did. There was a gutter at the foot of the statue that led to a tunnel that led to the sea. It was black and filthy and clogged with trash. She darted through it as quickly as she could—rotting vegetables; oyster shells; excrement; a living rat, which turned, red-eyed, and shrieked at her approach—and emerged like a bullet into the tide, shooting up through the spray and into the very first rain-drops that were beginning to fall.

She kept going. Kimber was no longer near, and neither was her priory. She punched through the bottom of a fat, salty cloud and used it as her cover, letting herself blow with the gathering storm back to land.

"They're gone," said Joan, lifting her head. She'd been lazing in a chair by the fire, her feet out with her ankles crossed, a fist support-ing her cheek. She sat up abruptly, looking around the room. "They Turned, just now. Did you feel it?"

"Yes," said Audrey, in the opposite chair, then muttered, "Lackwits."

Rhys had been pretending to be asleep on the floor by the hearth, a pillow stuffed under his neck. He'd unbuttoned his waist-coat and kept on his boots, his fingers laced over his stomach.

He'd felt them Turn. He'd felt Maricara's intention before it even happened, her eagerness to become smoke; it had washed over him in waves of lovely deep power, like strong spirits, like lau-danum. It had kept him locked in his motionless state; he'd wanted nothing to interrupt the sensation of her, even the sensation of her departure.

Joan tugged a hand through her wig, disgruntled. "Well, bug-ger. What are we supposed to do now?"

Audrey came to her feet. "I don't know about you two, but I'm taking the bed."

She stepped over his boots and walked to the bedchamber on a yawn, her tinseled skirts sweeping the floor behind her.

She went inland. Kim could tell that much. He caught the faint lure of her to the south, and so that was where he drifted, trying not to panic, to succumb to anger, or the fear for her that buzzed through him like atoms charged with the storm.

The rain began gently. It was a mist, and then a sprinkling, and it was no great difficulty to maneuver through it. Rain this sheer was more like a caress than a hindrance, especially when he did not fight it. He could be flat or deep, might or persuasion; the rain would let him know what he needed to do.

He blew past the last yellow-lit streets of the town, over darker cottages and orchards, steaming fields melting into moors of wildflowers and peat.

The rain picked up. It began to feel less like a caress and more like a great many tiny needles, but still Kimber stayed smoke.

That's what Maricara was doing. He could perceive it.

The thunder increased. Lightning forked the amethyst sky. The wind burned with electricity and traces of her, telling him, *yes, there,* or *no, you've gone too far, she circled back.*

There were farms below him. He sensed those too, the scant vibrations of humans in slumber, of cows and bulls and goats huddled in barns, or against tall trees.

He did not detect that sly, slight sense of dragon again. Not here. Not yet.

And then he lost her.

Just like that; lightning flashed, the wind slammed from the other direction, and all awareness of her was just—obliterated.

He pulled thick. He fought the storm and hovered in place,

seeking new clues. But all he got was rainfall and grass and dirt and leaves being washed clean of their daily dust. The last farmer's cottage he'd passed had a chimney that leaked the aroma of scorched peat—he still smelled that, for God's sake, and it was at least fifteen miles back.

Where had she gone?

The wind blew harder, ruffling his edges. He fought it a minute longer and then Turned to dragon, maddened, soaked instantly, straining against the blunt rage of the storm.

He dipped lower to the earth. Water sluiced off his scales and the dagger tips of his wings, down his claws. It stung his eyes and he narrowed them into slits; long, gilded lashes shielded him from the worst of it.

He skimmed a slow loop above the moor. Had there been anyone about it would have been suicidal; he was vividly colored, easily within the range of a flintlock. But there were no Others, no *drákon*... and no Maricara.

He kept on. Woods. Meadows. Ponds whipped to whitecaps, reeds bent in half along their shores. Alders and oaks with their leaves all pointing the direction of the gale. There came a moment when Kimber realized he was no longer entirely certain where he was: thirty miles inland? Forty-five? But if he turned his head, he could still taste the salt in certain raindrops. The sea would be behind them. So that was all right.

He kept on. And on. He wasn't going to give up, but he was starting to rethink his situation. What if she'd landed long ago, holed up in a barn or an empty silo? What if she'd doubled back to Seaham or some other town, if she had another hotel, another bed? What if—

Then he felt her. His body realized it before his mind did; he was already banking right, zooming in a long, straight line to minimize his friction against the headwind. His wings took the force of his turn with a straining hurt. His eyes shed tears into the wind.

A tingle like warmth along his spine. Gunpowder and flowers, a kiss of her perfume filling his muzzle.

She was there. He felt her like he felt the earth, like he felt the common elements of copper or wood, clay and quartz. She was there before him, essential and wild, a zigzag of sensation that washed over him, that bounced against his senses and led him east, where she flew. Where she dove and rose like a dolphin in the surf.

He first saw her in a burst of blazing light: a tiny dragon silhouetted against massive clouds, slicing through the rain in a frozen coil. The light died; his vision dissolved, but it didn't matter, because he knew where she was now, high above him, ripping through vapor with fangs and talons.

He used instinct to guide him. The rain intensified, striking hard against him, but she was still there ahead. Broken lightning revealed her like sketches in a picture book, wings open, wings closed, up, up, a long ripple down. She rode the wind like no one he had ever seen, diving headfirst into it, tearing against it, letting it flip her around and around. When he was close enough he could see the water shearing off her body, drumming the fine skin of her wings with a brutal, relentless rhythm.

He soared nearer. She didn't even seem to notice, caught in her loops and turns. Her eyes—almond-shaped, vivid silver—met his without blinking. She didn't try to flee, or Turn, or end her ballet with the storm. She only glided a moment, then tilted to her right into a slow, slow fall, one wing tucked in.

Kimber followed.

It was ruddy difficult. She made it look easy, every inch of her taut, only the mane down her neck flipping wildly with the velocity of her descent. As she drew ahead of him the pale, metallic tipping of her wings became the most visible part of her, silver tracings marking the points and bones of her grace.

His own wing began to ache. The ground was rushing nearer.

Still she held her form; together they corkscrewed in wide, flat circles, until a new gust of wind shoved him violently aside, forcing him to tuck and roll, to flap frantically to regain control. When he found his bearings again she was back above him, shooting upward in a curve. Kimber exhaled rain and air and once more began to follow.

She vanished into a cloud. He was right behind her, engulfed in the clogging vapor. Clouds were not meant for respiration. With every mouthful he felt his throat closing, his lungs shrinking, struggling for dry air.

He'd already lost sight of Maricara, who was pulling too far ahead. If he Turned to smoke, he wouldn't have to breathe—but dragons were swifter than smoke. And the wind would shred him to tatters.

He would not lose her again. Kim closed his eyes and let the animal in him take command, letting his dragon side have full rein.

Ah, yes. His teeth snapped closed, his claws clenched. The dragon knew what to do, how to slow his heart and strain the air, how to move through the thunderhead with its warmer jets and channels, let them push him higher, faster, to where she flew.

Mate. She wasn't far, female and slight. He didn't need to open his eyes again to see her. She was a clear vision in his mind, a very dark goal. And he was closing in.

The air began to charge, an unpleasant, electric itch crawling under his scales. It became pressure, and then pain: the lightning erupted as a shock, a column of power splintering feet behind him that singed his tail and jolted fire through his heart. Thunder swallowed him with it, grabbed down into the marrow of his bones and ripped him inside out.

It knocked him senseless. It sent him into free fall. He came awake with the clouds now a wall above him and the wind howling in his ears, his body trembling as he plummeted to his death.

No.

Kimber stiffened. He flipped upright, swerving drunkenly—black earth, black sky, fresh lightning to show him how close he'd come to annihilation—the flowers on the moor were visibly mauve and pink—

Rain hammered his face. He swooped upward, gritting his teeth and letting pain in his blood become an ally, become muscle and nerve. He was *not* going to fail.

He stabbed through the belly of the clouds. He tore a tunnel through the murk, gathering speed, gathering momentum, feeling that dangerous buildup of lightning again, prickling down to his claws. . . .

Kimber pushed harder. If he could have made noise, he would have been screaming, but there was only the cacophony of storm and thunder and the coming clap of fire—

He speared through the top of the cloud bank, breaking free to sudden silence: to heaven. To stars. To a placid ocean of air cooled with the night. His ears rang with the quiet.

And there she was, floating. Peaceful. As if she'd only been waiting here for him, silent as the moon. As if the planet below wasn't still a writhing hell, flickering with veins of purple light.

She did not glance at him. He soared nearer and she didn't pull away. Her eyes shone half-lidded and luminous; the light this high held a clarity that never reached the earth, undimmed with coal fumes or precipitation. Starlight defined each perfect scale along her body, each brilliant thread of her ruff, every eyelash. Her breathing slowed, and then slowed more; with every respiration she glimmered, ebony and silver, a flawless complement to the night.

He could hear her heartbeat. He could hear thunder below them and her heartbeat, strong and steady, and Kimber realized he had never heard anything so compelling in his life.

Mate.

All his worry, all his rage and pain seemed to soften, to melt.

Maricara lifted her head to test the wind and then flipped into a languid roll. He had a glimpse of her stomach, of shining black talons, and then she was right-side up again, still holding her sleepy, half-lidded look.

He edged closer. He came as near as he could without touching her, willing her to turn her head, to look at him again, but she didn't. So Kim opened his wings to lift above her, an easy thing, coming back down to touch his claws lightly against her back.

She accepted the pressure of him. She adjusted to it, maintaining her height, but that was all. They flew on, their movements now matched.

He'd never flown like this with anyone before, certainly not with any female. When the men of the tribe scoured the skies they tended toward isolation, unless on patrol. Younger *drákon* especially might game in the air, they might mock-fight, but there was never anything like this . . . this delicate and exquisite maneuvering, aligning his skills to hers.

She was warm. She was beautiful. She had abilities that he couldn't yet even understand, but the one thing Kimber absolutely understood was this: Maricara was his.

And in this star-crystalled moment, that was enough.

He wanted to descend with her and he didn't; they were alone here, alone in a way they would never be back in the human world. Kim was selfish enough to imagine what it would be like simply to keep flying with her, to let her guide him to the moon, or to cherry-tinted tropical clouds, to a place where there was no tempest or hunters at all. They didn't have to give this up just yet.

But Maricara dropped free of his touch. He let her go, keeping a few feet above her. When they hit the storm bank again he remained just as close, but she didn't attempt to lose him. She only kept going, steady now, and it wasn't long before they had sunk out of the haze and returned to the rain, ferocious water hissing off their backs.

She seemed to have a destination in mind, although there wasn't much below them but fields and what might have once been a grove of fruit trees, now spreading unchecked. When the next bout of lightning struck, he saw where they were headed, a ruin of some sort, an abbey perhaps, with half the stone roof sloughed away and high, crumbling walls enclosing chambers of weeds and stained glass.

Maricara Turned to smoke. Kim did the same, and the relief was nearly dizzying: The deluge slid through him; he didn't have to struggle to fill his lungs. She sifted down to one of the open chambers, through an archway of a loggia that still had its stone columns and a tall, peaked ceiling. Near its end she found a new room, also still with its ceiling, with a limestone floor, and blankets, a dark lantern and a pillow.

She became woman. Kim hesitated, lingering as smoke near a window of colored glass. And Maricara still didn't look at him, or even act as if she knew he was there. She walked to the blankets, drew them around her and sank to the floor. She picked up what he'd thought was part of another blanket—perhaps it was—but it was small, long and thin.

Like a blindfold.

She lifted it to her face. She used it to cover her eyes, tied the ends behind her head in a knot. Then she rolled to her side with her head on the pillow and let out a long, deep sigh, her shoulders at once going lax.

She was asleep.

It came to him gradually: She was asleep. Kimber materialized into his human shape, standing soundless in that corner. She didn't stir. Her respiration didn't change. Her lips were parted and her hair pinned with the cloth, fanning out in a dark glossy spill behind her. She'd cupped both hands beneath her chin.

He squatted to his heels, watching her. When the night finally gave him chills he crossed to her, easing down carefully at her back. He lifted the blankets, inching close, sliding an arm under her neck, letting the other rest over her waist, until her back was pressed against his chest and her legs lifted to tuck against his. She sighed again but didn't try to move away. To Kimber her bare skin felt like silk, like welcome.

She said something a few minutes later, a drowsy mumble:

"This doesn't change anything."

"No," Kim lied, very soft. He turned his face to her hair. "I know."

And she relaxed back into slumber.

He stayed awake, listening to the rainfall pattering against dirt and stone, his body alight, attuned to her every breath.

CHAPTER TWELVE

Birds were singing. She listened to them with something like wonderment; beyond the rare eagle or falcon that careened around the mountain peaks, Mari didn't know very much of birds. She'd hardly heard any songbirds over the course of her life. But there were two of them at least, their voices lifting and warbling, a question and an answer, intense, layered harmonies that tangled into beauty. It was a different sort of music from that of stones, she mused. More vibrant. More alive. They were notes that ached in her chest, they came so sweet.

But wait... she did know something about birds. She'd heard another one recently... what was it? A rush? A thrush.

Yes. A thrush.

And that was when Maricara realized that even though the

world was still dark, she was awake. On the ground. Enfolded in a man's arms. Everything smelled of rainwater and drenched moss—
—and him.

She sat up quickly, her hands rising to her face. She tore off the blindfold and blinked down at him, their hips and thighs still pressed warm together. Kimber gazed back at her with a look of calm green, folding his arms behind his head.

"Good morning," he said.

She couldn't speak. She stared from him to the blindfold in her hands, unable to make any sort of connection between the two— and those birds, still singing—

"I'd ask how you slept," he said, "but I already know."

She'd left him at the hotel. Hadn't she? She remembered it. She'd left, and he'd followed, but she'd eluded him, made it all this way—and then—

"My gracious," drawled the earl. "I never thought to see a woman look quite so appalled to discover me in her bed." He raised a knee to regard the brown woolen blanket that covered them both. "So to speak."

Her voice came on a squeak. "What are you *doing* here?"

"Regretting very much the lack of a mattress, thank you. Pity you couldn't manage to pilfer one along with the pillow. This floor is astoundingly hard."

She realized the blanket had dropped to her waist and snatched it up again, then leapt to her feet.

That, unfortunately, left him uncovered. He didn't seem to mind. She glanced around and discovered the other blanket behind her, kicked it to him. The earl caught it in one hand and drew it over his chest, not quite smiling, while the heat climbed up her neck and into her cheeks.

"No," he said suddenly, as she took a final breath. He sobered. "Don't Turn, Maricara. Please."

And there was something in his voice, a note so close to the sweetness of the birds...it caught her short. She wavered, staring down at him.

The day had risen clear and the monk's cell was suffused with light. Two glass lozenges from the elaborate clover-shaped window were missing but the rest flared crimson and gold, opulent colors lacquered bright across the limestone. A deep red edge fell in a line across his legs, switched to yellow over her feet. He sat up slowly and was caught in its bicolored brilliance; unclad, attentive, as if she might indeed lift to her toes and vanish should he make an untoward move.

She yet might.

"Do you remember anything of last night?" Kimber asked.

Mari didn't answer. Leaves from a sycamore outside the window made a gentle rustling; slender branches swayed between a broken lozenge and a whole one, emerald and sun in the corner of her vision.

She felt flushed and cold together, the scratchy blanket an exquisite torment against her own bare skin.

"Maricara," he prompted. "Anything at all?"

This time she managed to control her voice. "Did we have intercourse?"

His lashes lowered; the almost-smile returned. "*That* I hope you would remember." He lifted a conciliatory hand. "Relax. You seemed all in, actually. And it happened that I was somewhat tired myself. But if you're feeling rested—no, I'm not serious. Please, just...don't run." Kimber sighed. "I'm sorry. You can stand all the way over there, if you like. You can go stand in the walkway. But we need to talk. I promise not to ravish you. I believe I can manage to control myself that far."

So she took a step back, just one, and he gave a slight nod.

"How long have you been Turning in your sleep?"

She felt the blood rising again in her cheeks. The light from the window began to seem rather painfully bright. "Is that what happened? You found me—when I was in flight?"

"Eventually." He crossed his legs beneath the blanket. "You led me on a merry chase first, though, I can tell you that. There were a few somewhat...unsettling moments. I will admit I've developed a newfound interest in cowering indoors, possibly under furniture, during future thunderstorms."

She looked down at her feet. At her own rumpled blanket, her naked toes. A puddle of water shimmered flat on the floor not three paces away, pooled in the pitted stones beneath the window.

The earl spoke more quietly. "You're amazing. Do you realize that? I've flown since I was a boy, I've flown with the best of our tribe but you—frankly, I don't know anyone with skills to match yours. You've mastered moves I didn't even realize were possible."

Her eyes flashed to his. He wasn't smiling. His tone wasn't teasing, or ironic. His expression remained calm and courteous, as if he'd just complimented her on her coiffure, or her arrangement of flowers in a vase. The line of red light rippled down the muscles of his arm, melted into shadow against his flat stomach; the yellow caught the mussed fall of his hair.

"Well," she said, and nothing more.

"Perhaps, someday, you might want to share a few of your secrets with me. Just a few."

"I don't know any secrets."

"Oh," he said, "then perhaps you'd care to hear some of mine."

Mari chewed at her lower lip. Kimber leaned forward slightly, his elbows on his knees.

"I'm afraid of losing, Princess. I don't like to lose. I never have. I've been the best at nearly everything my entire life, and it's... exhausting. I think maybe you understand what I mean by that. Every man agonizes over failure, I suppose. We don't like to disappoint those who depend upon us, our wives, or our parents or children. But a king must trouble himself with much more than that. By his birth and his nature he is more than his family. He is his nation, and that's what we are, Maricara, both of us. We're kings, and so we are nations. When I fail as a king, when I lose, it's not merely I who suffers. It's my tribe. Those weaker than I, and less able. Every single one of them is dear to me, locked tight in my heart. They look to me for courage and guidance, and God knows I do my damnedest for them, but..." His voice trailed off; he shook his head, his mouth tightening.

"It's hard," she said.

"Yes."

Her fingers plucked at the nap of the wool against her thigh. "They can't do what you do. They don't have to, so they don't comprehend. Possibly...they even fear you a little."

"Possibly they do."

"But still you defend them. You worry."

"Exactly."

She hesitated, then dropped down in place, tucking the blanket beneath her knees. "So you're afraid of the *sanf.*"

"All evidence suggests I'd be an idiot to underestimate them."

"They're only Others. They haven't managed to eliminate us yet."

"Maricara," he said evenly, "should these particular Others come to Darkfrith, should they violate my land, harm a single innocent of my tribe..."

She waited, watching him search for the words, the fine curves and planes of his body shaped in red and gold.

"I'm not afraid of these hunters. I'm afraid for mankind. For what will happen to them. If the *sanf* declare war...I'm not going to lose."

"Yes," she said, and nodded. "I do understand."

"I know." He reached for her hand without hurry, giving her plenty of time to pull away. But she didn't. She let his fingers slip over hers, a light caress, gentle as the summer breeze that roused the sycamore leaves. Her hand was lifted; their fingers intertwined.

"What would you do?" he asked. "In my position?"

She thought of what she *had* done: warn her brother, flee the castle. At the time she'd believed it the best she could offer any of them. Despite her efforts, her people truly didn't want her among them. They hadn't for years. She'd tried leading them and protecting them, had tried carrying on the way the princes of *Zaharen Yce* always had, because that's what the Zaharen demanded, justice and power and wealth, the ingrained surety that they were better than all the fragile creatures crawling the earth. They were *drákon,* and so were better. And in return, the dragons of the mountains had gotten . . . a girl-child. A peasant who wore rubies and imported French fashions, who flew through nightmares every night and held on to her position by the skin of her teeth.

It had been easy to leave. If she had been a real princess, a true leader, she would have stayed even though they hadn't wanted her to.

Maricara spoke to their clasped hands. "Anything," she said at last. "I would do any terrible thing to save my people, no matter what came." She glanced up at him through her lashes. "In your position."

He regarded her gravely. Over the course of their talk he'd shifted more into the yellow-thrown light; his eyes held a strange, clear glow she didn't think she'd ever seen before. It might have been concentration, or relief, or anticipation. It might have been nothing more than the effect of the clover-leaf window, turning the pale green to greenish gold.

He was going to kiss her. She realized it; she held frozen for it; she could not move. She could not even try.

Kimber tilted toward her. His fingers curled over hers.

"You promised," she whispered, but she didn't really mean it. She didn't really want him to stop.

He came so close his face blurred, and then even closer. He traced words against her cheek, warm, almost inaudible. "This isn't ravishing." Slowly his lips moved to hers, touching, gliding: a languorous, sleek sensation. "This is merely seducing."

Mari found that she was holding her breath. "I don't..." He turned his lips back to her cheek, stroked the tips of his fingers in a line along her shoulder, up to her neck. She felt her eyes close and her head tip back in unexpected pleasure. "I don't perceive the difference."

"Ah." His other palm slid up to cup the back of her head. His legs eased around her hips. His lips brushed to her ear, the rough skin of his chin a surprising scrape against her throat. "For one thing"—his voice lowered to the barest, broken murmur—"with ravishment... there's less conversation."

And he bit her earlobe. Not hard, nothing painful, but it sent goose bumps along her arms and somehow tipped her head even more. With both hands in her hair he brought her mouth to his, this time without languor but with fire. With heat and intent, his body ardent, only blankets between them. He held her face between his palms and drew his lips back and forth over hers until she could not breathe.

She'd never known such a thing. She'd never been kissed in such a way. She'd had no idea that *kiss* meant this whispery, butterfly nervousness in her veins. The scent of him wrapping around her, filling her pores. Kimber's hand slipping under her hair, down her back, his fingers spread, urging her nearer. Her heart leaping in her chest. Her fingers against his arms, feeling the smooth flex of muscle and tendon, strength that pulled her nearer still, until their bodies grazed, because the blankets had somehow fallen aside.

His tongue brushed hers; he tasted of man and smoke. Their lips parted, clung, returned to delicious friction. The dragon in her woke to barbarous joy, lifting her blood into light, into fire—everywhere his skin met hers, every flushed, sensitive place. He made a sound in his throat and closed his arms hard around her and—

Maricara Turned to smoke.

She didn't mean to. It happened without her volition; one instant she was there with him, feeling her heart throb, feeling the butterflies rifle through her veins—and the next she was near the ceiling, no heart, no panic. Just vapor, diaphanous against the stone.

Kimber remained motionless below her, still seated on the floor with his legs apart, a very obvious empty space where she used to be. After a long moment he glanced up at where she lingered, then climbed to his feet.

"Come back," he said. No anger. No accusation. His voice carried a shadow of tension, but the chiseled contours of his face revealed only that same polite patience he'd displayed before their lips first met.

It was enough to give her weight, to let her trickle down to earth and pour into the shape of a woman.

She knelt and scooped up the blanket, wrapping it tight around her, her hair tugged in its folds. Kimber remained where he was, out of the light with his hands by his sides, looking at her askance.

"I'm sorry," she blurted.

"No, I'm fairly certain that's what *I'm* supposed to say. Poor princess, we keep going about this backward. First we kiss, *then* we sleep together..." He ran a hand through his long hair, pushing it from his cheekbones with a little more force than necessary. "It seems we were teetering at the edge of ravishment, after all. So. My humble apologies, Your Royal Grace." And he dropped his hand to execute a flawless bow, made only slightly unreal by the fact that he wore no clothing, not even the blanket any longer. And that he was still fully aroused.

Mari tore her eyes away. "I do not—" she began, and gave up, and started over. Damn it all, she was blushing again. "I didn't plan that. I meant no insult."

"Well, that's a relief. Never fear, I'm a thick-skinned sort of fellow. I've had far worse responses from the ladies fair."

She didn't want to delve into that, to wonder what *worse* might be, and what *ladies* he meant. She didn't want to think of him like that, or like this: charming and nude and impersonal, as comfortable in his own skin in this bare colored chamber as he was an earl in powder and velvet and pearls. She didn't want to feel that she had to explain herself, to speak of the butterflies.

But she was speaking anyway. She was wringing her hands. "You see, once I—"

"Please." Kimber shook his head, his tone now peaceful. "Lovely black dragon. It's forgotten. Look there, have you noticed the angle of the light? It's close to noon at least. If we don't get back soon, Audrey's going to accost every unfortunate pig farmer in the region, searching for us."

"Yes. All right."

But he didn't move, and she didn't. They only gazed at each other.

Mari broke it off first. She bent down, retrieved the other blanket, grabbed the pillow by a corner of its cover and placed them both by the lantern against the wall, out of easy sight. She found the blindfold she'd tried wearing for the first time last night and felt a new wave of embarrassment, crumpling it in her hand, tossing it on top.

She'd thought it would help. She'd thought if she could not see anything, if she couldn't actually open her eyes in the middle of the dreams—

"I suppose I can return for all this later," she said, knowing that she never would. She did not turn around. "Very well. I'm ready."

"Maricara." Still peaceful calm. "How old were you when you wed?"

She closed her eyes. He couldn't see her face; it didn't matter, but she did it anyway. "Nine years. Eleven months."

There was a pause. "How many days?"

"Three."

Outside the leaves kept up their quiet murmur. The day was warm and sparkling bright. The songbirds began again their ballad of bejeweled notes.

"Did he hurt you?"

She kept her tone untroubled. "I was a virgin. Doesn't every husband hurt his bride?"

"No," Kimber answered. "Not every one." Another pause. "You will return with me to Darkfrith, won't you?"

"Yes."

"Good. There's something there I think you'll appreciate."

She did look at him then, turning just her head, a quick glance from over her shoulder. "What is it?"

Kimber smiled at her, a true smile, and it was like watching the sun rise to paint light across the mountains. "A safe place to sleep."

She would fly there. There was nothing he could say that would convince her to cinch herself back into human clothes and climb into that coach for the daylong trip to Chasen Manor—especially with his sisters as company. She supposed she could have ridden in the second carriage, the one they had to rent to transport her safe, but the thought of trapping herself inside a tiny, enclosed space, jostling over ruts and ridges and mud holes for an entire day . . .

Far simpler to fly. Kimber knew it too. In front of his siblings he attempted to persuade her, but in the end, when it was down to just the two of them arguing in her antechamber as the others waited downstairs, he gave a shrug and began to remove his clothes once more.

He would not, naturally, allow her to go alone.

As if she hadn't spent her life that way. As if she hadn't crossed the world by herself, in moonlit dreams and awake. But one look into his eyes was all she needed to realize he would not be moved on this.

"The *sanf* are out there," he said flatly.

"I won't be going anywhere near them. They'll be roasting in the heat on the ground. I'll be high above."

"And I'll be right beside you."

"That's really not necessary."

"Indulge me. Consider it a favor. Just think of all the ways you might demand repayment."

He said it with a perfectly temperate expression. There was no reason at all for her gaze to drop to his lips, to remember in a flush of warmth their languid touch and taste, to feel that wonderful, awful nervousness wash over her again.

"I promise you'll get the chance," the earl added, mild.

Mari felt her mouth go dry. "Another promise."

"Aye. And if I break it, well...perhaps you'll be merciful. A man is only so strong."

She'd heard of chameleons, odd little almost-dragons that changed their skin to match every new environment. In the plaster-and-gilt civilization of the Seaham resort Lord Kimber Langford did no less. In nearly the same short amount of time she had taken to drag a brush through her hair and slip into a robe—she was going to Turn, after all, no matter what he said—he had transformed into someone new: his jaw clean-shaven, his queue tied neat, his coat of pressed silk redolent with something both musky and pleasant, like myrrh. Even the seams to his stockings were straight. By all outward appearances he was a wealthy, entitled peer of the realm once again, shining with silver buttons and garters.

Only his eyes betrayed what dwelled inside him. Against the glamour of the chamber they glowed cool, phosphorous green.

It was a Gift, a rare one. And it didn't manifest in their human shape without animal provocation.

She faced him squarely. "You were going to fly anyway. I overheard you tell your brother."

His mouth quirked; he draped his coat across a side table. "Resourceful. But didn't your parents teach you that eavesdropping isn't very polite?"

"My parents had no hope of it, I hear everything." Mari shrugged. "I can't help it. And I also cannot help but wonder why you'd take such a risk, especially given your aversion to being sighted in daylight as a *drákon* in any form."

"It seems prudent to have a guard in the air for the journey."

"Rhys could do that. Or one of your men."

"Yes," he said. "But they're not me."

Mari walked to the wing chair by the cold, swept hearth, arranged the folds of her maroon satin robe carefully and took a seat, relaxing back as if she were in no hurry to travel anywhere. She leaned her head against the cushion. "You're planning to hunt the *sanf* yourself, aren't you?"

"Not right now."

"Good. Because they'll be anticipating that. They'll be waiting."

"So I thought."

"If they figure out exactly who you are—"

"Maricara. Right now I'm trying to persuade you that the safest course of travel back to Chasen Manor is by coach, tucked nicely inside with my guard and my kin. That's all. Since I plainly haven't the slightest chance in hell of convincing you of that, I am simultaneously calculating the safest flight path home. A path that will lead us far from where we last sensed the hunters. I've no desire to greet them today. Certainly not with your neck on the line as well."

"Better to leave them behind here," she said, unconvinced. "Better to let them wonder and sweat."

"Yes." He moved away from her with a sudden, menacing grace, going to the window, tapping two fingers hard against the glass. He spoke in an undertone, the taps accentuating his words. "By all means, let them sweat."

"Return for them later, when you're better prepared. They won't give up so easily. They'll remain here at least a few more days. In fact, I'll come with you," she offered, when he did not speak. "We'll hunt them together."

"Two kings," he murmured—but didn't turn away from the window. His eyes reflected color off the glass, green against the bright blue sky.

"Yes."

"Smart kings let the peasants do the fighting for them," Kimber noted dryly.

"That rather works out, as I'm secretly a peasant."

"And I'm bloody George III. You've made your point, Your Grace."

She turned her cheek to the cool damask of the cushion. "Then we agree. Today we'll both go as smoke above the coaches. Two guards in the air, rather than one. Tomorrow . . . we'll be royal again."

The earl inclined his head, capitulation tempered by the sardonic curl of his lips. "Splendid. I cannot wait to hear my sisters' reaction to this."

"And your council's."

"Naturally, yes, the council. They'll welcome us home with banners and ballad singers." He glanced back at her; some of the dragon glow began to fade from his eyes. "You're deuced mulish, you know."

Mari crossed her left leg over her right, keeping the robe modestly draped across her lap. "I don't know what that word means. But I do know I'm doing exactly what you would, in my position."

"Pigheaded," he said.

"Precisely."

So they flew. Side by side, two gossamer-gray clouds that drifted high against the wind, and joined edges so often they began to seem melded into one.

CHAPTER THIRTEEN

At the wise and seasoned age of thirteen, Rhys had fallen in love for the first time.

Her name was Zoe. She was the daughter of the village seamstress. She had exotic black eyes and hair of the smoothest, purest ivory, and even though he'd known her since they were infants—since they'd been wet-nursed and day-schooled together—he realized one spring day that he was truly, utterly in love.

She wanted nothing to do with him.

Rhys fancied himself not ill-favored. Even then, he was beginning to show signs of the man he would grow into, and finding maidens of the shire to adore him had never proved a challenge before, except, perhaps, when he was compared to his brother. But Zoe Lane was resistant to his every wile. If he brought her roses, she said she preferred wildflowers. If he brought her wildflowers, she said she preferred them left to grow in the downs.

If he brought her sugar, she wanted salt. If he offered to read her poetry—poetry!—she claimed she'd rather go swimming in the lake.

With the other boys.

He'd fretted and stewed all summer, boiling in a sweat of unfulfilled adolescent desires. He'd tried everything he could think of, being kind, being mean, leaving her be, following her about, and one late night he was seated outside her bedroom window, eating blackberries and sucking the juice from his fingers while he tried to figure his next move, when her face appeared by the curtains, a pale oval framed with even paler hair.

They stared at each other; she was still the most beautiful girl he'd ever known. His stomach got upset just looking at her.

"You're really not going to quit, are you?" She kept her voice low, because, he knew, her mother slept quite near.

"No," Rhys said.

She nodded, vanished, then came back. She beckoned to him and he'd trotted up to the sill just like an eager puppy.

"Stick this needle through your earlobe," she said coolly, holding it up between her thumb and forefinger. "All the way through. Then I'll believe you love me."

The consequences had been instant, and rather immense. He was already supposed to be confined to quarters from eight at night till eight in the morning; Zoe's mother had complained more than once about his behavior around her daughter, and he'd been forbidden by the marquess even to speak with her for a full month. But there was no hiding all that blood. It had flooded his clothing and risen up around him in waves, spreading its scent like the worst sort of alarm, and Rhys never knew if it had been luck or planning that his elder brother reached him in the grand hall of Chasen Manor just before his father did.

He remembered Kimber's face, how his eyes widened as he stepped around the stairway and caught sight of Rhys trying to slip in unnoticed. How he stopped at once, and then turned as Rhys did to see Christoff emerge from his study.

A line of little red dots followed him like a trail along the floor. Rhys stood in the study with one hand pinched to his ear, trying to catch the rest of it so the carpet wouldn't stain.

His father had studied him a long while without speaking, tall and nearly frightening in his severity, candlelight dancing hellish bright behind him. It had *seemed* long, anyway, damned long, and it was all Rhys could do not to fidget while his fingers dripped and his mind raced through excuses.

"There was this needle—" he began.

Christoff interrupted in a deadly soft voice. "I thought I made it incontestably clear you were to stay away from that girl."

And then Kimber took a breath.

"Please, sir," said his brother, standing behind him. "It was my fault."

The marquess's gaze flicked to Kim.

"I dared him to pierce his ear," Kim lied, the golden child, the Alpha heir. "I didn't think he'd really do it."

Rhys snapped his mouth closed. He tried to look innocent.

"May I inquire why?"

"I was bored," said Kim. "And I wanted to see how much it would hurt."

It hurt, as it turned out, a very great deal. But somehow not as much as seeing Kimber punished in Rhys's place, confined to his own quarters, meals of bread and water for three full days and a formal, written apology to his brother for his part in the wretched matter.

When Rhys had tried to sneak meat up to him, Kim had refused it.

"They'll smell it, you dolt," he said through the door.

When he'd asked, softly, why he had done what he did, Kim had answered only, "Because."

Because he was Kimber. Leader, protector at all costs. Because whenever Rhys had fallen—in love, to his knees, into the worst of plots and plans, even at school—Kim was there to help him back up.

Kimber was always there. Rhys tried to admire him for that.

From his vantage now atop the carriage rolling back toward home, he watched the princess flow as smoke across the sky. Her grace, her thrilling beauty, all that defined the best of their kind... and Kimber there, always there, just beside her.

He felt that familiar, unhappy clench in his stomach.

Despite the fact that the sun shone very bright, he found he could not look away.

Kim had sent a man ahead to alert the shire they were returning, to carry the news that there were enemies lurking nearby—only that. He hadn't informed his guard of the thin-blooded *drákon,* the *sanf inimicus.* He hadn't wanted a full-scale panic at Chasen before he was there to contain it.

Tensions had been festering all summer. Before that. Before Maricara had arrived, before Rue and Christoff had left. The tribe's perfect mask had developed its first fatal crack back with that letter from Lia, describing a castle and pebbles and dragons that lived free under the stars.

She, too, is fully one of our kind.

Nothing had been the same since. Nothing had been as safe, or as good. The heat and oppression of this summer had only intensified everyone's tempers. Spats flared more easily and were ended more often with fists. The village tavern was filled to overflowing every night. Creatures designed for glorious flight and battle turned to gin and petty squabbling instead. The number of feuds Kim had had to settle in the past few years had been steadily escalating, most over field boundaries or imagined insults. A few over more serious crimes, like theft. Vandalism. Runners.

With every new disagreement, with every new *drákon* attempting to flee the shire, the old men of the council grew more entrenched behind their beards, hunkered deep into their soft, carved chairs. These were their ways, and that was that. They would *not* be modified, the tribe *would* fall into line, and there would be no debate about it. This is how it had always been done. This would be their gift to the future as well. The traditional laws had more than sufficed all these generations. They were the only solution. Loyalty to the tribe above all.

There had been nights Kim had fallen asleep with his hands actually pressed to his head as if it was trapped in a vise, cursing his parents, cursing his position, the seasons, Lia, the Zaharen. And then he'd wake up the next morning and get dressed and go tackle it all over again. Someone had to.

In fact, the only fine thing to emerge from this disaster, the only filament of luminous clarity, Kim considered, was Maricara herself.

She was all they had for information at this point, his lovely, night-flying princess. Unfortunately, she would also be the only person the tribe would connect with these part-dragon *sanf;* she was of the foreign tribe; the hunters were of the foreign tribe; unspeakable catastrophes were about to unfold, and who had caused it all to come about? Kim could all too easily imagine the council's reaction:

You've brought an ancient enemy to Darkfrith. You've caused the loss of at least three good men, you've flown in daylight as a dragon, you've defiled our rules and traditions and imperiled our very survival and oh, yes, welcome to your new home. We look forward to the wedding. Would you mind very much just stepping into our prison?

Or, even worse:

What's that you say? Lord Chasen described it as a fine place to sleep? Certainly it is. We'll even provide you both a bed.

Better to face that moment, too, in person.

So when they reached the manor house at last, Kim was hardly surprised that there were no singers awaiting them, no banners aloft, nothing remotely festive beyond the desperate flowers and shrubs progressively scorching to a crisp in the gardens. There was, instead, a line of ten unsmiling men standing in the drive beyond the main doors, ignoring the pair of carriages rolling up the wide, roundabout path, staring up instead at the sky.

They wore wigs, every one of them. Even in this weather, the formalities held.

If Kim could have sighed, he would have. As it was, he glided against the velvety edge that was Maricara one last time, then twisted down into man against the hard heat of the earth.

Evening fell. She observed it from a bench nestled beneath the coppice of willows she had once run through to reach Kimber's home, what seemed like ages ago. The mansion was towering walls and windows this close up, mellow stone that sang mellow songs, half-obscured by leaves that never moved, because there was no wind.

She sat alone. Kimber was nearby, Rhys was nearby, the sisters scattered, a thousand heartbeats, a million breaths, all the English *drákon* pulsing life through the Darkfrith twilight in heady, invisible waves.

Some of them were more visible. There were faces to be glimpsed past her little enclosure of willows, people walking in the woods, people staring from behind the beveled windows. There were bright, serpentine dragons floating through a sky of darker green and blue and purple above her. They cut in silence across the pinprick stars, sending them winking.

She was not tired. Not tired enough. She'd eaten as much as she could, she'd taken no wine. She'd asked to be alone to watch the moonrise.

Crickets began to wake. Maricara heard them in the far distance, pockets of chirping buried within the forest. The moon began as a halo of white light against the black rolling horizon.

Around and around the dragons looped overhead.

The place where Kimber wanted her to sleep was called the Dead Room. She'd overheard a pair of footmen whispering the name between them, their voices surprised and hushed. The earl had said only that it was a chamber within the manor designed to contain dragons—full-fledged dragons—to defeat smoke and keep whoever was inside it safely contained.

The Dead Room. No subtlety there, no mystery, for all their mock-human ways. She could damned well figure out what the place was actually for.

Mari gazed at the ascending moon. It shone like a drop of sweet cream, round and fat with the edges nearly misted, so much softer than at home. Everything in England was softer, the air, the savor of wildflowers and wood, the deep indigo night. Even she had become softer, Maricara realized. If she had an ounce of sense or self-preservation, she would Turn and leave this coppice, fly up and out and away, far from any room meant to imprison her kind. Kimber had claimed she was skilled at flight; she didn't know how true that was. She'd been flying since she was a child, going nearly where she wished, when she wished. Surely she could outrun all these cautious, curious *drákon* above her. After all, she'd done what she could here, what she'd come to Darkfrith for. They knew they were hunted now, and they knew by whom. She had no real reason to stay.

She could go anywhere. She could actually wander the globe, with no obligations to anyone or anyplace ever again. She was finally, truly free.

But for him.

But for that kiss, and the butterflies, and the stroke of his fingers along her bare arm.

Maricara closed her eyes. She exhaled a long, steady breath and began her sliding descent into dragon-perception.

Time slowed. The air pressed against her dampened skin. The fading colors of the sunset flared once again but now as vibrations, humming echoes of light that spread through her senses, burgundy, saffron, lapis blue. The crickets roared into lions, deafening; buried minerals beneath her feet chanted and moaned and pleaded for her touch. The paths of the *drákon* soaring above shone like concentric rings behind her lids, every one of them a brilliant link to a chain, repeated over and over again.

Kimber was inside the manor house, alone. In the music room, where they had first met.

She focused on that, *Kimber, music room,* letting all the other noises and rhythms and whispering songs sink away to unimportance, the moonlight gone, the stars swallowed, until there was only him, his quiet breathing, the rustle of his clothing and the press of his shoes into the woolen rug as he shifted forward into a step.

She heard a single note from the lyre. It came again, muted, as if he did not wish to pluck the string but his finger had found the sound anyway.

Another note. Another. It was D, lonely and strange, the same steady tone repeated.

Mari opened her eyes. She rose from the bench and, with one last glance at the cream-drop moon, retraced her path back into the manor house.

The princess stood at the iron door in a *robe à l'anglaise* of French blue and wide lacy ribbons, unmoving. She looked both delicate and chary, her jaw set, her hands folded over her waist. Kim remained at her side, one palm still braced against the cool metal, waiting for her to go in.

He knew how it appeared: Spartan, cavelike, a chamber clearly at odds with the fine bed that had been hastily assembled for it, the Chippendale chair and satinwood desk and tapestries of unicorns and maidens that hung from the walls. Her valise had been placed in here, even her safe. The candelabra from the blue parlor had been set atop it; seven candles in their sterling cups were lit, flames casting shadows that bent and slithered along it all.

It had been named a room but was truly a cell of enormous stone blocks, seven deep in any direction except the ceiling, which had been reinforced with plates of steel. No windows, no vents, no vulnerabilities. The door was solid and barred from the outside; when closed, it met the stone so perfectly a human hair would not slide between them. Without its new furnishings the space was brutally plain—stark, actually. Before this morning it had held a cot and a lantern and nothing else. It had not been designed for comfort. It had been designed to contain outlaw *drákon* in their final hours before being put to death.

And so, beneath the honey of melting wax Kim imagined he smelled sweat and desolation. Behind the thick woven tapestries were last words carved into the walls, good-byes, recriminations, faint tracings he had long ago memorized as a child with cold shivers crawling across his skin. He didn't think there had ever been blood spilled on this floor, at least not in his lifetime. But with a little effort, Kim could smell that too.

Fixed at its brink, Maricara let her gaze travel the chamber. Whatever her thoughts, she kept them to herself.

He felt the will of his people pressing against him. The council members, banished to the outer halls with the servants, waiting, everyone waiting for the last female who could Turn to take that little step.

"Lord Chasen," she said, without looking away from the cell.

"Yes, Princess."

"I'm going to require more than just a promise now. I'm going to require your oath."

"Yes?"

"Swear to me you'll let me out again in the morning."

"I swear," Kim said.

"On the lives of your people," she continued quietly, gazing at the bed. "On the future of your tribe. Your children. Their fates."

"Yes," he said again. "You have my word on it."

The hallway here was plain stone as well. He heard the reverberations of his voice diminish down into nothing. She tilted her head a fraction and glanced up at him. In this light her eyes held no color; he gazed down into bottomless depths.

"Someone once told me I'd be a fool to trust you."

"Who was that?"

"A man who knew you."

Kim dropped his hand from the door. " 'Once' is a very tricky word, Your Grace. It implies things shouldn't change, but they always do. I *will* let you out again."

"Shall I believe you?" she murmured. "Shall I trust you that far?"

"I'll stay with you, then. I'll sleep in the chair."

Her lips curved, just a fraction. Her lashes lowered. "It looks very uncomfortable."

"I admit, the bed would be nicer."

"I don't require quite that much sacrifice. Find your own bed. Come open this door again in the morning."

"As you wish," he said.

But now that he had her here, exactly here where he needed her to be, Kim found himself perversely reluctant to let her go. He meant to release her in the morning. He did mean to. But the thought that she would be trapped down here, in that bed, alone, when he had already held her at night and warmed her body with his and kissed her shoulder in her sleep . . .

"Good night," Maricara said, and passed the threshold into the cell.

He didn't move. The train of her gown made a wide, blue circle upon the stone. She paused at the foot of the bed, her face angled back toward him, her head slightly bowed. She did not speak again, but only lifted a hand to unlace the stomacher to her bodice, using her finger and thumb to slowly draw the ribbon free.

Kim closed the door. He heaved the iron bar into its braces across it, then turned the iron key in its single-sided lock.

"Good night," he said.

It was foolish of them to put all these pretty things in here with her. It was foolish to try to make a prison into anything but what it was.

She sat at the end of the bed and eyed the ornate woodwork of the chair.

It would snap into splinters.

The candelabra—mashed flat. Wax smeared upon the walls.

The tapestries shredded. The desk torn apart.

Only the safe looked like it belonged. It was ugly, the largest, most sturdy block of metal she'd been able to find. It might survive the night.

Her back ached. Her feet hurt. The candlelight burned her eyes.

She crossed to the flames and blew out all but one. Then she Turned to shed the gown, too weary to bother with the corset and tapes, and left it all in a heap where it fell. The valise contained her nightgown. It sifted like a white cloud down her body.

Barefoot, unthinking, she pinched out the final candle and realized at once that the English had not been so foolish after all. Without the candles, the Dead Room plunged into flawless black.

She might walk in her sleep, she might rage. But she would not be able to Turn.

Mari began to laugh. It was small and painful, a bubble in her chest that somehow turned into a smothered sob. She held it in by pressing her hands over her face.

In time, with her arms stretched out before her, she fumbled her way to the bed. It was not as soft as it first appeared; the sheets were cotton instead of satin, and the pillows gave off an aroma of long-deceased fowl.

None of it mattered. She closed her eyes and let the blessed darkness sink into her skin.

She slept without moving. He could feel her stillness, the solemn night wrapped around her, her absolute quiescence. The Dead Room was three floors below his own and half a wing over, sequestered from any other useful part of Chasen. It had been constructed near the heart of the house but sunk into the earth; the closest public space was the wine cellar. The hallway that led to it also led to the back gate of the manor, to a certain path that wound through the woods. Following that path for nigh an hour would lead to a field of bones at the end of it, bones charred and buried, the final remnants of the *drákon* outcasts strewn far from the tribe.

The princess took her rest in a cell brimming with ghosts, gone to her dreams with a peace that eluded him. He imagined her there on the bed he'd helped set up, between the sheets he'd smoothed flat with his own hands.

Rhys shifted beneath his covers, too hot, too aware. The down mattress felt suffocating. Her endless silence drove him mad.

He stared up at the ceiling of his room and wished for the same oblivion that had taken Maricara, or the outcasts.

His body would stop burning either way.

CHAPTER FOURTEEN

We do not have any legends of brothers at war. Perhaps in our history there have never been any. Perhaps if there were, the results were too dreadful to give voice. Our magic is in words and song and flight. Our savagery could rend the very fabric of the sky, sending the sun and all the bright galaxies spilling away like pirate's treasure poured into a white-frothed sea.

We were not meant to fight each other. We were not meant to use our Gifts in such a way.

But what better way for the Others to use *us*, to force us to work against ourselves? Without the *drákon*, all the precious stones and thick veins of gold, all the glories of the land and the blue promise of heaven would become theirs.

Such small, bitter beings. I don't know why we call them delicious.

CHAPTER FIFTEEN

The first child went missing that night.

Save the farms, most of the homes of the tribe were clustered in or at least near the village, which was the core of their commerce and community. It was large enough now almost to be called a town, but it had been known as *the village* since the beginning of their time, and no doubt would continue to be so, even if it ever rivaled London in size.

The girl's name was Honor Carlisle. Her father managed the silver mines that brought so much of the wealth to the shire. His name was Gervase; Kim had known him all his life. The Carlisles lived in a large, Elizabethan brick structure that used to be the gamekeeper's quarters, farther from the village than most. Honor was their only child.

According to everyone he spoke with, the girl was quiet, she was studious, she was obedient. She had few friends, but those she had swore they had not seen her. They also swore she had no special beaux, *drákon* or otherwise.

There had been a time when the notion of a maid of the shire linked in any romantic sense to a human male would have been almost unthinkable. But the way their traditions had been crumbling lately . . . he had to be certain.

Darkfrith had had no rain, but the dawn had come clouded, and the ground was dewed. The girl's footprints revealed she had left by the front door of her home, had crossed alone the long slope of the yard that ended at the road. The grass had grown brittle at its tips, slightly too long. It was easy to follow her trail that far.

The road led in one direction back to the village, and Chasen Manor beyond. The other direction led to the banks of the great River Fier, wide and flat and feeding fish and silt and swirling leaves all the way to the North Sea, miles distant.

Her scent said she walked to the river. And from there, she was gone.

She wasn't a child, really. She was almost fifteen, at the brink of the Turn, should the fates so choose to grace her. By the time Kimber had tracked her as far as he could, had convened and reconvened with the council and the elders and her panic-stricken parents, the sound of Maricara's relentless pounding against the door to the Dead Room hammered like a cold, hard knell throughout the mansion.

No one else had a key. There was but one, and Kim had put it on a ring, on a chain at his waist.

As he passed through the doors of his home, the longcase clock in the vestibule began its noontime chimes; it remained four seconds fast, no matter how it was wound. It was followed at once by all the other clocks in all the other chambers, forty at least, one after another. He'd wanted for years to put away at least some of them, but his sisters had protested. The servants were used to them; Chasen was the seat of a proud and noble family; all the best people had clocks. Better to keep up appearances, especially with the marquess and marchioness gone.

Their combined, jolly melodies going off every three hours made a mess of sound, rebounding off the marble floors and walls.

Maricara's fists striking her door nearly managed to drown them all out.

The majordomo hurried over to him across the black and white tiles, inclining his head.

"My lord, we attempted to contact you—"

"No doubt. I've been outside the shire."

"So we were told. I beg your pardon, Lord Chasen, no one was certain what to do about her. You did convey orders to leave her strictly alone, and without the means to open the door—"

"Yes, it's fine. Thank you."

Kimber did not rush to her. There were more servants watching, pale and observant, and he was Alpha, and so Kim did not rush. But he did make his way straight there, smoothing a hand over his hair as he walked, brushing an errant leaf from his coat.

He'd been dragged from his bed at daybreak. He'd thrown on clothes in the dark without waking his valet, and had been searching for the girl ever since. He was half-surprised to see he even wore boots of a matching color.

Closer to the Dead Room the noise evolved into something more like a muffled boom. There were no bulges in the door from her fists. It was four feet of iron, and even the strongest of *drákon* would have a hard time punching his way through that. But he could only imagine what the other side looked like.

Or, he didn't have to imagine. Kim hoisted the bar free, found the key on his chain, inserted it into its socket—the last *boom* echoed away—and pulled open the door.

She stood with her hair disheveled, two spots of pink high on her cheeks. Her eyes were glittering, her feet were braced apart—she wore a nightgown of sheer muslin; he could clearly see her figure beneath it, the colors of her dusky nipples, the dark triangle between her thighs, tantalizing curves—and in her hand was what had once been the smartly shaped cabriole leg of the chair, snapped clean at its base.

Maricara drew straight, her arm still cocked.

"Good morning," Kimber said. "Won't you join me for breakfast?"

She took a deep breath and spat something in that language he didn't understand, clipped and fluid, her chin rising.

"Kippers, I believe," he said. "And eggs, if you like. I'm sure there's some poached salmon as well."

"Bastard!" *That* was in English. "I trusted you!"

"It does seem to be a few minutes past morning—"

"A few! I've been trying to get out of here for hours!"

He lifted his hands to her, palms out. "I apologize. Deeply. If you wish to Turn into a dragon and bite me, I won't stop you. I only request that you don't maim me first with the chair leg. It's been—a difficult morning."

He stepped back from the doorway. He made certain she could see she wasn't trapped, that the corridor was empty behind him, the faint tinge of daylight from the main hallway beyond lighting the minute cuts and grooves of the stone.

A shade of the hostility faded from her posture. Slowly her arm lowered, until the curved wood of the leg brushed the side of her calf.

The daylight didn't reach far into the Dead Room. Everything behind her was charcoal dark, the bed, the tapestries, the floor. In her gown of floating white, her tumbled hair, her porcelain skin, she gathered the light, became nearly incandescent.

"Or," he went on, because she wasn't speaking and wasn't

moving, and he had to do something to distract himself from going over to her, from pulling her into his arms, "if you really must hit me with that thing, I suppose I can take it. Please not the face."

Her lips twitched. She actually seemed to be considering it. He chanced a quick glance at the back of the door; there was definitely a series of fresh dimples across the surface.

But after a moment she only said, calmer than before, "I didn't see the point of ruining my hands."

"I'm glad. They're lovely hands."

"Where have you been?"

Kim shook his head, looking down at his boots. Blades of grass still smeared across the leather. "Will you come eat with me? I could use your counsel. King to king."

At least a half minute passed. When he angled his gaze back up to her Maricara met it, shrugged, then dropped the wooden leg with a clatter. "All right." She turned around to walk back into the chamber, going to where her open valise had been placed against the wall, yanking free a frock in a sudden flash of vermilion.

"No fish," she said, from over her shoulder.

"Agreed. I'm a beef and gravy man, myself."

"Remain in the hallway. Do *not* close the door."

He complied. He leaned his back against the wall and then his head, closing his eyes, listening to the quiet, quick sounds of the princess dressing, seeing in his mind's eye the ravaged faces of the parents of Honor Carlisle, begging him for her safe return.

How Gervase's hands shook when he spoke her name. How his wife stared straight at Kim with intensely blue eyes, fierce with unshed tears.

He'd tried his best. He'd made promises he shouldn't have, *of course she's fine, don't worry, we'll have her soon,* he'd rallied his people; he'd searched and searched. He would search again.

He wasn't Christoff, legendary Christoff, or even bold Rue. He was just their son, doing his damnedest to hold back the swift, black edge of the oblivion that had risen to rush toward his tribe.

Bastard, hissed the dragon inside him. *Do not fail them.*

She had asked where he'd been, but she already knew. Everything about him whispered to her of the outdoors, the silken curls that escaped from the ribbon that tied his hair, the fresh air that lingered on his cheeks and clothing like a lover's last glance. The boots, clearly. The loosened cravat. He looked as roguish as a storybook corsair, and just as reputable.

But something was wrong. There were lines around his mouth that had not been there yesterday. There were shadows in his eyes.

It had hooked her heart in some silent, poignant way, and like a trout on the line she didn't know how to thrash free. She'd seen him kind, and she'd seen him arrogant. She had yet to see him truly troubled.

Maricara felt an odd, instant empathy. She knew troubled, all too well.

The hallways down here were more narrow than the rest of the mansion; the earl walked ahead of her a few paces. From time to time he'd glance back as if to make certain she was still there, even though she had not the slightest doubt he could sense her in every single way.

She was vivid enough in her red silk gown. She was sick of dark, sick of deadened air. She needed color like she needed that taste of brisk morning that clung to him, and so when they passed a set of garden doors she merely turned to them, opened them, and stepped out into the day.

It wasn't sunny. It was cloudy, the sky a lovely jumble of blue and purple and slate. A fine, thin haze misted the air, not strong enough yet to be rain or drizzle.

"We should break our fast here," Mari said, lifting her arms to the mist.

"Yes," agreed the earl, not even sounding surprised. "Good idea."

There was a Greek pavilion set atop a very gentle hill nearby, the woods spreading dense and mysterious beyond. It had tall marble columns stained with green lichen, and benches beneath a wide, vaulted roof. When she looked up she saw the ceiling had been set with tiny glass tiles, thousands of them. As she tilted her head, light glistened along the concave curves, revealing colors undimmed by time or weather. It was a mosaic to represent the four seasons.

She took her seat under Autumn. It had the best view of the forest.

Kimber was still standing on the grass below, speaking to one of the footmen who had followed them out. When he was done he ascended the stone steps to the pavilion and found his own seat. Winter, just next to hers.

For a while they did not speak. Mari was concentrating on absorbing the day, on unlocking that small, evil knot in her chest that had budded as soon as she'd opened her eyes to a black morning. That had grown with every hour that passed while she'd remained alone, her voice unheard, her calls unanswered.

But it was better now. She could uncurl her fingers. She could relax her shoulders. She'd returned to the light.

No crickets chirped today, no birds, no dragons watched from overhead. It was more than peaceable. It was carefully, unnaturally calm.

The earl sat with his arms crossed, his profile sharp against the green and gray and marble day. He kept his gaze fixed on some distant point of the horizon, his brows drawn flat and his mouth faintly grim. Only his hair moved, rebellious still, stirring with the mild coming rush of an afternoon rain. He seemed both part of this moment and alien to it; a fixed force within a man, beautiful in the way that some men were, without embellishment, without kohl or padded coats or jewels. He was solid as the carved pillars, scintillating as the glass tiles. And Mari knew, deep down, that he was also as dark and deep as the forest that tangled over his land. In his heart, just as untamed. Beyond this manicured place, beyond the sun or moon or any confines of civilization, dwelled the true creature inside him. A hidden shard of some secret core of her seemed to throb to life every time she looked at him.

So she looked away. She looked at the lawn, at the waves of shadow and shade that rippled across the grass with the racing clouds.

It occurred to her that although she had flown with him, and Turned with him, and slept at his side, she didn't know what he looked like in his animal form. Surely he knew how *she* looked, but all Mari could recall of Kimber Langford was man and smoke. She frowned to herself, struggling for an image, anything, but all she could summon were a pair of blinding green eyes—human or dragon, she could not tell.

"I wonder," he said suddenly, lifting a booted ankle across his knee, "Maricara, King of the Zaharen. Who do you feel right now in the shire?"

"Who?" She dragged her thoughts back with a guilty start, swiping at a lock of her own hair that had begun to tickle her neck. "What do you mean?"

"Can you feel everyone?"

"I could hardly know that. If someone was here whom I didn't sense—"

"Yes, yes, I understand." The earl flicked hard at some grass stuck to his boot. "I suppose what I'm asking is, is it possible for you to sense a *drákon* you've never met? To pick her out?"

"Her," said Maricara, feeling her heart hook again.

"A girl. About fifteen. She disappeared last night."

"Oh." And then, more softly: "Don't you really mean to ask me if the *sanf* are here?"

"They're not. There are no human men in this shire. I'm damned certain of that."

She lifted her face to the air, closing her eyes. "Yes, I agree," she said. "No Others. No animals. Not even the thrush, not any longer."

"And no missing dragon-girl."

"Can you describe her to me?"

"Somewhat. I've met her, of course, but there are quite a few maidens in the tribe. Let me think. Strawberry-blond hair, pretty face. Roundish. Blue eyes, like her mother...mostly I know her scent. Here." Kim reached for the square of cloth he'd tucked into his coat pocket.

Mari accepted it. It was a buffon, ordinary in the way that most handkerchiefs for young ladies were, stiffened muslin edged with lace, lacking even her initials embroidered upon a corner. The edges were deeply wrinkled, as if she'd had it tucked into her dress just the day before.

"I've got men hunting up and down the shire," Kimber said. "I've got Rhys and the council spread out to the nearest towns. But I thought..."

Mari raised the muslin to her nose and winced, looking back at him from over the wilting folds.

"She likes vanilla."

"I noticed."

Clouds, moisture, day: everything as it should be atop the surface, everything ordinary. The pulsing *drákon* of the shire, the sultry warmth of the unseen sun, the alloys and rocks of Chasen Manor and the ground beneath her feet. The sickly sweet extract of vanilla syrup flooded her senses; she had to work around it to discover the more subtle nuances. Young woman. Starch and innocence.

Maricara closed her eyes and once more lifted her chin. For an instant—the briefest flicker of a second—she almost caught something new...a hint of something both disturbing and known...a person? A stone? It swept over her in thin eldritch notes, a thorn in her memory. When she turned her head to hear it better it vanished as swiftly as it had come. Try as she might, she could not pinpoint it again.

She felt nothing of the maiden who had worn this modesty piece. Either she had managed to hide herself so completely that even her emanations were disguised, or she was well and truly gone.

Mari shook her head, lowering the cloth. "I'm sorry. I don't think she's anywhere nearby. Not for miles and miles."

Kimber nodded politely, rising to his feet. He stood motionless, gazing at the same far-off, cloudswept point, then bent down and picked up the heavy marble bench behind him with both hands and threw it against the nearest pillar.

It exploded into noise, taking out half the column, everything shattering into pieces, chalky dust, minuscule chips that ricocheted back and stung her chest and arms. She made no sound; she did not move except to save her face with her hands.

When it was over she lowered her fingers, glancing instinctively up at the roof, but nothing there toppled. No creaks or groans. There were seven more pillars still to go.

The dust settled around them like thin, glinting snow, sifting back into that unnatural silence.

"Imre had a temper." She spoke indifferently, shaking the grit from her hands, and then her skirts. "He very much enjoyed flogging the serfs whenever the notion took him."

Kimber gave a small savage laugh, his lips drawn back. "Charming fellow. I'm sure we'd have much in common."

"Only me."

He glanced back at her, his gaze still a little too green, a little too feral. The mist beyond his fine, darkened figure began to thicken into raindrops, silvery blue, just as a line of footmen emerged from Chasen, carrying a table and baskets and covered salvers, winding toward the two of them like determined, gray-powdered ants.

She said, "Perhaps the girl ran away on her own. She's young, fair, with all her shining years ahead of her. Who knows the story of her heart? Perhaps she fell in love, and ran away."

"Perhaps," he said.

But the rain wept down, and they both knew it wasn't true.

CHAPTER SIXTEEN

Three days of rain, steady, driving rain, that obscured any foot-prints through the mud or long-stemmed meadows, and buried the aroma of *drákon* and houses beneath that of drenched wood and sodden earth. It barely even managed to lower the tempera-ture; it felt like steam more than rain, as if Darkfrith had become enmeshed in some odd, equatorial confusion, and somewhere down near the middle of the planet was a tropical jungle enjoying clear English days and kind balmy nights.

Kim knew those days and nights very well. Every able-bodied adult of the shire was involved in the search for the missing girl; everyone understood what had been stolen from them, what they had to get back. They worked in teams, men above, women below, and the children, the elderly, confined to their homes with sen-tinels stationed in the streets.

Except for Audrey and Joan. And the princess. They flew with the men.

Every night, Maricara retired voluntarily to the Dead Room. Since it could be neither opened nor shut from the inside, Kim would escort her there, thank her for her help, and bid her a civil good evening. He did not kiss her again. She would look at him with her grave shining eyes and he did not even try. When he fell asleep at last he would dream of that look, over and over. He would dream of her lips on his, and her breath, how she'd melted in his arms; he'd wake so rigid and ready for her that his body cramped in actual pain.

Every morning at precisely eight o'clock he'd stop what he was doing—flying, speaking, striding through his fog of fatigue—and let her out. A bow, good morning. No kiss.

He would not frighten her again. He would not descend into violence without provocation, he would not be unchaste. He was not her former husband, but her next one. He was a goddamned bloody saint.

Outside the manor house Kimber didn't try to pair with her too often. She made it clear she was used to hunting on her own, and God knew he wanted success however it came. But he stayed near as he could without hovering. He couldn't help that; she soared and the men of the tribe Turned with her. She was smoke, she was dragon. However she traveled, she carried a halo of distant admirers like stardust around a comet.

At least he knew she was well watched. If she should need him, if she should happen to discover that one tiny clue that none of the rest of them could . . .

But she did not. There were no clues left to find. There was only the rain, storm and the moon or storm and the sun. If there were *sanf* nearby, those strange, partial *drákon,* none of them detected it, not even Maricara.

The most trusted of his men had been allowed to branch out

into the cities. On the fourth day one of them flew back from Harrogate as smoke, telling Kim he thought he'd felt something there, something of a dragon-girl. Alive.

It was Rufus Booke, one of his father's old cronies, stout and wily and not prone to exaggeration. Kim had immediately accompanied him into the air.

Less than a league out, with the sun beginning to slump from the thickened sky, a band of sullen yellow marking the thin, watery brink between heaven and earth, a new twist of smoke drew near.

Kimber knew her, of course. He knew her every shape, how she slipped along the wind—easy, lovely movements, feminine still, even when just a sheet of vapor. He knew her awake and asleep, because even as the tribe verged upon panic, even as he pushed and pushed to find the girl, to find a solution to the *sanf inimicus* and the prospect of extinction—she was there with him. She was always there, in his thoughts, if nothing else.

Kimber had been Alpha heir his entire life. Speculation on whom he would wed had dogged him all his years. The girls of the shire sent him long, improper looks from beneath their very proper lace caps, every one of them alluring, every one of them like him. Striving to lead. In their sharp-edged beauty and sugary sly ways they intimidated him, just a little. He wasn't truly chaste; he'd dallied aplenty before that letter from Lia made its way into his hands. But dalliance wasn't love, and it wasn't matrimony. And the maidens of the shire made it awfully clear to Kim that when they said, *yes, touch me there,* or *oh, how your lips are soft,* they actually meant, *we will wed.*

He'd been away too much, perhaps. All that schooling. All those stays in London with his parents, learning the glamour and falsehood of the human world. The young ladies of the *ton* giggled and smiled behind their fans and held his arm while they pretended to trip across some invisible stone, so that he might catch them.

The young ladies of Darkfrith dispensed with all that. They mouthed invitations to him from across crowded rooms. They met him in the woods. They begged him to Turn so that they might ride to the moon atop his back, clinging to his body with warm, strong thighs. Dragon-girls, every one. Their eyes glowed and their lips were carmine, and he had knelt to them and admired them and failed to fall in love with a single one.

He tried. He knew his duty and for years, he tried. With every new face, every stroking caress, he'd ask himself, *This one? Is it she?*

But his heart never answered. Kim would slip away again, time after time, ever alone.

Discovering Maricara had seemed to take the matter out of his hands entirely, and frankly, he'd been relieved. The subject was closed; he could stop trying to feel things he'd never comprehend. Romantic love was for Others. *He* was to wed a princess. It was his fate and hers, and they would spend their days together leading their people and raising their children and creating new strength for generations to come. It was logical, it made sense for the tribe; he hadn't been able to think of a single argument in opposition to it when the council raised the vote.

Maricara of the Zaharen.

She was a name on a piece of paper. He'd had no idea what she looked like, how tall she was, her favorite color, the pitch of her voice. If someone had said to him: *mirror eyes; to your nose; royal blue; husky sweet,* they still would have been merely words.

The reality of her was beyond that. There were no words significant enough for her. There was sensation. There was excitement; the tidal rush of desire, drowning deep.

She would not be the grinning girl astride him as he launched into the night. She would be the beast on the wind beside him, teaching him new loops and tricks, seeing the world just as he did. Sovereign, seizing the sky.

For the first time in his life, Kimber was beginning to understand something beyond duty and carnal pleasure and devotion to his kind. He was beginning to understand his own self. She'd emerged from the shadows that very first night and where before there had been emptiness in his chest, now there burned a white-hot spark. His heart spoke at last: *You've found her.*

She was a miracle. To know of her, to touch her in the flesh, a princess with wings . . . a miracle.

By the oldest laws of his kind, they were already wed, Alpha to Alpha. The ceremony would be merely formality. It was why Rhys stayed away, why the other men were careful to give her a wide berth even as they were drawn to her. Kim rather thought that Maricara knew it too. It was why she had let him kiss her. Why she wasn't letting him do it again.

Through the darkening dusk now she raced beside him, smoke and beauty, following him south, no doubt feeling his urgency, trailing thinner and thinner with speed until she was little more than a wisp against the blue-gray gloaming.

Booke kept the lead. Kim felt the last hidden sliver of the sun disappear. The ground grew dim and flat. The forest gave way to meadows and fields again. Small, cloistered villages, mills and viaducts that shone silver with water as they flashed overhead. Flocks of sodden sheep.

Harrogate emerged as a veil of light upon the horizon, a misty thin glow that resolved into crooked medieval streets and very modern buildings. The rusty scent of dissolved iron struck him from miles away, followed at once with that of sulfur; it was a spa town, fashionable and rich, with Turkish baths and steam rooms and more than a few people Kim might know taking their leisure there. It wasn't as large as York, but it was far bigger than Darkfrith. If he was careful, he needn't run into anyone at all. Especially since he would be naked.

And so would his bride.

Booke took them perilously close to the main square, where riders crowded the streets even in this weather and shops lured customers with lamps set in glinting windows. Beneath the sulfur stench rose more human smells, wet clothing, tea and gin and a bakery of meat pies. He heard men laughing. He heard fiddlers, and the slap of cards on felt.

As mist they began to drift more slowly, plainly caught in the illumination of the candle lanterns. Horses shivered directly below them, shaking off raindrops. Pedestrians cocooned in capes and hoods rushed along the sidewalks, darting from awning to awning. A few miserable footmen carrying sedan chairs kept their hats pulled low as they attempted to trot through the crowds. No one looked up.

Booke skirted the main boulevard, drifting over a sprawling garden of flowers. There was a building directly ahead of them, facing the garden—one of the spa hotels, Kim realized, constructed in the Eastern style as a palace, with everything scrubbed blinding white, the piers and carved marble filigree at every angle, the magnificent onion dome dominating the roof. Enormous statues encircled the dome, gods or Romans, who knew.

Candlelight hazed warm from the lower windows, revealing the patrons within. A pump room, a formal dining chamber. Dressing rooms. The baths themselves, set beneath the central dome, slitted skylights fogged with steam incised in curves along its base.

Booke turned into man on the walkway that circled the dome. It was closed and narrow, clearly meant more for ornamentation than practicality. There were no people nearby, no lanterns, only braziers, and none of those were lit. He took shelter behind one of the oversized statues, eyeing the slow-dropping smoke that was Maricara.

Kim Turned before her. He walked to the next statue—Athena,

without question—and lifted a hand, waiting until the princess slithered down to his side. She Turned behind the goddess, her fingers becoming flesh over his, slipping free. She leaned her head past the stone hips to see them both. Rain slid down her hair, soaking it instantly, blackened strands clinging to her cheeks.

"What is this place?"

"An excessively malodorous hotel. Sir Rufus thought he felt the girl here." Kimber looked back at his man. "Booke?"

"It was beneath us, my lord. In the pools, I must suppose."

Kim shook the water from his eyes, trying to concentrate. It seemed an unlikely location to bring a hostage, especially a well-bred, unwilling girl . . . but perhaps there were secret rooms. A basement of natural caverns. "You're certain?"

"Aye. I don't feel her now—but before. Aye."

Kimber reached out. He sought the girl, and when that didn't work, he sought *drákon,* anything of them. He felt foremost still that heavy rich iron that swamped the air, and then the people below them, bathing, drinking, chatting with cups in their hands, sophisticated accents, trilling voices . . . songs from a thousand gemstones, smaller and larger, bright and clear; a more subdued energy beneath it, the spa workers, the great sloshing pools, pipes of thermal water, the rocky ground, fissures in the stone . . .

"No," he said, on an exhale. "I sense nothing. Maricara?"

Her brow puckered. Her eyes took on a distant, glazed look; water dripped in a tiny stream from her chin. She curved a hand around the folds of the marble tunic. Her nails went bloodless; she pressed hard—too hard. The stone began to crackle.

Kim touched his fingers to hers. She blinked and came back to him, thick wet lashes, her hand dropping free.

"I don't know," she said, hesitant. "I thought there was something . . ."

"*Sanf?*" he asked instantly.

"No. A few notes, indistinct...almost eerie."

"Only that?" demanded Booke, also soaking behind his god. "We all hear songs, gel."

"This one I last heard when you handed me the kerchief of Honor Carlisle, Lord Chasen."

Kim nodded, turning back to the panes of a fogged skylight. He bent to wipe a hand across the beaded surface, glimpsing colors and shifting darkness inside.

"Then let's go in," he said.

It was her idea to steal the clothing. Although the baths themselves were curling with steam, the rest of the spa remained a bright, luxurious building, with tall, tall ceilings and Italian-looking frescoes, and Baroque gilded flourishes plastered along the walls. Exquisitely garbed dandies and gentlewomen were sauntering up and down its halls, carrying teacups or tiny glasses of port, their wigs slowly gumming in the humidity.

Nude people would be noticed, Mari pointed out. So would smoke. The antechamber beyond the main baths was lined with dressing booths, women on the left, men on the right. They could float in and walk out. It would be easy.

They stood debating it, the three of them, in the darkest, deepest part of the waters. There was a tiled dividing wall separating the ladies from the men; Mari didn't have to raise her voice to be heard across it, and neither did Kimber or the older man. They could whisper to each other and catch every word, although she was gathering some startled looks from a few of the other women bathers.

A pair of rouged matrons in voluminous black swimming costumes stared at her from across the pool. It seemed unlikely they'd noticed her materialize a few moments before; the chamber was vast and gloomy. But Maricara bent her knees a little more, so her bare shoulders would not show.

"You know, some people say it's wrong to steal," murmured the earl, with a very dry undertone to his voice.

"Hang that," muttered the other man. "We'll give it all back."

"*À bientôt,*" Mari said, and ducked her head under the water.

It was nasty, really, stinking of sulfur and metal, and she couldn't imagine why anyone would want to bathe in it, much less imbibe it as they were in the other part of the spa. But all she had to do was Turn beneath the thick waters, smoke again, pushed up in her lighter state to the air, rising like the rest of the steam in lazy fat rolls.

She made it over to the booths, past the bored maids seated in chairs along the side, past the heavyset footmen sweating at the pillared entrance to the baths. Mari spread sheer, and slid over the nearest door.

She emerged wearing a stylish ensemble of pearl-gray silk and jet-beaded trim, her hair piled up precariously with the few pins she could find. The slippers were loose on her feet, and she hadn't taken the wig or any of the jewelry—a fob watch and a wedding ring, a silver brooch; there was a placard posted inside the booth declaring METALS IN THE WATERS WILL TARNISH FOULE—but this would do.

She hoped the woman who owned this dress enjoyed the fetor of sulfur very much.

Kimber was already waiting for her in the shadow of the portico just past the footmen, wearing a coat and breeches of black and faun, striped stockings and heels of red leather. He slanted her a look beneath his lashes that brought blood to her cheeks.

The gown was a size too small. She'd had to hold her breath to get the corset tight enough.

His gaze roamed her face, lowered with deliberation back down to her bosom. "I retract what I said before. We should steal more often."

She tugged at the bodice. "From larger people."

"Or ones of slightly better fashion." He smiled, gently cynical. "I'm far from an erudite judge of ladies' couture, but there's typically a scarf or a tucker draped across the neckline, is there not, Your Grace? Was it missing?"

"It itched," she said shortly.

From the shadows he was dragon and man, his voice dropping soft. "Lucky me."

A hot agitation stung her skin, embarrassment, the stink of the room becoming astringent. She angled her face away from his and lifted a hand to the nape of her neck, feeling it burn.

"We shouldn't dally here."

"I'm perfectly amenable to dally with you wherever you wish. Ah, Princess, such a killing look. If only you could see how fetching it—never mind. We lack only Sir Rufus—excellent, there you are. Don't we all look nicely legitimate. Shall we have a stroll?"

And they did.

The place was crowded. They decided to make their way to the pump room first; it held the most people. Kimber walked at her side, the man he called Rufus following behind. Try as she might, Mari couldn't sense Honor or those strange, hollow notes, but she knew what she'd heard. Something here was amiss.

The earl cupped her elbow with the lightest of grips. He looked quite at his ease in these lavish surroundings, ambling just as idly as all the rest of the polished, aristocratic throng. At times he nodded to the Others who greeted him by name, smiling, enigmatic. A few clearly desired to stop and talk—their eyes would light upon Mari and then her décolletage; she now regretted sharply leaving behind the scarf—but with his gilded charm Kimber simply pushed by them, hauling her slowly yet inexorably with him down the hallways, not granting anyone time actually to address her directly. No one was so brazen as to demand her name, at least not to the earl's face. They wondered aloud aplenty as they were left behind, though.

She should have realized how completely he would slip into this world. She should have realized how effortlessly he would become one of them.

She felt conspicuous in her borrowed gown. She noticed how the women they passed glanced at her tumbled hair, her clean cheeks. How the men were glancing lower than that. No doubt on its owner the gray silk was perfectly respectable. On Maricara it became something else, soft gleaming material that bit into her skin, that forced her into small, mincing steps and sent a barb into her ribs with every breath. She could not bend in any direction. She could not lift her arms above her breasts. She felt her hair threaten to topple all the way down her back every time her hips swayed.

"By God, if you keep doing that, I'm going to have to secure us a room," Kim muttered, staring straight ahead. They crossed into, and out of, an oval of flickering light.

"Doing what?"

"Holding your breath like that. It makes your chest swell magnificently. Kindly cease."

"I can't *cease*. I can barely inhale."

"Then next time," he said sweetly, "steal a bigger gown or use the damn tucker."

They were at the entrance to the pump room. Instead of an actual pump, there was a fountain in the middle of the chamber shaped as a scalloped bowl, a bronze pipe sprouting from its center, burbling water. A string of adolescent maids in mobcaps and aprons stood in a circle around its base, ready to offer glasses of murky liquid to the men and women around the chamber who lifted hands for it.

The tables were adorned with lace and fresh flowers, nearly all occupied by laughing, chattering people. Waiters clipped back and forth with tea sets and wine and plates of warm food, their mouths pinched, their buttons and polished shoes reflecting the gleam of the brass chandeliers above. The floor was hardwood but every walkway was beautifully carpeted; a great many portions were spotted with water. The pungency of damp wool overlaid that of the iron and sulfur, noxious.

"There is a table over there," said Kimber's man, still behind them.

Mari shook her head. "I am *not* drinking that water."

"No," agreed Kimber. "Let's avoid poisoning ourselves if we can. But if we wish to remain inconspicuous, we can't remain standing here. At least seated we can get our bearings."

The *maître d'hôtel* was already coming toward them, bowing low, bidding them forward. Kimber drew her along with him again.

The table was close to the putrid fountain. One of the serving girls rushed over with three glasses as soon as they were seated. Kimber and his man nodded their thanks as she bobbed a curtsy. Maricara only pushed her glass away.

"We're inconspicuous," reminded the earl, with a pleasant smile. He pushed the glass back toward her. "You don't have to drink it. But try not to look as if you want to throw it at me. I know at least ten couples in this room, and they'd all give a guinea to have a savory bit of gossip to take with them back to London."

"I'd wager they've already got it," offered the other *drákon,* staring down at the glass he cupped between his palms.

"True. Most young ladies dining out with me for the evening don't look quite so murderous."

"We're wasting time here," Mari said. "We should be searching for the child."

"We are." Kimber draped an arm over the back of his chair, revealing a waistcoat of startling bright blue. "You're seated now near the center of the entire spa. If she's here in any direction, this will be the best spot to tell. Do you feel her?"

"I cannot feel anything but an impending headache. This place reeks and the noise—"

"My love," interrupted the earl, soft. "Beautiful dragon. Please try."

She closed her mouth with a snap. Her gaze flicked to the other man—still staring down at his glass, his cheeks and jowls growing flushed over the flowing ruffles of his borrowed jabot—and then back to Kimber. He waited, not moving, not even smiling now, only watching her with a calm and steady expectation.

Mari leaned back. She turned her eyes slowly around the bustling room, taking in all the faces, all the colors, lush textures and cascading voices, and then tried to let them sift into frequencies, letting them fall away one by one, until she heard only what she needed to hear, until she caught the echo of those notes, and they seemed suddenly very near—

"There he is! There, right there, by the fountain!"

The exclamation was extremely loud, louder even than the general commotion of the chamber; in her heightened state it jolted through her like a knife. The man who had made it was standing by the entrance, portly and quivering with emotion, dressed plainly in black breeches and a shirt that didn't quite fit, one arm lifted dramatically to point straight at Kimber.

No—at the other man. At Rufus.

"That blackguard stole my clothing!" The man glanced wildly at the two human males beside him, both well dressed, both clearly management. "What manner of establishment is this? I demand satisfaction! You there, sir! Ho, you! Where the bloody hell do you think you're going?"

The portly man began to trot toward them, followed by the other two. But Sir Rufus was already away from the table, moving with surprising speed toward the wall of folding glass doors that led to the outer courtyard.

"Blast." Kimber pushed back his chair, reaching for her.

"No," she said quickly, and rose to hasten the other way, still speaking, knowing he could hear. Other people were beginning to stand up; the angry man had veered toward Kimber, his voice rising to a bellow. "There will be empty rooms at the top of the hotel, farthest from the stairs."

"How do—"

"Because there always are." She took up her skirts with both hands, dodging tables, the servants trying to speak to her, not running yet, just walking faster. "If nothing else, there's the garret. Don't get caught. *Go.*"

She was nearly to the folding doors; the footmen were distracted, and there were a great many people gaping and pointing at her, behind her, and through all the ruckus and rising voices she heard it again—the eldritch sound. The soft, dreamy reflection of notes—only now it was practically at her side.

Maricara, startled, turned her head, and met the gaze of the woman falling into step beside her. Blond hair, brown eyes, dragon grace and poise and a face Mari instantly recognized—

The other woman grasped her hand and took the lead, guiding them both to the doors, to the dark outside.

CHAPTER SEVENTEEN

I t's time I explained *Draumr* to you, Child of Mud.

Some of you will have heard of it already, of course. Some of you are well studied in our ways, and to you the word *Draumr* might as well be *salvation*. Or so you would think.

The dreaming diamond, the lost blue gemstone. For centuries it haunted our kind, born *as* we were amid magma and comets, *where* we were at the mystical brink of mountain and sky: a perfect, fatal counterpoint to all our strengths. *Draumr* was a monstrosity rejected by the cosmos, disgorged to earth. Exquisite cold, wicked with song, it crystallized into a drop of unblemished evil. It was never meant to be.

Because it was the only stone ever that had the power to enslave us.

Yes, well might you prick up your ears at this news. It had that power. For centuries it was kept locked in *Zaharen Yce*, hidden from everyone, even ourselves. It sang a song so enticing there could be no denying it; you drowned in that stone. You lived with its opium saturating your blood, and it was like floating through a waking dream, breathing thick honey, adrift in blissful clouds. Under its spell you had no troubles, no will, no resistance. Defying it was unthinkable. So human or *drákon*, whoever held the diamond could command us utterly.

We did our best to annihilate it. Even so, twice it nearly destroyed us.

Well... could you do it? Could you bring yourself to crush the most powerful object of pleasure known to your kind? The gem that had but to hum a single, perfect note in your ear to send you reeling into gentle oblivion?

You have your drugs. You have gin and laudanum and all your fine fermented wines. You crave their relief; perhaps some of you, a small fraction, might understand why we never demolished the stone.

We kept *Draumr* in a vault, in a dungeon, in our castle named after ice and tears, atop its barren peak. We kept it very well until it was stolen from us by a human.

But we got it back.

Some of it.

CHAPTER EIGHTEEN

He waited for her in a room that had not seen the light of day for at least a season, he would reckon, although there was still a faint lingering of honey citrus rising from the polished wainscoting. All the windows were shuttered, and there were sheets across the furniture. The bed was unmade. Kimber didn't bother to make it. He only snatched one of the sheets and shook out the dust, then wrapped it around himself like a toga, falling back into the chair it had covered.

He'd had to Turn to avoid being pinned by the hotel's overzealous managers. He'd been doing all right until then, summoning all his charm and an entire fiddle-faddle of lies, gradually managing to extricate himself from the most brightly lit sections of the pump room. But the man missing his clothing had also lost Rufus Booke. He wasn't about to lose his other quarry. He'd cornered Kim and right away tried to wrap a meaty hand about his arm. Kim had remedied that with one quick, hard grip of his fingers, still smiling.

The man had paled and Kim let go; after all, it really wasn't his fault, and Booke *had* made off with what the fellow swore was his new Italian coat.

Kim hoped wherever Booke had managed to leave it, the coat would be recovered unsullied. And quickly.

One of the more uncommon Gifts of the *drákon* was that of Persuasion, the ability to temporarily command Others, to get them to do whatever they were asked to do. To believe whatever they were asked to believe. It was a notoriously tricky Gift, and although Kim had inherited a trace of it, convincing an entire babbling chamber full of people of his innocence was proving a shade beyond his talents.

So he had offered to take their business out into the hallway—the less illuminated hallway—and in the ensuing argument and bustle had found just the right second—only that, a bare second—when all four of them had paused by the shadow of another marble god, and none of the Others were looking straight at him. He had said, very calmly, "You will not notice me," had stepped back against the statue and Turned, abandoning his own purloined garments to the floor.

He had not dawdled to listen to their eventual exclamations. If he'd had money, his own belongings, Kimber would have bought his way out of it all; there were fine advantages to being rich. But he could hardly afford to have another fuming, ill-dressed man stumble across them as they negotiated. He'd managed thus far not to mention his name or title. There were plenty of people present, however, who would have been delighted to mention them for him.

It was the devil's choice: Turn to escape, or get snared as the earl.

So he'd Turned, in public, potentially in view of half the *ton*. It was one of their most hallowed rules, one that might as well have been tattooed across his body, *Thou Shalt Not Turn before Humans,* and he'd done it just to save his own arse because he couldn't think of a better or more expedient way to escape the situation. When the council found out, there was going to be hell to pay.

It was all a right mess.

On top of all that, he'd lost sight of Maricara. He didn't know where she went, or how she went, only that by the time he'd evaporated into smoke, she was no longer in the same space.

Nor was she anywhere he floated. It wasn't easy to be inconspicuous as smoke inside a closed building. She'd been absolutely right about that. With the slanting rain outside, all the windows were shut tight. It had taken bloody forever to find a door that even had a decent crack around its jamb.

At least most of the Others roaming the spa were downing liquor instead of the water. Tipsy humans tended to excuse most anything.

Kimber scrubbed his hands over his face. She'd been right about the empty rooms, too. There were three of them; he'd invaded the farthest one. He let his arms drop, hanging over the arms of the chair, and gusted a sigh.

If she didn't show up soon, he was going to have to go get her. Under no circumstance was he going to simply wait for her to come to him, not with all that could yet go wrong. She'd said there were no *sanf* here, he himself felt nothing like that, but still. . . .

He was weary. He couldn't recall the last night's decent sleep he'd had. Days ago. Weeks ago. Before his lovely, troubling, tempting, maddening-beyond-reason princess had shown up, that was for damned certain.

Kimber sat up in the chair. It was dim in here, only slivers of rainlight slanting past the shutters, but his eyes were adjusting. He stared blankly at the wall before him, the cornflower-blue-striped paper, a framed watercolor of coy hares and leverets cavorting in a field of strawberries. He felt the dust of the room in his nose, the threads of the satin in the chair against his forearms . . . the beech floors, oak joints behind the walls . . . mice, rapidly scattering to the other end of the hotel . . .gunpowder and summer flowers, a subtle wafting through the air.

The dragon in him blinked awake. He let it flood his heart, quickening. Let it singe his blood.

She was close. She was here.

Kim cut his eyes to the door. Smoke was curling through the keyhole.

She Turned in midstep, pacing over to a dresser, whipping off the cloth that covered it in an arc of grayish white. She wrapped it around herself just as he had, flipping an end over her shoulder.

"Pleasant," she said, glancing around.

"Adequate," he responded, and gave a narrow smile. "How good to see you, Princess. Any lasting repercussions?"

"No. A gentleman stopped me briefly in a hallway with his hand upon my arm, but he apologized profusely when he realized I wasn't his wife. It seems she has a gown exactly like mine. By the time I made it out to the courtyard, your squire was already gone. And you, my lord?"

"Nothing I couldn't handle."

"They didn't catch you?"

"Not for long."

"I see." Elegant black brows lifted in what might have been astonishment, or just plain amusement. "You're shedding your vaunted rules like last year's scales."

"You do seem to have that effect upon me."

She gave a bow in her sheet, as natural as any man. "*Merci beaucoup.*"

"Oh, you're most welcome. It's remarkable how easily nearly thirty-two years of hard-won wisdom and restraint are tossed."

"Was it easy?" she inquired, interested. And then: "You're thirty-two?"

"Thirty-one, and yes, extremely. I enjoyed immensely putting myself on display for all and sundry like the village poacher neatly pilloried. No doubt everyone was greatly entertained."

She went to the bed, perched upon the bare mattress and leaned forward with her arms on her thighs. Her hair slipped over her shoulders, a velvet-dark shadow covering her chest. "There," she said softly. "You see? Freedom is pleasurable."

"So is survival," he said, curt. "So are a few other activities I can think of. Perhaps we might engage in some of those instead."

Her head tipped, her lips still smiling. "Sir Rufus is currently downstairs, loitering in the garden as smoke. Don't you think you should go fetch him? He won't know where we are."

Kimber stood. He stared at her another long moment. Slowly her brows arched again.

He Turned. He left the way she had come in.

Mari made up the bed. She'd never done it before; as a child there was no bed to make up, only pallets, and as a princess there were always servants. Servants to tidy the rooms, servants to help her dress, servants to do her hair, and bring her food, and polish her jewels, and watch her with hawk-bright eyes when the prince was not at her side.

So she didn't truly make the bed. She only found a bureau stuffed with clean linens and tossed those over the lumpy mattress. There were no coverlets or even blankets stored anywhere else in the room, but there were five sets of sheets, and that seemed sufficient. It was warm still and she wasn't planning actually to sleep. But she could at least be comfortable while she waited for the earl to return.

She crawled to the center of the bed. She lay flat on her back with her arms out and stared up at a ceiling of smoothed plaster. She did not feel tired. She felt very, very awake.

Rufus Booke was not in the garden. Not as smoke, not as man—not as anything. Nor was he in the sky. Kimber hunted for him a good two hours, going back into the town, even back down to the pools of the spa—closed this late, the water lapping in tongues against the tiled stone, not even a single lamp for light—but Sir Rufus was no longer anywhere nearby.

Kim wasn't worried. Not yet. Booke was a good man but, more important, a cunning one. If he'd gone to ground, there would be a reason for it. Chances were, however, he'd only gone back to Darkfrith.

It was where Kim was going with Maricara, as soon as he could fetch her. If Honor Carlisle had ever been here, she wasn't now. He would have picked up something of her by this point, even if it was just the princess's mystery song.

But there was nothing. And as Lord Chasen, he could no longer afford to remain publicly.

He maneuvered down a thinly smoking chimney near her end of the hotel, emerged at a grate clutching the remains of a smoldering log and burnt tinder. Embers brightened and broke apart as he sighed past, but there was nothing of him to ignite. Kim poured away untouched.

A woman slumbered in the wide, curtained bed. Her maid was on a cot in the adjoining room. Both of them snored.

He glided out from under the door.

The room that held Maricara was still unlit. Even the rainlight had darkened to ash. He stood a moment in stillness by the window, letting what light would come fall across his skin, so that she could see him.

But she was also asleep.

Maricara did not snore. She was on her side amid a swirl of sheets, her hair a sable slash across the cambric, her arms folded and her legs bent. It was how she had slept in the abbey.

She had been naked then, too.

Kimber crossed the chamber without sound. He tested the mattress with both hands, then eased atop it. She shifted with his weight but did not wake, so he moved closer, settling down in front of her this time, his head upon his arm, examining her face.

They were so beautiful, all of them. He'd never thought on it much before, but the truth was, it might even be considered a weakness of their kind. Their unblemished bodies, their thick locks, the inches and corners and shimmering colors of them that all joined to create a being beyond simple man: It marked them for what they were. Not human.

He'd long ago grown accustomed to it. In fact, Kim vividly remembered his first impressions of London as a boy. Rooted in the city odors and noises and violent eddies of disorder were people, real people, who were very plainly a different sort of species from his own.

Their skin pocked with disease. Their teeth yellowed, and fell out. Their heads were shaved to stubble beneath their wigs and still they swarmed with fleas and lice; they smelled of their food, and their sweat, and whatever refuse they had last trudged through. Some of them were kind and some of them were not, but to a young, wide-eyed lad, their state of constant human decay had been both repellent and fascinating.

Retreating back to Darkfrith was like stepping into an alternate world, one in which everyone he knew lived suspended in their own unique perfection. No filth, no lice, no gap-toothed, drooling grins. His kin were born to a certain hard grace and they died in the same state. In between, they ruled the stars.

Maricara was no different. In rest, in lightning or candlelight or splashing rainfall, she remained lovely. His hunger for her, the craving that ate through his bones, was as fierce as ever; in her every form, in her every motion, he responded.

The tribe had an overworn adage: *Uncover the heart; wed the fire.* Kimber had always assumed it was an oblique reference to the *drákon's* legendary passion. But it was about love.

This sleeping young woman—clever, mysterious, royal and obstinate—was his fire. She had been for all of their lives, and it was simply a whim of the fates that it had taken exactly this many years for their paths to wind close enough to intersect.

Perhaps it was another weakness, this desire to love and be loved. This profound and ardent recognition of what was meant to be for the course of their lifetimes. Kim didn't know. Right now, on this bed with her, he did not care. Come hell or high water, come *sanf* or extermination, he could not let go of her. Even as she scorned him, even as she ducked and turned away, he could not let go.

He'd been lonely without her. It seemed now so patently obvious a child could have pointed it out to him, but he hadn't known. All his years alone, witness to the matrimony of his family and friends, and he had been lonely. He'd had his responsibilities to fulfill him, his position as leader and lord. He was Alpha and godfather and uncle; he was heir to a great tradition and estate. For some reason, he'd always thought that that had been enough.

Certainly these things had consumed his days and many, many nights. He had labored at each role, grasping at duty and honor to guide him when he needed them, emerging back into the light as he could. He'd thought he was content. That, somehow, all that had made him content.

But it wasn't so. He'd been missing something so powerful, so basic, Kimber had never even guessed at its enormity; it was like trying to comprehend the diameter of the earth just by measuring a single grain of sand.

He'd been missing his mate. His helpmeet, his partner. His destined wife.

No more, he thought. It was a notion both so foreign and so true that he whispered it aloud.

"No more."

Kim lifted a hand, tracing his fingers above the contours of her face. He did not touch her skin. He didn't need to. He could feel her without touch, the curvature of her cheekbone, her fine nose, her full lips. Winged eyebrows. Lashes over closed lids.

Maricara came awake. Her eyes did not open, but he felt that as well, her sudden awareness. Her body didn't even tense.

"I want to kiss you again," he said quietly.

Her lashes lifted. She gazed at him in the dark.

"Will you let me?"

The fingers of one hand curled a little tighter beneath her chin. "Yes," she said.

So he lowered his fingertips to her cheek. He stretched closer, because she did not move either toward him or away, only lay there in her bed of sheets, the linen rucked up between her knees, her arm and shoulder free.

Her skin was cool, much cooler than the air around them. He traced the corner of her mouth with his thumb, her lower lip. She continued to gaze at him, her eyes a smoky reflection of the last light of the chamber. He touched his nose to hers, exhaling as she exhaled, allowing their breath to mingle. Her lips turned up. She began to lower her head, to pull back, so he spread his hand behind her neck and brought his mouth to hers.

She stiffened. That was fine; he knew what to do. He knew how to taste her, to be as slow and gentle as she needed, massaging lightly the tension in her neck, until the tightness under her skin began to slip away like the water down the glass windows, and the sound of the storm became a drumming in his veins, her heartbeat, his desire. She was smaller and slight and not the same as him; and yet she was the same, because her lips parted, and she began—tentatively—to kiss him back.

Kim drew nearer. He lifted one leg and hooked it behind both of hers, letting his fingertips now discover the delicate path of her spine, following it down beneath the sheets. Oh, she was warmer there, so soft. He sucked at her lips and smoothed circles at the small of her back, his every motion tugging at the layers of cambric that pulled between them.

Her lips grew less tentative, her responses longer, deeper. When he opened his eyes he found her watching him, intent.

He rolled on top of her. Without looking away from her face he found a loose corner of one of the sheets and tugged at it, then tugged harder.

The linen ripped easily, threads popping like paper along a seam. He was left with a long, frayed swathe, a weightless floating in his hand.

Kimber drew them both upright; Maricara's arms swiftly crossed her chest to keep the sheets in place. He brushed noses again, moved his mouth to her cheek, her eyes. He waited until her lashes fluttered closed and then took the blindfold he had made and placed it around her head with both hands.

She held motionless, wet lips, clenched fingers. He sat forward on his heels to tie the ends behind her, loose enough so that she could pull it free if she wished. Tight enough so that she could not see. When it was done he nudged aside her hair to press a kiss to her throat, fleeting at first, then harder, opening his mouth to savor the faint trace of salt on her skin. Pulling her closer. Marking her with his teeth. He felt her hands become fists against his chest.

Fire.

He smiled against her, drew his tongue up the flushed heat of her neck to her earlobe. Her jaw tipped away from him, allowing him more, so he took it. He tasted her and breathed her in and listened to the anthem of her heart pumping, rushing to match his own.

With his arms hard around her, they lowered back to the sheets. Maricara licked her lips, dark and luscious red, the pale blindfold a tease and a foil, his safeguard for this moment, for kisses and stroking and the luxury of her flesh against his.

He pressed his hips to hers; they sank deeper into the feather bedding. She was slim and real beneath him, unbelievably real. He'd imagined her for so long, dark nights of sweat and longing and dreams that wrung him dry. To have her here at last, their bodies clinging in the humid warmth, her thighs parting under the last wisp of sheet between them—

He started to move, small thrusts, urgency singing through his blood even as he forced himself to be careful, to be measured and deliberate. But she brought her hands up to his hair and pulled his head to hers. She said his name against his lips.

Caution began to crumble, tiny pieces of him falling away down an endless steep cliff. He pulled the sheet from her in a long, languorous slither, revealing the wonder of Maricara in parts: right breast, left; deep pink nipples. Her rib cage, lifting and falling. Her belly. Lower than that, the curve of one hip . . . soft dark curls; he dragged his fingers through them and nearly could not breathe with want; she made a whimper in her throat.

Kim bent his head. He let his cheek graze one nipple, turned his lips to it, a lap of his tongue. She hardened instantly, an exquisite puckering in his mouth—and the sound she made now was purely erotic. He did it again while pressing the heel of his palm against her mound, feeling her arch. Her fingers twisted painfully against his hair.

"Maricara."

"Yes?" Her voice came thin, breathless. It broke with the stroking of his tongue.

"*Ma belle dragon.*" Another kiss, his fingers slick. She lifted her hips as he bit gently at her lips.

"Oh—yes. What is it?"

"Just so you know"—he slid a finger inside her, God, so hot and wet,—"*this*...is ravishment. And you're doing—a wondrous fine job of it."

She began to laugh, tiny hitches of sound, still breathless and a bit uncertain. Kim took away his hand and lowered his body, nestling against her smooth folds, probing, pushing into her; the laughter abruptly died, replaced by a swift gasp and then...yes, then, her arms sliding to his back and her knees drawing up, taking him deeper.

He put his forehead to hers, finding the fabric that hid her eyes, closing his own so that he would be blind too, so that together they could just feel.

She did feel. She felt things she'd never before guessed could exist: a man's hands on her with reverence, caressing her, strong fingers cradling her head, holding her for his kisses.

The way his body filled hers, no pain, but a rising thick pleasure, an aching that spread from the core of her to lick along her senses. Butterflies transformed to scarlet bright flame.

Movement, their dance together.

His weight upon her, welcome and taut, every muscle, every ragged breath.

The hair on his arms, his chest and legs. The smooth, strong planes of his back, the hard curves of his buttocks.

His face to hers. Her name, other words, English and softly slurred, caught between a whisper and a groan.

Mari didn't need sight. What she needed very desperately she could not even define—relief from the flames, release from the aching, the joy that was coming up hard to consume her. And she didn't know how it happened: One instant she was woman beneath him, stretched and amazed and afire. In the next she shattered into sweetness, a terrible bright bliss that lifted her body and drove shock waves to her atoms and sent her spinning up out of control to heaven, to him. And she never Turned at all.

Kimber caught her there in his arms, roughly, and pressed so hard into her that it hurt. But she wanted it, she reveled in it. As he shuddered and gasped into her hair, Mari felt herself smile, ferocious. Her legs lifted to cross her ankles over his waist; he could not escape. Her arms clasped him tight against her.

She rubbed the blindfold off in her dreams. He lifted it carefully from her, let it fall from his fingers to the far corner of the bed.

Her head lay at his shoulder, her hand flat over his heart; even though he'd tried to move as gently as he could, he woke her. She shifted a little, stretching, then settled back warm against his side.

Kim thought she'd sink back into slumber. Instead, her hand began a slow drift down his chest, to his stomach, drawing lazy, featherlight patterns across his skin that brought him wide awake.

Her voice came scratchy with sleep.

"What sort of dragon are you?"

"Large," he breathed, and used his hand to push hers down farther. He felt her smothered laugh.

"I meant, what colors?"

"Ah. Hmm." Her fingers closed over his shaft. He lost his breath with the sensation. "Red and blue. Some gold."

She began to stroke him, up and down, squeezing, releasing. She used her nails to lightly score his tip. "Will you show me someday?"

"I think it's safe to say—you'll have ample opportunity to—see me as dragon."

Her hand stilled its astonishing torture. He felt her head tilt as she looked up at him.

Kim lifted up to an elbow, reaching for her hip. "Black dragon. I plan to ensure it."

CHAPTER NINETEEN

The sound of the rain peppered her dreams. They weren't truly dreams, more like colors and perceptions and meandering thoughts. She slept in a haze, never fully surrendering to the depths of complete silence, struggling to remain at that cusp of awake: the scent of sulfur and storm in the air; her cheek on his chest; his breath stirring her hair.

It was strange. It was extraordinary.

It had been so long since she'd been with a man. She'd forgotten this, the intimacy of a rainswept night, entangled legs, the weight of a masculine hand upon her waist. But then, in the slow-moving fog of her thoughts, it seemed to Mari she could not have forgotten what she had never before known.

She did not feel anxious in her repose next to him. She felt secure. She felt as if his heat and his embrace and his torso pressed to hers were all things that had been conspired to be—for ages, for her lifetime. She felt that she could sleep like this forever.

And that, of course, eliminated her last hope of real slumber.

It was not yet dawn, but she'd always been able to see well at night. In the deep quiet light that latticed the chamber Maricara studied Kimber Langford, curious.

It was odd to see a man so relaxed around her. No one relaxed around her, not really, not even Sandu. On occasion she would pass one of the looking glasses hung in the castle and catch a hint of her own reflection: silvery hair, silvery eyes, gowns of deep color and skin paler than the moon. She was a winter beast hidden behind a human face, a piercing gaze, a ghostly peril. When she smiled her lips curved cold and beautiful, no matter how she tried to warm them. When she lifted her hands they gleamed with rings and the fluency of her movements; she could circumvent neither.

Before her marriage, Mari had been a brash, grubby maiden, her hair escaping from scarves, her skirts a muddy mess, as delighted as all the other children to romp through the hamlets and meadows. But as a wife...

No wonder her people would not drop their guard for her. The grown woman staring back at her from mirrors with creamy shoulders and plucked brows didn't look anything like Maricara. The creature there shone clear-eyed and diamond-hard, and looked fully capable of devouring man or cattle alike. It rather frightened her as well.

Ah, but this man...this powerful, lovely man, was not afraid of her. He was also a beast and an earl, which seemed to be something like a prince in this country, and he was not afraid. And he was tender, and he was strong, and he was *drákon*.

She touched a hand to her mouth, observing his. She pressed a kiss to her fingers, remembering how it felt to kiss him instead. She followed the contours of his eyelashes and remembered the intensity of his gaze, the last thing she had seen before he fixed the sheet around her eyes: his own, alight and brilliant, green cool depths and a hunger that had stilled her to the bone.

She'd let him blindfold her. She'd trusted him, beyond the Dead Room, beyond her body and her sight. She'd trusted him, and he had risen to it.

This wasn't love. It was new and unfamiliar, but she had seen love before, and this had to be different. It was lust, certainly, and the inevitable collision of their dragon natures. It was pleasure and astounding satisfaction; every time he touched her, every place, she felt a physical, hot delight. Tangible, like dipping her fingers into the gold dust that lived in the rivers of the mountains, spreading their glimmer across her skin.

Love wasn't glimmer. Love was struggle and anguish, stratagems and long nights of weeping into pillows. Every legend of the *drákon* involving love ended in full-fledged tragedy; even Mari knew that.

Her parents had scoffed at it; Amalia and Zane had been fully snared. A handful of *drákon* from the villages professed it, but traditional marriages were arranged. Love might come after that; it might not. Most people trudged on with their lives anyway.

Every now and again flared some great, feverish ardor between a young Zaharen couple, but they always gave the impression of being more miserable than not, prone to sighs and dramatic gestures and extravagant public declarations such as *I will surely die without him.*

She, on the other hand, wasn't going to die without anyone, and that was perfectly acceptable. In fact, it seemed to Maricara that falling in love was perilously close to what the *sanf* were so eager to do: rip a hole in a *drákon* chest. Steal from it the beating flesh of the soul.

Just like her own, Lord Chasen's heart was veiled. All she had glimpsed of it was a knot of thorns and passion. That was also acceptable. She understood knots, and quite enjoyed passion. She had no wish to delve deeper than that.

Power. Position. Desire. She was comfortable with these things. They were surely enough to keep her content.

But...

Kimber's palm shifted against her. He sighed and whispered something in his sleep and slid his hand down her arm.

... he was so very like her, more than anyone she had ever met. And so *very* beautiful.

Mari closed her eyes. With the earl's face turned to hers, she allowed herself gradually to lapse back into that place of rain-scattered slumber.

When she looked next around the room the light had shifted, a gray so dense it was like peering through cheesecloth. Nothing much was clear, save the man standing over them.

Rhys.

Their eyes met. He wore no clothing; his face was expressionless. Without the emerald or hoop in his ear he seemed nearly without life, another specter from her dreams. His hands were loose at his sides.

His lips made a taut smile. His eyes followed the shadowed lines of her figure entwined with Kimber's; the night had been warm and then they'd made it warmer, and together they slept atop the covers.

Mari was a panther, she was a king. She let Lord Rhys's gaze rake her body and did not move.

"Countess," he murmured, and inclined his head.

Then where there had been Rhys, there was smoke, and then simply air. But for the slight creaking of the door upon its hinges, she might have imagined it all.

They flew back to Darkfrith in silence. The clouds had roiled and thickened into a mantle of cotton by the last magenta flare of the dawn. The air still felt of rain but none fell; below them the earth awoke beneath a trillion liquid drops, each one catching the reflection of the sky, the pair of dragons that pierced the pinkened mist in a line, appearing and disappearing according to the whorls of the clouds.

Well, one dragon. The other remained higher, better hidden. Mari wasn't so incautious as to fly openly through the morning. But she did, at times, allow a claw or her tail to reach down and break the vapor beneath her, leaving a furrow of clarity in her wake that nearly at once puffed and amassed and rolled back together again.

Kimber kept within a wingspan. When she'd Turned to dragon after their ascent he had done the same; they both knew he wouldn't be able to keep up otherwise. But Mari hadn't Turned for speed. She could pretend she'd done it because she needed to, because it had been too long since she'd knowingly scraped the atmosphere with her body, and all that was true. Existing strictly as woman or as smoke denied the most important part of her.

But beyond that, beyond speed or function, she'd done it because she knew it would be forbidden. And she wanted to see his reaction to that.

He gave her none. As a dragon he only flew extremely close, so close she could make out the fantastic etching of his scales, rich metallic hues of sapphires and the ruby sun, his eyes brilliant green and lined with gold.

His head lifted. He snorted a breath that made the illusion of smoke, blowing clearer air through the mist, baring his teeth afterward; it looked like a grin.

She grinned back. She closed her eyes and navigated by her senses, the world below and him above, the flavor of morning bright in her mouth.

There were no men waiting for them this time. None of the council lined the drive; there was no one at all nearby, in fact. Kim took Maricara into Chasen the same way he used to go back when he was younger—much younger—and needed to slip inside unobserved: through his far bedroom window. He'd figured how to secure a thin metal strap across the sash, thin enough to remain unobserved from the inside. Protruding just enough on the outside to prevent the lock from clicking fully into place.

It entailed that he Turn human to pull at it. There was just enough room on the ledge to keep him balanced on the balls of his feet. Half the time he'd ended up tipping backward anyway, Turning at the last second to save himself a bruising against the ground. And in *none* of those times had he tried this in broad daylight, in full view of the lawn and gardens below.

His quarters faced east, toward the woods and the first handsome lanes of the village. The burn of the sun on his back was nothing to the heat flooding his face.

How incredibly sophisticated: the Earl of Chasen, squatting bare-assed on a window ledge of his august and stately home, yanking at a weathered tin strap that did not want to give. He could have simply gone to the front doors—

The strap broke; Kimber fell; the window tugged open.

He entered first, Maricara twirling behind. There was a definite gleam to her eyes when she Turned in the middle of his bedroom.

"Don't say anything," he warned, and went to her before she could give voice to that gleam, taking her by the shoulders to kiss her on the mouth.

"I was merely—"

"No." He kissed her harder.

"—searching for that—"

He brought his hands up into her hair. He felt its weight, cool between his fingers.

214

"Indelible," she gasped, when he broke for air. He pressed his face to her neck. Her arms came up around him; he felt the laughter rocking her. "The perfect English word. I believe I have it right. Indelible. I'll never, never forget—"

"Splendid," he muttered. "Tell everyone, why don't you?"

Maricara spoke with measured consideration. "I doubt very much I could do the scene justice. One really had to be there for the best effect. Do you have a gown anywhere in this chamber?"

He did not. Even Lia's quarters were a floor away. If it were not for the fact that the day was passing, and people would be looking for them, and the sun sloped bright across his rug from the newly washed sky . . .

He left her in his dressing chamber, running her hands over rows of shirts, strolling slowly alongside the faceless wooden heads that held his wigs. One entire cherrywood closet was devoted to everything bejeweled, coats and waistcoats and buckles and fobs; his last image of her was of her standing before it, her hands clasped behind her back, her fists locked above her hair. Slowly she drew a foot up and down the back of her calf, her toes curling.

He left while he was yet able to leave. He would find something of Lia's, it was closer than the Dead Room, and then he'd get back to her. It wasn't quite yet noon. There were voices echoing in and about the mansion, but the tones were low and muted. They carried no urgency. Kimber's door had a good lock.

He found a frock of his sister's in her dim, dustless room. It was steely blue and frothy white and looked like something he'd seen her wear to tea a few times; it hardly mattered. It would fit Maricara, no doubt a damn sight better than that gray thing she'd had on last night.

But as he was leaving, closing the door carefully behind him, Kim registered that the voices he'd been hearing were becoming more distinct. They were more than the usual background of questions and commands of the servants, a gentle swell of sound he typically managed to disregard in any case. These were the voices of men, about twelve of them. The council had convened.

He found them in their splendid chamber, not yet seated. They stood in clusters, grand old dragons with their hands on their hips, a few holding glasses from the sideboard. They were stout and gaunt, perfumed with oils and powder. Their tones struck a chord that carried all the way to Kimber by the door: heated, quarrelsome. In the stark light from the world beyond the windows they stood rigid and muttering, eleven men shining with pearls and gold, the sun sparking rainbows off their crystal cups. The richly fruity aroma of port spread in eddies throughout the room.

The longcase clock struck noon. All the others joined in, all the songs, the ticking seconds banged out in a wild Babel of chimes.

Kimber wanted, for one very vivid, very heart-stopping instant, to back away. To ease one single step away, and then another. To disappear into the warren of the house, to take the hand of the princess and vanish.

Like his parents had done.

He stood frozen with it. He was split into two, half-in and half-out of the doorway, and then Rufus Booke glanced over at him, his heavy face lighting, and the instant passed. The last chime died away, and Kim took his step forward, into their midst.

A honeybee was trapped in the silk folds of the window curtains. Mari opened the window, pushing with both hands, then pinched the edge of the curtain up high between her fingers to free the bee. It flew in a dizzy circle, bumping once into the glass, then found the fresh air and rolled through the opening, a noisy black dot vanishing against the green.

She leaned her forehead to the pane in front of her, enjoying a long, deep breath tinted of apples and flowers and elm. It was odd that the heat didn't bother her quite as much as it used to. In fact, right now it felt very good, casting color on her white skin, revealing in intricate detail the fine weave of the shirt she'd donned, the diminutive twists and coils of the lace at the cuffs.

She might go down as smoke to fetch her own garments. She told herself she did not because she had no reason to think the door to her cell would not be closed and locked; there would be no entry without the key. She would wait for Kimber. She would laze in the sun, and wait.

With her arms at her sides, the lace spilled past her fingers. The Earl of Chasen was larger than she; the breeches she'd pulled on were too big as well. She'd had to roll the waist over twice just to get them to stay up.

Maricara tipped her face to her shoulder and inhaled. She thought she might be able to smell him in the linen. She might even catch the scent of their coupling on her skin—though that was imagination. The sun addled her brain.

She was addled. It was the best explanation for this astonishing, scotch-warm feeling in her chest. The butterflies of before gathered and thickened into anticipation, into joy and light. When she concentrated on him it only intensified: his face, long brown lashes and crystal-green eyes; the smooth-muscled curve where his shoulder met his arm. The touch of his fingers, slow and soft, or firmer, more urgent. His dragon grin. His human smile.

She had her own secret smile; she kept it as she drew a cuff in to tickle beneath her nose, and took another deep breath.

A pair of children emerged from the break in the woods. One boy, one girl, both about ten years of age. Her skirts were beige and blue and rumpled. His collar and knees were smeared with mud. They were arguing about something, a stick and ball, the river that had taken the ball . . . Mari listened to them without moving.

She remembered a time when she had been that girl, and Sandu had been the one ever scolding her. These children were tow-haired, and their words were foreign, and the place was foreign too.

But they were the progeny of her kind. As if they'd practiced it, at the precise same moment both of them glanced her way, found her framed in the window and in light, even from such a distance.

The girl lifted her hand in a wave. After a second, the boy did as well.

Mari raised her hand in return. She pressed her palm to the glass as the pair of them walked on, still arguing.

And there were more voices arguing. There was her name, her title. The words like a cold splash of water in her face: *imprison her.*

She cocked her head. She pushed away from the window and looked back quickly at the doors that led to the sitting room, that led to the hall. Both remained open.

Too much a risk.

Despite its size and maze of hallways, it wasn't hard to find her way down to the main level of the mansion, where all the men were. She felt them, of course, but they weren't even bothering to keep their voices low.

The soles of her feet felt very warm against the marble floor.

Can we even trust her?

She walked by three footmen without pausing. A scullery maid hung back in a corner of a gallery, a mop in hand, her face down-turned, still dipping a curtsy as Mari passed. No one looked directly at her. Like mice pinned between the paws of a cat, they were frozen, trepidation and an acrid tinge of fear shrouding them like a cloak.

After all, Kimber, we don't know who she really is.

This was an ominous, familiar dream: a giltwood mirror hung by the master stairs, her own reflection a brief moving shadow. She glanced over and there was the princess once more, pale and ghostly, cold and bright. Her hair was a rough black streamer down her back. Her eyes were dragon eyes, liquid silver. Glowing with radiant light, they dominated her face.

Where her loyalties lie.

She did not realize she had that Gift. No one had ever told her, and she had not known. It gave her the look again of a beast behind a mask. No wonder the little maid would not lift her head.

She is my wife.

No, my lord, she isn't. She isn't yet.

As Mari reached the portal of the room that held all the men, the conversation choked into silence. She breached the entrance, standing alone before them.

"Good afternoon," she said, and even her voice sounded different inside her head, smoother, darker, with a song of menace and despair lurking beneath her words.

She found Kimber in their midst at once, his face and body half-angled to hers; no doubt like the rest, he had felt her approach. In the next instant he completed his pivot, coming to her in a quick, easy stride. He took her hand in his own. She allowed him that, keeping her focus now on the other men in the room, their faces and closed, defensive postures. They were grouped *en masse* in a block of unvarnished light; when one turned his head to steal a glance at the man beside him, his wig let loose motes of flour, bright as snowfall in the sun.

Their square of tables was just behind them. It was littered with papers and empty cordial glasses. A scribe sat there staring at her, his quill pinched between his fingers, too gone to his thoughts even to rise to his feet.

"Your Grace," the earl said. "I apologize. I have a gown for you."

"No need." She freed her hand, smiled at the standing men and watched two of them rock back on their heels. "As you can see, I've made do."

"Maricara."

"Yes."

Kimber waited until she looked at him. With the daylight shining behind him he carried a nimbus, his face in shadow, even his eyes cast dark. He made a short motion toward the table. "Sit down."

"No," said one of the men, and broke from his pack. "Begging your pardon, Your Grace, but this is a private meeting of the Council of the *Drákon*. We permit only members to attend. Perhaps the princess would care to retire to the—to the chamber we've prepared especially for her."

"Not really," she said, still smiling. "Why? Do you imagine the princess cannot hear you from there?"

"Madame, I don't know what you—"

"Since you are discussing me, my loyalties, and my future, I believe I'd like to have a say. If there are accusations to be made, I'd enjoy the opportunity to respond. Or are you not so enlightened as that? In my land, even the lowest of serfs may lay claim to the right of defense."

The man who had tried to get her to leave spoke again, shaking his head. "This is not a trial."

"No," agreed Mari softly. "It sounded far more like a conviction."

Another man pushed through the others, stomach first, and this one she recognized. It was the squire from yesterday, Rufus, the one who had fled into the night.

"Who was that woman you were speaking with in the spa?"

Mari regarded him evenly; the earl remained a shadowed presence against her shoulder. "What woman?"

"The blonde one. The one you met after that bloke began yelling. In the pump room, before the doors."

He did not appear to be in jest. He stared at her with bushy gray brows and blue-sharp eyes, his hands holding hard to the lapels of his coat.

Maricara lifted a shoulder in dismissal. "There was no woman."

The squire shifted his gaze to Kimber. "You saw her, my lord."

"No," answered Kimber carefully. "I did not. As I mentioned before, I was busy dealing with the man and the hotel workers. I didn't see the princess escape the pump room."

"There was no woman," Mari said again, stronger. "Why would you fabricate such a thing?"

"Fabricate!" scoffed Sir Rufus. "Indeed! I know what I saw."

"And I do not."

"Blonde woman! Tall! Green frock! She wore amethysts. She had you by the arm."

"I'm telling you all, that did not happen."

"Then you, Missy, are a liar—if not worse."

She kept her expression serene. She kept her feet rooted to the ground, to the rug, the cut pile rough against her toes, as the dragon in her rose and rose.

A hand came to rest upon her shoulder. A voice spoke through the buzz of rage in her ears, low and sleek.

"Have a care, Booke. You're treading deep waters."

"Great God, man," burst out the squire. "Open your eyes! She's bewitched us all! You see a female who can Turn, you see a bride, but she's an outsider to us! She's a threat! Use her, yes! Wed her and bed her, aye, but have a dram of faith in our ways as well! We don't know her. She left that room with a stranger, I swear it, with a woman wrapped in odd music. I saw them both! And then together they were gone."

Mari was beginning to shake. She thought to conceal it; she hid her hands behind her back and the grip on her shoulder squeezed and tightened and shifted to her arm. But no one was looking at her anyway. Everyone was looking at the squire.

"First our scouts disappear, then *she* shows up, fills our heads with some nonsense about human hunters, works us up and then vanishes herself—it's all been a game with her. One of our gels is missing, and *this* creature is off cavorting with strangers. Look at her, my lord. *Look.*" From across the chamber Sir Rufus gestured to her with a flat, open palm. His voice went to gravel. "Does she look like *anything* we can trust?"

She stared back at them all, her spine straight, refusing to lower her gaze. One by one she held their eyes until at last her gaze moved to Kimber, to the earl, standing at her side.

But she could not read his face. He was golden and beautiful. He had stroked her bare body, had wooed her and kissed her lips and found his rapture inside her—but she could not read him.

His lashes lowered. His hand dropped from her arm.

Mari lost herself then. She lost the feeling of *princess,* of winter-cold beast. She felt her heart become lead in her chest, a solid dead-weight.

"There was no woman," she repeated one last time, straight to him.

The squire's cheeks grew very red. "Aye, and isn't this what we've feared all along? I told you, Chasen. I told you *and* your father. This is why we needed to get to them first, before they tried any trickery—"

"Booke," Kimber said.

"Why we needed to see this Zaharen castle for ourselves, to study the land and the people before we moved to occupy—"

The earl did not speak again. From the corner of her eye he only moved his hand, a quick downward slash of his fingers, but it cut the squire visibly short.

"Occupy what?" Mari asked.

No one answered. Even Sir Rufus seemed to have recalled his wits, his mouth thinning into a narrow dour line.

"Occupy *what?*"

She looked up at Lord Chasen, who had shifted from her side—at the light that lifted colors from the rug to emphasize the shape of his chin, his cheekbones and brow; at his eyes now very visible, glacial pale.

He slid a step from her. With a sudden formality he offered her a bow, though it wasn't deep, and his hands remained at his sides. "Your Grace. Would you do me the honor of leaving this chamber? It is a closed meeting of the council, and we have much to discuss."

"Yes," she said thinly. "I see."

She did not rush, she did not tarry. In his shirt and breeches she only turned around and walked away, the rug beneath her feet giving way to buttery wood by the door.

CHAPTER TWENTY

S o here is the scene you missed, you *delis:*

The Princess hurried toward her escape. The glass doors were already ajar, because the fat elder dragon-man had already pushed through them—roughly, mind you; he had broken a fine brass latch to do so—and so they stood cracked, with a nick of cleaner air from the garden beyond pushing wet into the odors of the pump room.

The Princess was swift. Her slippers barely touched the floor. She moved like a dancer in ethereal gray past the slow and startled Others; the surest way to follow her was by the jet beads fringing her gown. They shone in black winking tears, and clinked and rustled and sang out with her every step.

That was how the other female dragon found her, and was able to take her by the hand. With that one single touch their minds fell into harmony. Together they flitted past the glass doors and became seamless with the night.

This other dragon was no princess. But she was yellow-haired and fair and born in a mansion of clouds and light; let us call her a lady.

The lady also winked with stones, mostly amethysts that moaned a curious song about lakes and caverns, and geodes breaking apart into sparkles. About the lady's neck was tied a velvet ribbon, and from it hung a pendant shaped as a heart. Embedded in the pendant were three shards of diamond, each one of them shining pale, evil blue.

The Princess looked at the lady, and the lady looked at the Princess. The rain fell upon them in hard silver pins, biting at their skin.

The diamonds lifted and joined to weave a chorus of blinding noise; it was all the Princess could hear, and all she could fathom, until the lady said:

"Go, Maricara, and forget me."

And the Princess did.

CHAPTER TWENTY-ONE

She had traveled across a continent without accompaniment. She had crossed the skies, and bathed in secluded tubs, and supped on cold meats and cheesecakes and slices of gingered pineapple, delicacies all purloined from the finest of houses. She had been alone, and not lonely.

But Mari had accompaniment now. Oh, they were not so bold as to follow her openly, not even the footmen who had dashed ahead to open the main doors before she reached them, or the gardener and his assistant who glanced up from their bed of mulch to watch her stride past, sweat-dripping faces beneath the brims of straw hats.

Not the three young kitchen maids, also in the garden, clipping herbs and whispering behind their hands. The gathering of boys behind them, holding baskets.

There were *drákon* everywhere in this shire. They trickled through the woods still, clouded the cobalt sky. They watched her without approach. They waited, she knew, for the order from their Alpha. That was all that held them back.

The air felt opaque. It felt so heavy and wet she could hardly force it into her lungs.

Mari angled toward the staggered break of trees that marked the forest closest to the manor. She crossed a bed of violets and pinks, crushing perfume beneath her heels. The shade of a chestnut dappled her shoulders and dazzled her vision, and the chestnut touched branches with an elm, and the elm took her into the real woods, and then she was inside them, and the air was cool on her face, and she could draw breath again.

She set her back against a rowan. A copper-winged butterfly zigzagged through the holly and bracken; she closed her eyes against the matted green leaves and summoned the cold.

Snowstorms. Winter.

Mountains and boars and white fields. Frost rimming windows; icicles frozen from eaves.

Zaharen Yce.

It had been raised in crystalline towers and wide, high terraces, a true sanctuary for dragons. Only later did it grow walls and an armory, transforming with deadly grace into a plain sound fortress. It could withstand cannons and cascades of flaming arrows. The portcullis was of iron. The oaken doors still held the indentations of a battering ram wielded four centuries past—the doors had not yielded. Time had proven again and again that humans could not breach the castle.

Dragons, however . . . oh, dragons could.

She brought her fists up to her eyes. She felt her lips pull back in a grimace of a smile and did not know if she should scream or weep.

An occupation. They planned to occupy her home—to invade

it. They had planned it all along, perhaps for years. Perhaps from the very first. And the Zaharen—proud and cloistered and unwary—the Zaharen would fall because these dragons were stronger than her kin. By Gifts and wiles and smiling false diplomacy, they were stronger.

Damn them to hell.

And Kimber . . . Kimber . . .

The shaking that had taken her in the council's chamber stole up through her limbs once again, bleak and icy, colder even than that snow she remembered.

In her darkest musings she had imagined something like this. It explained their repeated requests for her location, to come to her or have her come to them. But she'd also thought that these English *drákon* would be more like her own folk, remnants of a once-mighty race, with pockets of power and a majority of thin-blooded people. Before coming here, Lia had been the only one of them Mari had ever known, and certainly Lia had been formidable, but no more formidable than Maricara herself.

Even if her worst fears proved real, she'd thought the Zaharen would prevail. They had the castle and at least a hundred good strong men who could Turn, and so would prevail.

But she had been wrong.

Darkfrith, a haven, was far larger than she'd imagined. There had to be close to a thousand here who could Turn.

A thousand.

It would be a massacre.

She would leave, then. She would fly home. She belonged to the Zaharen, by birth and by marriage, and this time she would not abandon them. Let the earl and his English kin come; her people would still fight. Let them see what might there was left in the Carpathians.

She shoved from the rowan in a surge of determination. Another butterfly shivered up and away, but Mari barely heeded it. She took two steps into the dark humid forest, her power cresting—a mere second from the Turn—

But then she heard music. Stone music—not the notes from the spa—she had no idea why the squire would invent such nonsense; it was surely just another part of their plot—but this was something broken and queer and hauntingly familiar. Mari knew this song. She knew that melody.

Through the sultry heat a chill crept over her skin. She paused, rubbing her arms, glancing around at tree trunks and wildflowers bent double to rest their heads upon the ground. A breeze stirred the rowan and quieted the song; she waited until the air settled again, listening. And then she began to walk.

It was such a slight, unsettling thing, so faint beneath the other sounds of rocks and metals and running water that she lost it three more times. And there were twigs and bugs and she should not be walking, but she knew if she Turned now, she'd have the immediate attention of all those not-clouds dangling above her. Mari had faith enough she could escape them when the time came. But first she just wanted to see...

She walked a good while. The sleeves of Kimber's shirt caught against the brushwood, and once she splashed into a flat little stream throttled with muddy debris. After a half hour her feet were filthy and perspiration had the linen clinging like translucent skin to her torso and arms, but the notes were getting clearer.

The forest opened up into a meadow. It was sprinkled with scarlet campion and bluebells, a good many of them flattened to the earth. Dirt had been kicked up. The smell of man and steel sopped the air. And blood.

Sanf inimicus.

She moved cautiously into the grasses. She glanced up and around and stepped sideways like a crab, unwilling to keep her back fixed to any one spot, even though the scent of the *sanf* was hours old.

There was the blood, a few drops, nearly the same color as the campions they decorated.

And there was the song. It was an emerald, buried beneath a clod of sticky brown dirt. She crouched down and dug until she found it, two halves of uneven green, a gold wire hoop that had been mashed into a lump.

Rhys's emerald. Rhys's earring. She touched a finger to the petal of a campion and felt the small, electric thrill of dragon blood, freshly dried.

Mari stood. She rubbed the pieces of ruined emerald between her palms, gauging grit and music and sharp edges, and blew the air between her teeth. The canopy of trees above her head made a skein of branches and leaves without a single nest of any kind, not from birds or squirrels.

This was not her concern. None of it was. Not any longer.

But the broken flowers ruffled with the breeze. A cricket nearby began a tentative creak, and then one more. Within three chirps it was joined by a fellow; together they made a low, urgent sawing.

Mari plucked the blooded campion. She wiped the moisture from her face with the cuff of her sleeve and began the trek back to Chasen.

She came upon the gardener first. She walked straight to him—he had moved from the bed of mulch to the violets she had trampled, resettling the stems—and watched as his gaze lifted from her feet to her bare scratched shins, to the oversized breeches and soiled, transparent shirt. When he reached her eyes she held out her fist to him.

"Here," she said. She dropped the earring and wilting campion into his hastily lifted hands. "Take these to your lord. Tell him I found them in the woods, about five miles distant. And that now I am done."

Night fell. It was moonless, no clouds, only stars to pierce the inky black—stars and torches and lanterns. Voices that did not call out, but whispered like a river running constant through the trees and darkened lanes. Voices that purled, *They're here, where do we hide, whom do we trust?*

The *drákon* searched for their missing in silence. They sent out parties in groups; no one traveled alone. Not any longer. Men went to smoke to curl stealthily through the forests; women blocked all openings to their homes, their children confined to parlors, bright eyes fixed on doors, carving knives and loaded pistols kept like embroidery on their laps.

Their domain had been breached. A young prince had been taken. Mari knew he wasn't a prince, not really, but to these people, Rhys Langford was as near as they would come.

She remembered the flaxen-haired Englishman found dead in the mountains, the particular gray tinge of his skin. She remembered the man in the mines, the rigid curl of his fingers, the gape of his mouth. She thought of Rhys and his pirate's grin and wished that of all the people she had met in this place, it had not been him.

From her seat against the polished glass dome topping the manor she watched the many dots of light that illuminated Darkfrith, stars tilting above, bobbing flames below. She sat with her arms wrapped around her knees, still dressed in Kimber's clothing, because she would not risk going down to the Dead Room, no matter the wealth and memories she had stored in the cell down there.

She did not think any of them could sneak up on her. But she was unwilling to be proven wrong.

At least the night was cooler than the day. The glass kept a pleasant heat against her back, not much, only enough to keep her comfortable. She leaned her head against it, watching the man drawing near across the slate tiles with half-lidded eyes. The roof of Chasen Manor was unlit and so was he; as he walked toward her the curve of the dome sliced across his body, blurring, a figure of shadow and sheen.

The entry to the roof was on the other side of the dome. She'd chosen this spot in particular so that she could see him approach. So that he would not have to Turn, and come to her as any other being but the earl.

"You're still here," Kimber said.

"As you see."

He stopped at her feet, balanced on the slope with one boot above the other.

"Twenty men," she commented, without moving. "Would their time not be better spent searching for your brother, rather than wasting the night hovering around me?"

She couldn't make out his smile but she imagined it, thin and sardonic, with no humor behind it. "Will you give me your word you won't attempt to leave Chasen?"

"Absolutely. As many words as you wish."

"Why, thank you, that's most reassuring. Isn't it delightful to discover we understand each other so well. I've four times as many men searching for Rhys. And I do not consider it a waste in any sense to ensure your security." The earl paused. "Do you feel him anywhere?"

"No," she answered, with real regret.

Someone Turned to dragon overhead, silent, falling and rising. Mari lifted her head, squinting until she found the shape of the beast against the sky, a black winged rope beneath a blacker heaven.

"Do you think I can't elude them?"

"I think that if you could, you would have already done so, Princess."

"Perhaps I was only waiting for you."

Kimber climbed closer, then eased down beside her, crossing his legs. "How fortuitous. Here I am."

"I've been thinking," she began, angling her gaze now at the glow of a lantern that marked a slow, wavering trail through the forest. "About what your squire said."

She felt his attention, although he watched the lantern too.

"I cannot . . . actually recall leaving the pump room."

"Oh?"

"I remember leaving the table. I remember the husband stopping me in the hallway afterward. But in between . . . there's nothing."

He turned to look at her.

"I wanted you to know that before I left. I wasn't lying before; I'm not like you. But I realized—later on—that I did not remember." She shrugged. "Perhaps there *was* a woman. Perhaps it was your missing girl. I don't know. It's a mystery for you to unravel after I'm gone."

"Maricara . . ."

"And I wanted something else. Something to take with me."

He shook his head. He was at the ragged edge of his restraint; she felt it. She heard it in the tempered tightness of voice. "What?"

"This."

She lifted a hand to his face. She found his cheek, unshaven, and the heavy warmth of his hair, unbound at his shoulders. With her other hand she held him steady and brushed her lips to his.

He allowed it. She'd feared he wouldn't, that in his state of hunt and disquiet and eagerness to shackle her to the ground, he would be in no mind for kisses, not even this one, soft and in the dark, and with her eyes closed, so that she could not see even a hint of his features.

He covered her shoulder with his palm. He held very still, and when she pulled away, he said only, "Was that supposed to be a good-bye?"

She felt herself color a little.

"You're very young," he said flatly. "And for all your worldly ways, I fear more than a little naive. From the moment we discovered your existence, Maricara, there became no question of our people joining into one. You've seen the life we live here. Our foundations in this society, our careful disguise. Without the Zaharen, our survival was sustainable. But *with* you, with the very fact of you, everything must change. You will change, and I will change. For the good of us all, we're going to unite. We will have rules and opinions and I don't expect we'll agree on a great many things. But this is how it will be. As my wife, you're the perfect liaison for all the *drákon* living in Transylvania."

"I don't want to be a wife," she said, her hand still cupped to his face.

"I'm sorry to hear it. Because it's going to happen one way or another."

"My people will fight you. We are ferocious fighters."

"I'm sure you see that that would be a great waste of lives. Even counting your kin, there are so few *drákon* left. I'd hate to lose more of us in fruitless battle, especially with the *delis inimicus* panting at our heels."

She dropped her hand. She sat back again, propped her head against the dome and looked up at the stars.

"Is this truly how you want our futures to unfold?" she asked quietly. "War and bloodshed. You're determined?"

"Let me you ask *you* something, Princess. Why did you come here?"

"You know why."

"A letter would have sufficed as warning for the *sanf.* The rings were ample proof. There was no need for you to show up in person, unless you had another motive."

She was surprised into a laugh. "You think I came here to marry you?"

"I think," he said, "that somewhere in your heart, you knew where your fate would lie. That there was no *drákon* of the Zaharen who would match you as I would. You were wed to an Alpha because that's what that black dragon simmering in your blood demands of you. You will wed an Alpha once more. *Pendant que nous vivons, ainsi nous devons être.*" The warmth of his touch modified, became lighter, a bare stroke down her arm. "I regret you heard what you did with the council. I regret there isn't more time to convince you that I'm right. I'm not your enemy, Maricara. Like it or not, for better or worse—I'm your husband, and your mate. King to king. Soon you'll be a queen as well. Neither of us can change it. It *is* why you came to me. Why fight what's over and done?"

Her throat had gone dry; she swallowed and looked away, and was glad he could not see her face. "How romantic. I'm quite swept off my feet."

Kimber's fingers tapped lightly against the backs of her own. "I can shower you with rose petals if you'd like. I can feed you Swiss chocolates and bathe you in French champagne...but you'll have to come with me inside for all that." He looked at her aslant. "Will you?"

"No."

The stars glinted silver and blue and gold and pink. Clouds of smoke drifted above, tails and twists of deep charcoal.

Mari said, "You can shower me with petals up here."

She felt him change, felt that edge of frustration in him sharpen and splinter, transforming into something else.

"I'll wait," she said.

It was no time for dalliance; she knew it as well as he. No time for anything more between them but the end rushing closer, enormous, inevitable. She had come to this place and brought with her the devil's wind, a searing ill harbinger of exposure and death and everything hazardous to a people woven from fiction, from threads of mist. She had not meant to do it, but it was done.

Yet the Earl of Chasen only fixed her with a hot, intent look she didn't even need to see to feel. Then he was gone, his clothing settling down to the roof with a sigh of cotton and leather, his boots falling over to lightly strike the tiles.

After a moment, his voice floated up from beyond the edge of the parapet.

"Great King. I'm afraid you'll have to join me down here, if it's petals you require."

He would not be able to bring them to her as smoke; she had no idea how he'd manage it as a dragon, either.

She Turned, following the scent of him to the garden, to a corner of arbors and pergolas and long, sweet grasses, and rows and rows of windows shining black above them.

He stood in the shelter of one of the arbors, a profusion of vines and red roses tumbling from the wooden slats. Fragrance twirled around him with honey-slow leisure; her first breath as woman was spiced and pungent, nearly too strong. It made her head spin.

She had Turned right against him. She had taken that breath and then leaned up to him with her bare body and kissed him, hard and open, her hands clutching at his shoulders. He caught her to him, returning her hunger with his own. She heard the rustle of rose leaves, the shifting of gravel beneath their feet that felt hard and real and wonderful all at once, like him.

He drew her farther with him into the arbor, shadows so thick she lost the image of him entirely; he was heat and muscle and touch. She felt his arms lift, held above her: rose petals floated down, patting her nose and her chest and her arms, skimming the surface of her hair. A few still clung to his palms as he lowered his hands to kiss her again; one trembled at the corner of her lips; another at her collarbone, a perfect fit to the hollow at the base of her throat.

"There," he murmured. "There. You look like…"

"You can't see me."

"I can." His mouth found the petal at her lips, his tongue tracing its shape, tracing her. "Lovely girl, I can."

Mari closed her eyes and caught her breath, tipping back her head. "Like what, then?" she whispered.

He smiled against her. "Like an elfin queen. Like a dragon king." *Like mine,* he nearly finished, but kissed her full on the lips instead.

He wished for light. Torchlight, sunlight—to see her openly again, beyond the gleam of milky skin, beyond the dim luster of her hair, the gray-night shine of her eyes. Her lips were dark, and her hair was dark, and her nipples, God, her nipples were dark and plump and hard against his palms. He opened his mouth over her pulse, the tender column of her neck, dragging his lips lower, half-crouching to rub his face to her chest. Lifting her, hearing her low gasp over the drumming of her heart. But she was light in his arms, hardly a weight at all, and his mouth found one perfect tip, warm and puckered. He suckled her, and heard her gasp become his name.

He needed this. He needed this moment—not very long, not forever, just enough to wipe clean his worries right now, to bury the weight of his title and honor and the bitter fear for his brother in the lush promise of her body. In her kisses, and her taste, and her legs wrapped hard around him. There was a terror running through him so raw and deep it made him tremble; he was a leader and man, and he stood at the ruin of all he loved—and he just needed this one stolen moment with her to forget—

Deep, deep inside him, in a place so hidden and quiet he didn't even have a name for it, Kimber knew that the terror was winning:

He was quaking apart. He could not think of his brother without anguish; it was a pain so profound, so vast it seemed to transfigure his very blood. He seemed made of lead now, not flesh, lead that was both numb and slow, useless against the vicious cold eating away at him from inside and out. He was desperate to help Rhys and could not. He was desperate for his tribe. Whenever he closed his eyes the image of the broken emerald burned like a brand behind his lids. The shattered stone. His little brother dead. Tortured. Rhys's heart—his *heart*—

If he came apart, Kim honestly didn't know what would be left behind. Nothing good. Nothing of use to the *drákon,* or his wife.

Perhaps Maricara sensed his secret trembling. She was mystic and surprising and when she looked up at him now, surrounded by roses and night, Kim actually felt like he was drowning, surrendering to her mysterious depths. He grasped at that, grateful. Aye, he could drown in her, and be free. There was nothing he wanted more in this instant than that.

Her legs lifted to encircle his waist. Her fingers clenched against his shoulders. She arched back and for one glorious instant he saw her gently silvered in the starlight: her throat and jaw and shoulders, slender muscles held taut, and then he'd swung her back into the protection of the roses and the subtle dark, giving his back to the barbed canes. Kim raised his head to nuzzle her neck and lowered her onto him.

He found her entrance. He was eager for her, he was aching for her, to the point where he nearly forgot where he was, forgot the garden and the manor and the *drákon* all around them. The dry leaves of the roses sketched patterns on his skin. Thorns pricked, drew blood. He didn't care.

She was here. She was ready. She kissed him with her tongue in his mouth and took him inside her and all thoughts of *location, discretion, smoke,* blew away, incinerated. He heard a noise, a deep visceral sound of pleasure, and realized it had come from him.

Maricara answered it by parting her lips and sinking deeper. Her arms cradled his head; his hands supported her buttocks, cupped her to him, lifting and helping her. They rocked together, and she was wet and stretched and velvet around him, her heels pressed to his spine, her fingers twisted in his hair. He'd never felt anything like this, never known he could make love to a queen in a garden and think, *Yes, this is what I need, this* and *her.*

He felt her body begin to tighten. He felt the coming of her release before she even caught her breath, before she stopped breathing entirely. She stiffened against him and made the smallest, most amazed little noise—it finished him. He squeezed her bottom and pumped into her and felt the bounce of her breasts against his chest. He thrust up and pressed her down to him so hard it felt like pain, the best pain he'd ever felt. Maricara jerked against him, coming again. And Kim spilled his seed in her, and let the roses have his blood.

That, she thought, still clasped to him, sated and sore, the floral scent of the garden now overwhelmed by frank musky sex. Mari let her head rest against his, her lips in his hair, tasting salt and satin. She closed her eyes, learning the curves of his skull beneath her fingers, precious and new.

That was good-bye.

She fell asleep standing against him. He was holding her upright with one arm around her waist and the other crossed behind her head, keeping her close, her temple to his shoulder, her long hair brushing his hips, his back bloody and stinging and his dragons above them both flitting silently back and forth, night terrors on the wind.

He had to leave her. He had to rejoin his kin in the sky. Even the time he had taken to find her on the roof of his home was precious seconds leached from Rhys, but Kim had done it anyway, and now he had to go.

He'd not parted well with her this afternoon, and it had bothered him. He'd spent the day and evening remembering that, the expression on her face, as he'd plunged into the search for his brother and Honor and tried to let the hunt consume him, as it should.

Shock. Hurt. And then, worst of all: detachment. She'd lowered her eyes and shut him out and walked away, and even though he'd known she would not be able to get far—he'd placed guards on her with just the sweep of his finger as she'd stalked out the manor doors—Kimber regretted wounding her.

Because she was his wife. His fire and his heart. She was.

And he'd truly not wanted to hurt her.

But he couldn't leave now without knowing she was safe. He had to know that *someone* he loved was safe.

Kim turned his face to hers, closing his eyes, his lips to her forehead. She roused a bit, lifting her head, and blinked and looked around them from the circle of his arms. In the waning starlight the roses bloomed wolf-gray, textured petals above them and surrounding them, and sprinkled at their feet.

"Beloved," he said. "Come inside with me."

She brought a hand to her face, pushing back her hair. "No, I . . . I don't want to go back there."

"To the—to your room?"

"Not alone."

"You won't be alone. I'll come with you," he temporized. "For now, at least."

She sighed, a rush against his skin. "No."

"You're exhausted. You need to rest."

She tipped her face to his. Her eyes had that hollow cast he'd last seen over dinner in Seaham, uncanny weary and bright. "Not yet," she said, and took a longer breath. "I'm not tired enough yet."

He said, soft: "Mari."

"Not yet," she repeated, her voice breaking. She pulled from his arms.

"I'll be here, black dragon. I'll be your anchor. I won't let you fly."

She made a sound like a laugh, but it was small and turned into a yawn; she smothered it with one hand. Kim found her other, lifting their joined fingers to point at the balcony outside his chambers. "There. Do you see it? The window to the far left of the gargoyle, the one with the beak and the feathered wings—it's open. That's where we'll go."

He went to smoke on nothing but faith that she would follow; after a few seconds, she did. Together they wound through his bedchamber, over to the bed. Room after room was unlit, not even the golden lamp of Moorish glass on the nightstand left to gutter. Every *drákon* of the shire had a role to play this night, and none of them was of servant.

His sheets were soft, washed with French soap, dried in wind and flowery heat. He flipped them back for her and waited, and the lovely blue haze that was the princess coalesced, became form and corporeal beauty. She regarded him from the other side of the mattress, frowning a little, swaying very slightly.

"I'll be here," he said again.

She climbed into his bed. She pushed down between the covers and closed her eyes, one arm flung across the pillows.

Within seconds, she was asleep.

He meant to stay beside her only a short while. There was so much he needed yet to do, so many urgent things, and, when he'd lain atop the duvet at her side, comfort swept over him like a sweet, sweet narcotic; he'd meant it to last only so long as to ensure she knew he'd kept his word.

She slept. Kimber kept watch, or he thought he did. He was studying her—what he could see of her—in the vague dark of his canopied bed it was more like the notion of her, the curving line of her chin, the smoothing of the night along her upper arm—and when he next looked up, the sky beyond the balcony had brightened into green, the cumulus clouds just visible at the edge of his windows stained orange and deep cool orchid.

It was dawn. He awoke alone in his rumpled bed.

Maricara was gone.

CHAPTER TWENTY-TWO

She did not fly east. They would be expecting that, for her to head toward *Zaharen Yce*. West was Ireland and ocean, and north was the rough drab land of the Scots. So she ducked and circled and finally went south, because that was the direction that made no sense. South would lead her only deeper into England.

She left behind the hills that sheltered and isolated a foggy, leafy shire. She left behind the mansion of windows and dulcet songs, and her gowns and jewels. She left behind the *drákon* and their leader, the man who had managed, despite all her very best efforts, to discover the map of her heart. Who had pinned her with a cool green gaze and passed his hand over her chest and scorched a hole in her center without even trying.

She'd see him again. She didn't like to think how.

Mari used the same trick to exit the shire that had gotten her in:

She soared straight up like a rocket, as high as her wings would carry her and then more, snarling with effort. The air waned so thin she worried they might hear the rasp of her breath, but the majority of the Darkfrith dragons were intent on different prey. The *sanf* were largely human and could not fly, and Rhys Langford, wherever he was, probably could not either.

The ones who'd been guarding her, however, followed at once—twenty-three, actually, smoke as she was smoke, dragon as she was. But the somber gray minutes before daybreak were always the best time for an escape; she'd known that since she was a child. Eyes were fooled. Senses were smothered. One by one her pursuers fell behind.

Two proved to be extremely persistent, obviously skilled trackers. It took a good ten miles before she was able to lose them above the meandering elbow of a great river, wheeling low again to let the freshwater obscure her scent, and the colors of the woods blurred as she blurred, and within a quarter hour she'd lost them both.

Maricara pulled high once more.

Everything slipped beneath her like that river. Like rain, land and lakes and towns, places passed over so quickly she barely registered them. She flew until the threat of the sun became burgeoning peach and gold, and the anvil of clouds swelling ahead shone beryl in its middle and caramel along the edges. She found the sea, a sudden uprush of brine in her nose—and then stunning, scintillating light, foam breaking ivory around rocks of small islands, and ships that dotted the blue-green waves.

She narrowed her eyes, considering. The water would be wide here, with scant place to rest should she need to, and she didn't like to swim. She'd do better farther south—as far south as Dover, if she dared. But as she glided along the brink of the coast, Mari found herself gazing and gazing at the thin, ambered line that split the salt water from the horizon, envisioning wind-scoured alps instead, glaciers and edelweiss. Timberline. The crisp chill of mountain mornings.

Waking nude atop the tower terrace. White quartzite, and hay that poked at her skin. Suckling pigs devoured in the night. Belfries.

She missed having a home. She actually mourned it; she imagined that in her sleep, in her flying dreams, she was searching for it still, that place where she could be accepted and whole, where she could rest at last. Perhaps the Zaharen would never truly welcome her, but the castle was hers as this isle could never be. She had spilled blood for it and reached adulthood in it, and she had as much right to defend it as anyone else.

Her wings crooked. She began to veer east just as the first sheer notes of music lifted from below her.

Eerie notes. Notes that spoke to her of a girl named Honor, and a vanishing.

No. Mari flattened her ears and stretched her body thin, going faster. She wasn't going to listen to it. She wasn't going to turn around. She didn't care how mysterious those notes floated up to her, how powerfully they called. She didn't want to know what made them. She had a mission now. She had a duty.

Oh...but it was beautiful. The smallest of canticles, beckoning, a melody at once so simple and so profound that, when she blinked, teardrops scattered to the wind behind her; she found her wings arcing once again, her body tugged right, back to land.

No, no.

But she was going. She was circling around; the sea flashed; a loose cluster of terns low, low against the ground bunched and then shot inland, vanishing against the buffed cliffs and dunes.

The song was wistful and poignant and still so familiar. It pulled her over the cliffs as sure as if she wore some stretched, invisible leash, over trees and the pointed peaks of a village over a league distant—but the song was not coming from there. It was coming from a clearing, trees chopped raw at their bases and dying leaves still littering the ground.

Someone was burning the trees. Smoke—real smoke—boiled and clawed at the early-morning sky.

At the edge of the clearing was what looked like a ramshackle shepherd's hut, still half-enclosed with woods. The smoke rose from behind it. She went to vapor, blending with the black-burnt sap of the trees, gliding down to a moldy thatched roof, the heavy branches that supported it split and bent with time. A bed of gnarled white geraniums still struggled to bloom between the weeds beneath the only window.

From within the hut the notes sang *yes, yes, come in.*

Mari sank between the thatch.

He was awake. He could not recall coming awake. Hell, he couldn't recall going to sleep. He'd been in the southern woods; he knew that. He'd been walking, pacing off the agitation that burned in him, following the faint press of a deer path and mist that broke around his feet into the heart of ash and wych. He must have fallen asleep. He had no memory of that. But he was awake now, excruciatingly awake, and somehow between that time and this the world had gone blind and reeking.

He wore a hood. He was on his knees in dirt, because the chains were that heavy. He couldn't even rise above that, and he was strong, so whoever had bound him with the chains was clever enough to know his strength. They had been here moments ago. Although time seemed an uncertain thing to him now, Rhys was fairly certain that was true. They were men plus another who was not a man, and they spoke a language he did not understand—not French or German, or anything so logical as that; these words blended into rhythms he could not follow, and his head ached like the very devil when he tried—

Yet they were gone, fled in haste. He knelt alone in a room of some sort. There was an odd music in his head, and his hands and feet felt frozen, even though the air was too warm. Something wet trickled down his neck, saturating the cloth where it was tied against his throat. He thought it was probably blood.

A new sense of warmth gathered above him. It was soft and sly but very there, a presence that pressed into his muffled world, cautious, feminine.

He knew her. He lifted his head, his mind breaking clear of its miasma with a sudden crystalline horror. He felt her Turn before him, dropping down, her hands clutching hard at his.

"Rhys," she said.

His fingers curled. "*Turn*," he croaked—but just as he'd suspected, the Others were never far off at all.

For thirty-one years, the sum of her life, Audrey Langford Downing had been one-half of a whole. She had not asked for it; the *drákon* were prone to twins and even triplets, although it was true that in recent years single births had become far more common than not.

She was born second, which might have rankled, but more significantly, she had been born a girl, and that meant she would have been second even had she been born first. But Kimber was eldest, and always had been. It was as if he'd come squalling into the world with the knowledge of his place in their society already embedded beneath his skin. As long as she could remember, he'd been quick to lead, quick to decide, quick to dismiss. Had he been of smaller mind . . . had his character been a whit less generous, she might have grown up resenting him. After all, he had everything he desired, and always had. He was handsome and charismatic and well-favored with the tribe. He was Alpha heir and then Alpha, and she'd spent years watching him accept the favors of their people with an untailored sort of graciousness that always, deep down, managed to astonish her.

She might have hated him. Sometimes when they were younger—when Kim smiled his comely smile and spoke blithely of London and balls and the royal court, places she'd never go, dances she would never dance—Audrey thought perhaps a wee part of her did. But it was Rue who'd shaken that seed of spite from her daughter's heart. Rue, who would not abide shame or dishonesty from any of her children—although her definition of "dishonesty" was somewhat unorthodox, to say the least.

Her mother was the one who found Audrey early on the morning of her seventeenth birthday. The celebrations had started the evening before, fireworks and raucous dancing in the tavern; blue-and-gold ribbons festooned the village shops and houses, fluttered pretty along the lanes. There was to be a soirée at the manor house later that night for anyone who might care to come. An evening of more genteel cake and music and punch in the ballroom, perhaps even a quadrille.

And it was all for him.

Yes, Audrey happened to be born on the exact same day, of the exact same parents. But it was for Kimber, ever Kimber, that the tribe met to celebrate.

She'd not yet been able to Turn; that Gift hadn't come for another quarter year. So when she'd slunk from Chasen Manor she'd done it the human way, by foot, wearing black. She'd made it as far as the circulating library in the village before Rue smoked down to catch her.

The circulating library, at four in the morning. She'd been leaning with her back against the bowfront window, staring down sullenly at her feet. Nearly everyone was asleep at that hour. There were people still in the tavern, but they were drunk and it was at the opposite end of the village, and, as usual, no one noticed her.

One of the ribbons was torn free of its mooring; it made a very fine snake against the paving stones. She stood there, watching it flip back and forth with the breeze near the hem of her skirts. She was thirsty already, and she'd forgotten to bring anything to drink.

"It's late," announced her mother's voice, tranquil and just beside her.

And because she was thirsty, and because her little moment of rebellion had been quashed just that quickly, Audrey had sneered, "So?"

"So, nothing, actually." Rue kept back in the shelter of the awning above the library door. "I've always enjoyed the night myself. Quite useful for stealing about. What an interesting gown. It looks very much like one of the maids' uniforms. What did you do with the apron?"

"Nothing," she muttered. After a moment: "I'll sew it back on."

"Better you than I," said Rue, cheerful, because everyone knew how she hated to sew.

Audrey lifted her chin. "Well? Aren't you going to punish me?"

"I?" replied her mother. "Good heavens. What have you done?"

"This." She made a curt gesture to the village, the shuttered windows. "Running away."

"Ah. Do you consider this running away?"

And there was something there, some careful compassion in her voice that made Audrey's temper snap. "Yes, I do. Certainly it's nothing compared with *you,* the glorious Smoke Thief, but I daresay this isn't allowed—I pulled that banner down, yes, and I fully plan to pull down all the others, as many as I can—and I guarantee you that if I had an *ounce* of your Gifts I would have left this place in the *dust.*"

Rue said nothing. Audrey was breathing hard through her nose, humiliatingly close to tears. The darkened street before her wavered and the music from the tavern became heavy with French horn.

Audrey had already extinguished the candle lantern in front of the library by the simple expedient of one well-aimed rock. When Rue stepped forward, it was into shadows.

"Do you imagine it will be easy for him?" she asked softly, placing a hand on her daughter's arm.

Audrey twitched free. "I don't care to discuss it."

"It won't be, you know. He's strong, and that's a very good thing, because being the leader of our kind is a burden that devastates the weak."

"Oh, yes indeed. Poor Kimber!"

"No. Poor Audrey, to have to watch and realize that she's as smart and as strong as her brother, but she'll never be allowed to live his life. She will grow into a beautiful young woman. She will fall in love and wed. She'll learn to fly—yes, my dear, you will; we're very alike, and I've given you that much, I don't doubt. But you will always be female." Rue lifted her hand to the night, examining the tips of her fingers, the turn of her wrist. "And perhaps—someday—Audrey will become more than the rest of us. Perhaps she will convince her clan that the womenfolk deserve a firmer place than they have now. Perhaps she will succeed where her mother has not." Her arm dropped. "Kim's world is both less and more than yours. He'll never struggle as you do. He'll never learn as you. When your father was his age he'd already been forced to publicly kill two of our kind because they were threats to the tribe. To our survival. Is that the role you want?"

It was true; Audrey knew it was true. She glared down at the ribbon twisting over and over itself and shook her head.

"Your brother doesn't want it either," said Rue simply. "But he will do it. Violence, assassination. Lying, cheating, death. Whatever he must. Much like his twin, he was born with a tender heart, and the path ahead of him will do naught but darken it. I don't think you should envy him that. I don't."

All these years later, her mother's words echoed in her ears, Rue's matter-of-fact tone, her fleeting touch. Audrey looked at her twin standing now in the grand black-and-cream ballroom of Chasen Manor, bright with the fretwork of amber inlay and leafed gold and the faces of their kin, as many as could cram into the chamber, and that was a great many.

One-half a whole. He stood atop the musician's dais—the very dais where a quadrille had once been played, fourteen years before—and spoke words to the tribe, words that Audrey did not really hear because she was concentrating on the man himself instead.

This man wasn't Kimber. He didn't look like Kimber, and from this distance, he didn't feel like him. He was ice and marble and someone new, someone she'd glimpsed once or twice before in the most fell of extremities, but that was all.

A darkened heart.

His lips moved. He wore clothing she'd seen countless times: a starched shirt missing its waistcoat, buckskin breeches and tall brown boots. The sun angled in from the west and lit his plain country attire to gilt and fire. His hair was undone. In the natural light it shone every rich shade of blond. It was the only aspect of him that still appeared—human. Every atom in the chamber seemed drawn to him, charged and bright and dangerous, and only a dragon could do that.

His face was drawn in planes, harsh and bleak; his figure fixed as if he grew upright from the dais, from the manor house itself, and the wild sky and the trees and the blood of the earth. His gaze raked the crowd with an intensity that had more than a few of the younger maidens enthralled with wide-eyed dread.

Rue was gone, no longer beside her second-born child; Joan

was with her now instead, and together the sisters clasped hands and watched as what was left of their eldest flaked away, an imaginary skin that frosted and cracked until only the Alpha stood before them, an animal that never raised his voice, never shifted his stance. He held the tribe rapt with just a few soft-spoken sentences.

"Our time is come. Assume any strangers in the shire are *sanf,* no matter what they say. Slay them if you must or save them for me."

A pair of starlings winged across the vista behind him, blackened and swift, falling from sight against the backdrop of verdant woods.

The Alpha said, "Do not hold back."

CHAPTER TWENTY-THREE

I t has been a matter of some debate among the *drákon* today as to whether the stone *Draumr* ever truly existed.

It is debated with the utmost civility, of course. Dragon-ladies in lace and corsets sip their tea in fashionable parlors and keep their voices to a throaty murmur. They sit with their ankles crossed and smile at each other and occasionally show teeth that gleam very white.

Our men do very nearly the same, standing about in magnificent card rooms, rapiers of Spanish gold and gemstones affixed at their hips, their elegant hands weighted with rings of carnelian and topaz that burn with subtle song.

They reach no cohesive conclusions.

How could they? These dragons never heard the lure of the diamond, not truly. Every now and again perhaps someone will lift her head from the details of her day, her attention snared as a few languorous notes seemingly appear from nowhere to wrap around her, to twist into her bones with devastating bliss. Born from echoes, dissipating into echoes, they're gone nearly as soon as her lips form that first, delighted gasp.

She'll retire to her bed that night and ache as she remembers how it felt. She'll wonder if she's feverish, if it had been naught but a dream.

It *was* the dreaming diamond, after all.

And yes, it was real. So many of us no longer believe, but I was there. I fell prey to its malevolence more times than nearly any other of our kind, and by the very last time *Draumr* and I clashed, I had mastered it enough to wield its power myself.

Had I that diamond today—even a portion of it—who knows what I might do.

Ultimate pleasure is an eloquent motivator.

Pain, of course, is as well.

CHAPTER TWENTY-FOUR

This was London. She was sure it had to be although she never had a glimpse of it. She had been taken there in a carriage, pulled by horses that groaned and huffed every time she shifted against the squabs.

Her mouth had been gagged, her hands fixed at the small of her back with actual chains. Men had sat with her in the carriage, four men, their heartbeats fast and uneven. Three of them smelled like peasants, like raw onions and the fetor of unwashed bodies; they needed to bathe, and that was before the carriage even breached the outskirts of the city, when an entirely new layer of stink filled the air.

In all the hours of travel, those three never uttered a word. It was the fourth man who spoke to her, a whisper in her ear after they'd snatched her in the hut and jammed the hood over her head, and they'd pressed the blade of a knife into her throat until she'd felt the warmth of her own blood.

The man had knelt to where she lay in the dirt, put his lips to the hood, and murmured in French, "Do not resist. Do not speak."

And she had not. He was the one with the terrible music; he was the reason she lay here now in some unknown location—not a hut or even a cottage, because the scents were far more sophisticated than that. A place of narrow halls and many rooms . . . coals gone to ash and lukewarm brandy, faded opium and whale oil and cleaning chemicals laden with cologne. She had no shoes; as she'd walked to this chamber her feet met a series of carpets laid over a cool stone floor. She sensed no change in heat or light through the dyed hood, no resonance of glass against any slight sound; if this place had windows, they were probably bricked over.

London. Beyond the walls and corridors lifted the cries of street vendors hawking fish and sweet cherries and tea. More carriages rattled past, more than she could count, with dogs yelping and children begging, and the nearest clear conversation she could make out was between two men discussing trade winds and ivory and hemp. By slowing her breath and relaxing her hands she was able to focus enough to even hear the tiny, continuous slap of water striking rock walls and a shore, a great deal of water, and that had to be the Thames. She'd read of it in books, the mighty river of commerce, the merchant heart of England. Never, never once had she thought to be so desperate—

Never once had she thought to venture this close herself.

Her own heart was pumping far too fast. She obeyed the fourth man's commands; she could not speak if she wanted, and resistance truly seemed out of the question. At least right now.

Sanf inimicus. Fear and wrath settled into a queasy, cold knot in her stomach. If she had the chance to eat *any* of their hearts, she would.

Fourth Man had wrapped a blanket around her after the hood, fastened it with tin pins in some way so that it did not slip from her body. The material was coarse wool, cheap, like the other men. But it wasn't nearly as awful as the hood, which had gone damp with her breath and now adhered to her entire lower face, suffocating. It was black and tied under her chin. No doubt it was just the same as the one they had on Rhys.

Rhys. She'd been hauled from the shepherd's hut while he was still inside; she didn't know what happened to him. He was nowhere nearby now.

Perhaps they'd killed him. But she'd never smelled more than just a trickle of blood.

The *sanf* led her to this room, to what felt like a bed. Fourth Man helped her to sit upon its edge; the blanket rode up and began to separate along her lap. He tugged it back in place impatiently, tucking the folds of it hard beneath her legs.

There was metal on his hand, a ring. As his fingers grabbed the wool it must have turned against his knuckle, because she felt the brush of a diamond against her knee—not just any diamond.

This one burned her. It hurt—not terribly, because the stone was small—a deep angry prickle that set her nerve endings alight. A wave of intense dizziness rolled up to peak inside her head, black and blue fireflies exploding behind her closed lids.

It felt marvelous. It felt agonizing.

She knew that stone. And she knew now with complete, appalled certainty, who was leading those other three men of the *sanf.*

The Alpha went alone to the roof of Chasen. He went to the same place he had found her before, seated with her knees drawn up, her back against the majestic blue-water glass curve of the Adam dome. He knelt and placed his palm upon the layered slate at its base.

She was still there, traces of her. She rose up and surrounded him in soft welcome, phantom girl, sinking into his cells, linking, whole. His wife.

He did not shut his eyes. He lifted them to the edge of the shaped tiles, past the chimneys and carved limestone gutters, to the sight of the woods poking up, stiff-fingered, into the deep bowl of the sky.

Inhale. Exhale.

He knew her now. He knew who she was, and how she was. Fragility; wit; reckless valor. He knew the hue of her eyes by moonlight and by sun. He knew the softness of her skin, the shape of her breasts and belly. He knew how she felt inside, the vivid pleasure of her sex, and all these things united, became a key to the lock of the mystery of her vanishing.

He could find her. He could find her through the fires of Hell.

The diffusion of Maricara began to pulse, to become more than scent and memories, transforming into energy. Into color.

He'd experienced this before, only a very few times, times when the hunt for a runner had been so dire he'd lost the feeling of being human entirely. He was *drákon* now. All that, and only that; it was everything he needed. He knelt in a pool of gold and orange and violet that opened around him like a flower, slowly gathering streamers of light, the last living colors of the female he claimed as his mate. When he turned his head he saw her path with dragon eyes, a vanishing bright line headed south, glimmering and wavering like the aftermath of a sparkler on a dark Bonfire Night. He stared at it until his vision blurred, until he was absolutely certain.

Distant gunpowder rose on the wind. He felt her, small and rash and strong, and came to his feet.

The Alpha Turned into a dragon, pushing off the roof of his home, dislodging a flurry of slate that skipped and toppled and shattered into pieces against the earth below.

For the first time in a very, very long while, Maricara was aware that she was dreaming. It wasn't a nightmare, not yet; she wasn't flying toward anything in particular, or even away. In fact, she wasn't flying at all. She was walking through cool, shadowed hallways, places she'd never seen before, but at the same time she knew them, and knew them well. It wasn't her castle, it wasn't Chasen.

Voices whispered but she did not understand them; they drew her forward, deeper into that stonework maze of light and dark.

When she looked down, she saw her body garbed in a gown of cobalt, adorned with ribbons and gems and all manner of pretty human things. When she looked aside she saw her reflection in windows of chambers she did not enter: a dragon sleekly pacing, black-scaled, silver-star eyes.

She reached a convergence in the corridors and realized suddenly just where she was: at the priory in the English countryside. If she went left, she'd return to the ruins, to the warren of hallways and empty cloisters. If she went right, she'd enter the open-aired loggia, where, past the pillars, sun and comets and galaxies all glowed against a deep red sky.

A dragon flew against that strangely beautiful horizon. Lonely and distant, soaring, dipping. He was blue and scarlet and feral green eyes and he saw her, she knew. She walked up to the stone railing and pressed against one of the columns, watching him, how he danced and twisted and came no closer. Comets spilled from his wingtips. Galaxies spun in his wake.

He was leaving. He grew smaller, and turned his face away.

An unexpected anguish lanced her heart.

Wait. I love you.

She didn't know if those were his words or her own, but she knew that they were true. She lifted a hand to the creature in the sky, willing him closer, almost weeping for the lack of his touch.

I do love you, oh God, I do. Come back to me.

But he vanished without ever glancing at her again.

She awoke to the fact of tears on her cheeks and her hands and feet chained to the posts of the bed. The chains were short enough that she could scoot around only a very little. Mari pulled at them and felt the low, protesting moan of iron against iron, but nothing gave. When she yanked very hard the bed didn't even tremble. It had to be bolted somehow to the floor.

She stopped, sucking air past the gag, and began once more to assess her situation.

It was a prison of contradictions. The duvet was without question velvet, and a pile of furs folded at her feet felt like sable or mink. The air carried only those same odd scents of food spices and river water and bleach-based cleaners; she caught nothing of decay or effluent nearby. The worst smell still was the leftover stench of the peasants.

And the Thames. That smelled too.

But the bed would not move, and the chains would not give. She'd already rubbed her cheeks raw against the covers, trying to get the hood off. They must have used a cord of steel to secure it, closed hard around her neck.

Despite the voices in her dream, no one spoke in this place. They were more canny than that. She'd heard them walking about sometimes, crisscrossing the floors above, but that had been hours—hours?—ago. Now the rooms remained silent, so Maricara did the same, flat on her back on the very plush mattress, awaiting the return of the man with the tiny stinging diamond that burned her to the bone.

With *Draumr.*

She did not know what would come next: rape or death, her heart ripped out with her mouth still bound and eyes still covered.

If they didn't remove the hood before it was done, her very last sight in the world would have been of the wrong brother.

She tried to slow the panic in her blood. She thought fiercely of Kimber and saw that distant dragon instead, tilting away from her with wings of scarlet and gilt.

"We should kill them now," muttered the bearded Romanian. "We never thought to have two of them at once. Especially not *her.*"

He spat the last word with a great deal of disdain that was, Zane thought, meant to belay the fear Graytooth actually felt in the presence of Her Royal Grace the Princess Maricara. Had they still been anywhere near the building where she was being held, Zane had the notion Graytooth would fail to drip nearly so much scorn.

But the four of them were well over a mile away from the place they had secured her. Even so, they spoke in whispers, and everyone was careful not to use either Her Grace's or Lord Rhys's real names. One never knew who might be listening.

In point of fact, Graytooth was not the Romanian's real name either. His real name was Basarab, a convergence of syllables Zane found both slightly sinister and unnecessarily foreign to pronounce. *Graytooth* conveyed a certain elegance of imagery. It was also, not coincidentally, rather accurate.

England could claim a great many injustices in its treatment of the poor, but there was plenty of nutrition available for those with nerve enough to step up and snatch it. Yet in all these years of travel, he'd found that the diet of the Carpathian Mountains tended to consist of brown bread and cabbage and potatoes no matter where he went. No wonder these fellows looked so wan.

Zane was a man who enjoyed the more exquisite aspects of life. At this moment, that consisted of the cup of African coffee steaming fragrant in his left hand, and the lemon cream éclairs arranged neatly upon the plate near his right. He stretched out his legs and allowed himself the brief luxury of imagining that very first bite. The instant rush of sweetness on his tongue; the tart concurrence of lemon zest, silky filling and lightly fried dough—

It didn't seem so long ago he'd been one of the many starving urchins crowding London's streets, and sugar remained his weakness. He could walk away from platters of ham and beefsteak and marrow puddings; his body was one of his best weapons, and Zane kept it as fit as a wire. But sweets . . .

The éclairs were from a bakery set like a jewel in the exclusive heart of Mayfair, made by the very best French pastry cook the city had to offer. They had been delivered to this extremely innocuous and unremarkable safe house in Clerkenwell by means of a livery boy who'd accepted the five shillings Zane had tipped him and left without squeaking a word.

The boy was one of his own, of course, the son of one of his more prolific cracksmen. He'd never trust anything so important as this address to anyone he didn't control.

The fine fellows of the *sanf inimicus* had settled into the parlor of the house with hardly a grumble. They'd shunned the bitter strong coffee Zane favored and devoured the pastries until there were only two left.

They were both on Zane's plate.

He picked up his silver fork. With all three men watching

him, he used the side of the fork to slice into the éclair, speared it, lifted it with deliberate slowness to his mouth, and closed his lips over the bite.

Magnifique.

He hardly ever ate cream. Too rich, too intoxicating. But he needed to consider carefully his next move and so made certain to chew as slowly as he could.

Not that these men would leave him in any case. He was the *mágos* Englishman, the man who controlled dragon magic, and they had yet to unravel how he'd kept two of the most powerful of the *drákon* anyone knew in his thrall. But with their prey so obviously in hand, they might begin to wonder a tad about why Zane seemed so loath to make the kill.

He would, in their position.

The ring on his hand was solid gold, a significant weight, the diamond chips in its bed releasing constant slivers of pale blue brilliance. It was not a wedding ring; it had, in fact, taken the place of one, and it had been more difficult than he'd even imagined to remove that ring that had tied him to Lia, to wear this one in its place. This band never left his finger. He'd learned some time ago to sleep with his dirk clutched in that hand.

Not that he'd slept much lately. Bloody *drákon*.

"If we kill her right away," he murmured at last, "we lose a most valuable asset. She'll be mated by now. The English tribe will be searching for her; she's almost certainly the bride of their Alpha. They will be scattered, their defenses weakened. I've told you how formidable they are as a group, much stronger than the Zaharen you know. The longer we keep her alive, the greater our advantage."

Another difference between Zane and his new comrades was that of language. The very loose affiliation of the *sanf inimicus* relied upon a complicated patois of provincial French and

Hungarian for both written and spoken communications. It was jumbled and confusing and one of their first requirements into the brotherhood. It had taken him nearly eight months to master it, and for him, that was significant.

Zane's French was fluent. So were his German, Italian, and Spanish.

So was his Hungarian. And his Romanian.

No one else knew that, of course. He was ruddy good at keeping his mouth shut when he should. He would not make the mistake of underestimating any of them, not even Graytooth.

The *sanf* were exceedingly particular about whom they accepted into their realm, and their leader downright gave him chills. *That* was damned well saying something.

"It was a stroke of great fortune," he continued, sipping his coffee, "that she came to us as she did. No one knew she was so near, and we could not have asked for a better capture. Even if she wished to do so, she won't be able to pinpoint the location of the hut, or of Rhys Langford."

It was, in truth, about as much the opposite of good fortune as Zane could imagine. Rhys had been a planned capture, a deliberate calculation that flowed nicely into his hidden scheme of things. Maricara, however—

Trust the princess to scramble the works. She'd always had a way with surprises.

"I don't like it," said one of the other men. Clem, Zane had privately named this one, for the man who had once trained Zane in all the lovely dark arts of thievery—and subsequently did his best to murder him afterward. This Clem had the same guileless blue eyes and bluntness of features as the man from Zane's childhood. He could very easily imagine the bloke sticking a knife between his ribs in a moment of inattention, and Zane had enough scars as it was. Another reason to sleep with his dirk so close.

Clem never took those eyes from Zane's face. "They'll come for her whether she's dead or alive. She's a danger alive. Not so much dead."

"Do you truly imagine they can't tell if she's alive while on the hunt? That they cannot sense her heartbeat, or her breathing?"

"Then all the better—"

"No. We kill her now, they may steer off; there's nothing left to save. But they'll hazard a great deal if they know she's living. I can keep her tame enough until they come. They'll never Turn here in the city. You'll get your chance at them then, man to man. No more stealing about the countryside. No more hiding in taverns or barns. You'll deal a blow to their core like none other, the bride of the Alpha destroyed. When the rest of us arrive, imagine their faces as you show them the dragon hearts."

He could see how that appealed to them, these brawny, devious men. He could see it in the way they exchanged looks, in how they opened and clenched their fingers and shifted in their fine new English clothing.

"Think on it," he said mildly, and lifted his fork for another delicate, lemony bite.

"Good evening, Princess," said the voice. "I'm going to raise this hood enough to release your mouth. Do me the very great favor of not attempting to kill me as I work. I have a knife in my hand, and the edge is very sharp. So kindly hold still."

The thin, eldritch music punctuating his words ensured she did as told, stretched out on the bed, her hands curled into fists. The fresh air on her skin felt cool and wonderful; the diamond on his hand brushed her neck, and that felt like fire.

"It's time we talked," he said in a low rush of Romanian.

Mari licked her dry lips. "Speak English. I hate the sound of my language on your tongue."

Zane began to laugh. "Very well. I suppose I should have anticipated you'd learn English. You were a most precocious child."

"Lift the hood," she said, using her darkest voice. "Let me see your face."

"Alas, not that precocious, I must suppose. Persuasion, is it? One of my favorites. But your Gifts won't work on me, Maricara. You do realize that. And you realize why. *Draumr's* not quite what it used to be, but with enough of the pieces set together, it still does the trick of controlling unruly *drákon,* at least for a while. I'll tell you what, pet. I'll lift the hood. You will not Turn. Agreed?"

You will not Turn, echoed the remains of the diamond called *Draumr,* a spell sinking through her in rolling waves. *You will not Turn . . .*

"Yes," she managed, against that slow, dire ricochet of notes.

"Excellent."

The chamber was dim, with no visible outside light. It was done up in dusky, jeweled colors, the walls painted ocher, the furniture all gilded and flowered. Swags of cloth draped in billows from the ceiling down to the floor, tarnished gold and blood-red and purple wine; cheval-glass mirrors gleamed from every corner. An oddly sensible lamp burned atop a bureau, simple oil and brass, its flame so still it looked painted in place.

Above her, directly above, hung another mirror. The covers of the bed reflected deep velvet blue. There was a china doll chained to the bed, wrapped in a blanket. Her face and feet and hands poked out stark white.

"Do you like it?" Zane threw a glance to the mirror above them, amused. "A bit lurid for my tastes, frankly, but I purchased the entire lot from an old friend of mine and never got around to redecorating. Used to be what we'd call in the business *une maison de joie*—do you know the term, Princess? Yes, I see you do. Anyhow, no windows. Very handy."

He'd changed so little. His face was tanned and a bit more

lined, perhaps. A little more drawn. But his hair was the same color, rich tawny brown, and still much too long; it made a braid that fell over his shoulder and across his chest like a bandoleer. His eyes still shone cunning amber.

"It smells," Mari said.

"I beg your pardon, it certainly does not. This is Threadneedle. It's a most respectable part of town, I assure you. Even the rats here are spanking clean."

"Oh. Then no doubt it's merely you."

"Now, that's just unkind. I'll have you know I bathe every day. Nearly every day. Imported soap, too, pressed by the hands of the fairest of South Seas virgins, every one of them infused with tinctures of ginger and hibiscus. Try finding *that* in Transylvania."

She looked up at her reflection, the breadth of Zane's shoulders, the top of his head. "You're using the stone, what's left of the stone, to control us. You're leading the *sanf inimicus* straight to us. Do you despise us so much?"

Zane's voice became a soft slur. "The men with me know nothing of the diamond. You will not tell them."

Draumr settled beneath and between his words, binding them in her brain.

"Are we clear, Princess?"

"Yes." She moistened her lips. "Where is Rhys?"

"Away from where you last saw him, and away from here. He's really not your concern, you know. If I were you, I'd be far more worried about my own skin."

"You didn't kill him?"

His brows lifted in mock affront. "Please. He reminds me far too much of his youngest sister."

"What did you do with the girl? With Honor?"

Zane sat back a little, his smile fading. He looked down at his fingers, the dreadful gleam of little diamonds that stirred and murmured and slipped songs into her head. In the depths of the mirror, his braid rippled dark. "Honor," he said more quietly, "is safe. For now, she's safe. How much longer, I really couldn't say." His eyes lifted to hers. "She's with Lia."

Surprise kept her mouth closed. No doubt he read her expression anyway.

"You've seen her already, you know. You won't recall it, but you have. In Harrogate. That was a night, let me tell you. Between you and Chasen popping up like that, over a year's worth of plans were nearly demolished. But Lia found you first. She has her own pieces of *Draumr* she's been using to disguise herself from your kind. She told me she'd ensured you'd not remember your encounter."

"That was *her*?" She gave the chains a vicious tug. "Why would she hide from me—from her brother? Why not return to Darkfrith? Has she turned into a traitorous coward, like you?"

"My dear, such youthful venom! *Très charmante.* One might say many things about Amalia Langford, but she's no coward. She can't go back to Darkfrith because she swore to me she wouldn't. Ever. I don't care what she or her parents say, I don't trust their council not to enact their alarmingly medieval notion of 'justice' on a female who runs away—especially one with the audacity to wed a human. It didn't go over very well with her, but she needed something from me, something important, and that was the only way I would agree."

"What did she need from you?"

"The protection of her family. Did you truly imagine I would be here for any other reason?" He offered her his crooked smile, a shadow of pain behind it. "Love sends us down peculiar paths betimes. Lia dreams the future, you know. She foresaw all this—the *sanf,* your travels to Darkfrith. Rhys, poor lovesick bastard. This girl, Honor, who apparently has a very interesting path of her own ahead of her—believe me, I'd rather be just about anywhere else in the world right now, Your Grace. But Amalia sent me here. So here I am."

She gaped at him. "You joined the *sanf inimicus* to *help* the *drákon*?"

"Ironic, wouldn't you say?"

"You're a spy!"

He looked pained. "What a loud voice you have."

"Why did you—"

"As much as I'd love to delve into all the details of my admittedly fascinating life, I'm afraid there's not that much time. The people with me speak only a rudimentary English, if that, but they learn quickly. I'd rather..."

But he didn't finish the sentence; instead he sat back, his fine mouth tightening. From the shadows of the doorway stepped a new man, and then another, and another. Watching, alert. They were dressed better than she'd supposed they would be, not as peasants but as common Englishmen, with ordinary hats and coats and extraordinary, hungry faces. One was young and two were older, and all three stared at her spread-eagled on the bed as if she were that white-eyed ox tied to the tree. A creature moments from being devoured.

The bearded one said something in a language she'd never heard before; Zane responded from over his shoulder, brusque.

The Others inched closer.

Zane glanced back down at her. "They want to hurt you," he whispered, framed in velvet and gold. "You know that."

"Yes."

"I'll stop them as long as I can."

She felt her throat close and set her teeth against it. She made herself smile at him, made her voice flat, calm.

"Why don't you kill them instead?"

"Because, Princess," Zane said, "sometimes sacrifices have to be made. And as you've thoroughly mucked up my plans, this is the best I can manage at the moment. I'm sorry."

"That's quite all right. Kimber's here now, anyway." Mari looked him up and down through her lashes, holding her smile, then added softly, "You should run."

CHAPTER TWENTY-FIVE

He smashed through the roof. There was no real reason not to. It was the most expedient way in.

It was a wooden hip roof, sloped and tidy. He descended upon it in full form, hind feet first, his wings straight up behind him for velocity. Against the roar of wind and blood filling his head, the Alpha slammed into a new wave of sound: that of a thousand Others glancing upward, witnessing a dragon of blue and red iridescence descending from the dark evening sky, talons extended, eyes alight. Their screams bounced off his scales. He plunged straight through that shimmer of sound, hardly noticing the humans pointing and scattering along the cobblestone streets. Horses galloped madly away, taking riders and coaches along with them. Vermin and cats and dogs, birds and cattle, all of them shrieking, fleeing, with Kimber as the center of their panic.

The last thing he saw before hitting the roof was a woman in a wig and shawl shedding posies behind her as she ran, her skirts hitched up with both hands, a straw basket still tucked into the crook of an elbow banging against her side.

He tore through the shingles. There was a pair of chimneys, too; red bricks and splinters spewed outward like confetti, tumbling through the air. It was swifter than the blink of an eye and he felt no pain; there was only *her,* still below him, her colors and scent. A cloudy, curious song surrounding her.

He took out floors. Chairs, beds, chandeliers, tables. All of them empty of Others, because they were still below—and then he was there too, on the ground level, his talons digging into the floor as he skidded to a stop in a large parlor full of pillowed sofas, ripping up rugs and chunks of hardwood. His wings slashed furrows along the walls; paintings crashed; sconces shattered, pungent oil splashing in great clear drops across everything.

He lifted his snout and opened his mouth and revealed his fangs to the Other rushing at him from the doorway.

The Other had a pistol. Still running, he raised his arm and fired, a spark of molten heat that ripped high through Kimber's chest, embedding against something that crunched. A bone.

It was hardly a remarkable feat; Kim took up nearly the entire chamber. So all he had to do was wait for the man to sprint near enough, then bend forward and snap off his head.

The body ceased its forward momentum. It dropped to its knees, and then to its side. The Alpha spat out the head, stepping over the dead man and into the corridor beyond without a second look.

The next human also had a pistol, but he appeared older, more hardened, and he didn't waste his shot. Instead, he stood his ground as the dragon stalked forward, Kimber's tail whipping back and forth, taking out the plaster and walnut walls of the hallway in huge, concave holes. Only when Kimber was near enough to see the spittle on his beard did the man pull the trigger. Kim Turned to smoke, so easy, and then at once back to dragon.

The bullet passed harmlessly through him, thunked into a wall behind him.

The Alpha's lips curled back, the closest thing he could manage to a smile in this state. The *sanf* man shouted something then whirled about, retreating to a hall to the left.

She wasn't there. Kimber smoked by it—in case there was another gun—and found her chamber, ill lit, crowded with shadows and furniture. The shadows began to flicker; he Turned back to dragon and let loose his fury.

He tore the tops off the lower two bedposts right away. She thought it might have been his wings that sheared them off, but more likely it was his tail, thick and strong, a set of eight razored gold barbs lined neatly along its end. With the iron posts gone she was able to lift both her feet high, still trailing chains but no longer bound to anything fixed.

The chains at her wrist were too short for her to sit up. So Maricara drew her knees to her chest and flipped her body backward; it tore the blanket apart right away, the pins snapping free, dull silver sprinkled across the blue covers. She rolled until her feet met the wall behind the headboard and the chains slapped against the plaster. She used her momentum to finish crawling downward, until she could rise to her knees with her arms twisted before her.

Kimber was a spiral of color and stealth, a glittery reflection from every mirror. He radiated heat; he blurred with every sinuous movement, nearly too fast even for her to follow. One of the *sanf* still dodged him, though, grunting with effort—it wasn't Zane, who had apparently heeded her advice. He was no longer anywhere in view.

From the mess and confusion of man and beast, something hot struck her in a spatter across the throat. Blood. Kimber's blood.

In the very same instant, she saw him wobble, drop to one knee. His body struck the bureau with the oil lamp at last. It teetered and fell and shattered with a *pop* into a rosebud of flame, a bud that opened and spread into a flume of soft rising noise.

Both the dragon and the man leapt back. She saw Kimber shake his head in the bright new light, more blood shining slick down his scales. The man saw it too.

Mari gathered herself. She bowed her head and drew her arms inward, her breath held, then released—a groan that burned chest deep, the last two posts bending with her will, the iron screeching—

The links snapped, and she pulled free. Instantly she vaulted from the foot of the bed, found the *sanf* in front of Kimber—he held a sword, and the tip was dripping red—

She jumped behind him. She wrapped the chain still attached to her right wrist around his neck, and pulled as hard as she could. His back arched; he dropped the sword and began to gurgle, clutching at the links.

"You will *not* hurt him," she snarled in Romanian. "You will *not*—"

Voices were calling from some other part of the building. Human voices, coming closer, high-pitched. Flames from the broken lamp found a swathe of purple silk and leapt all the way to the ceiling.

Kimber Turned to man. He picked up the sword of the *sanf inimicus,* fire a glorious bright halo behind him, and pierced the heart of his enemy with one short thrust.

Mari released the body. She caught the earl by his arms and kissed him, a kiss so rough and sudden it hurt, and tasted of blood, and he wrapped both arms around her and kissed her back harder still.

A new human staggered to the doorway, a man in a uniform with a metal badge on his chest, his hand cupped to his face.

"Oy! You there! You two!" He glared frantically about the room. "You've got to get out of here!"

She pulled away, panting, her chest and stomach wet with the blood that still flowed from a hole too near his heart. By then the man had darted into the room, followed by another, both goggling from the lump of the fellow on the floor to the two of them, naked amid the flames.

"I can't Turn," she said to Kimber, under the gathering roar of the fire. "I've tried. I'm trapped like this."

"Come on!" cried the second man. He stooped to grab the body of the *sanf* Kimber had stabbed, dragging it along from under the arms. "Follow me!"

Kimber wiped a hand absently across his chest, smearing the red into channels with his fingers. He looked down at his palm with his blond hair in his face and then back up at her. Smoke lifted black and coiled around him, clouded into her lungs.

She coughed with both hands over her mouth, managing to ask, "Can you fly?"

His lips curled into something that was not a smile.

"Bloody *hell*," shouted the first man, back by the door, "what's the bloomin' *matter* with you two?"

The fire consumed the ceiling. It made a merry frame around the door. The man pulled back and vanished, and Kimber Turned, and Maricara climbed, chains and all, upon the powerfully broad back of her mate, the Alpha dragon, hooking her legs above the bones and leather of his wings.

She twined her fingers into his ruff. She clenched her thighs and ankles and hid her face between her arms as he twisted around with one smooth, powerful movement, his tail striking the outer wall.

Plaster sloughed away; burning embers whirled; brick went to dust. He hit the wall again, and again, and then there was a hole there, larger and larger, and fresh air, and the night.

Kimber clambered through it, his golden claws shining with firelight.

And all the people gathered around the blazing, elegant, gray-faced building set back on this mannered street in Threadneedle began screaming once more.

She kept her head down for most of their flight. The summer wind felt remarkably chill against her unclad body, but Kimber was warm, and that made it all right.

Maricara turned her cheek to his neck. She closed her eyes and traced her fingers along the pattern of scales that flowed from his jaw to his shoulder, discovering perfect symmetry, the rhythmic pull and release of his muscles beneath, magic made actual flesh.

I love you. The words circled through her, a magic just as potent as the body beneath hers. *You're strong, you're going to live. I love you.*

Drop by drop, one single splash of crimson at a time, his blood fell in silence down to the distant curve of the earth.

Such a silence also lived in the shire. It was as if with the loss of Kimber's blood—with the loss of his brother, and the maiden—nearly everything bright and vital had drained from the land as well.

The earl, naturally, did not die. His skin grew very pale; his face took on the smooth, hardened cast of ivory. He spent time alone in his quarters, more time than he clearly wished. She heard the servants whispering about it from their nooks and crannies in the mansion, how he directed the tribe from the darkness of his sanctum, how he would eat only sparingly, and sleep in short hours at a spell, day or night, in either his bed or hers.

She knew that already, of course.

He was powerful, and stubborn as she was, and he would survive. But he would need time for healing, and time had become the fresh new enemy of the *drákon*. No one knew when or where the *sanf inimicus* would next strike.

Darkfrith was a machine that slowly lumbered into gear for war, and Kimber still stood at its helm. The protections that had been in place before were strengthened, layered throughout the land from house to house and soul to soul. No one traveled alone here, not any longer. Not even Maricara. She'd told the earl and then his council of Rhys, and of Zane, and of Lia and the diamond. She'd even gone back to the place of her capture by carriage—she could not yet fly—but just as Zane had said, Rhys was gone. Neither she nor any of the *drákon* men with her had been able to unearth a hint of him.

And she had tried, more than once, to tell Kimber something else. Mari would sit opposite him in his bedchamber, the two of them dining by candlelight or daylight, or by the grace of the moon. Her head would lower; her lips would begin the words that had come so easily to her in that London dream of red sky and stars: *I love you.* But something always managed at the last second to strangle her short. She gave herself a thousand excuses, that he looked too weary, or too distracted, or that too many people interrupted them at all hours, family, physicians, council members.

And every time, it was as if he knew. She'd summon her nerve and lift her head and open her mouth and *every* time, no matter what he was doing, he'd pause and look back at her, fixing her with a gaze of light, fervent green—and her voice died in her throat.

She did not like to consider herself a coward; she'd said and done things far bolder than this, certainly. Yet the Earl of Chasen kept so beautiful, so somber and apart. Even as they shared a bed and their bodies, she felt the distance yawning between them, a chasm she could not manage to bridge, at least not with words.

There were occasions when she'd glimpse him in some ordinary moment—pulling on his coat; sharpening a quill with a penknife, tiny shavings curling paper-thin around his fingers—and feel as if she'd surely suffocate if she couldn't speak what was in her heart.

But she didn't. He never seemed to mind at all.

It took her nearly a week to regain the Gift of dragon and smoke. A week of being forced to travel only on human feet, to witness the mansion and the village and the woods from always this same human level. Mari walked whenever she could, burning off the restive energy that seemed stored up in her legs, swinging her arms hard with every step, letting the sun gradually heal the faint red lines that encircled her wrists.

It frightened her more than she would ever admit to think she would linger forever in this state. Whenever she attempted what had nearly always come so easily to her—*vapor, animal*—what happened instead is that the faint, sultry notes of *Draumr* resurrected around her, sent those tendrils of music to sink into her once again, binding through her until her very cells froze solid.

Zane was gone. *Draumr* was gone, both consumed by flames or the anonymous London night; none of the *drákon* sent to the city afterward had been able to discover a trace of them, either. But it seemed that neither man nor stone would let her forget that instant in the brothel, four languorous words spoken nearly under his breath: *You will not Turn.*

It was somewhat ironical that now that the dragons of Darkfrith soared with less secrecy than ever in their history, Maricara was kept fettered by her own body to the ground.

Damned Zane, and damned diamond. In fact, damn the whole world. All she'd ever wanted was to be free. And now, with Kimber secluded and her talents no longer so wondrous and rare, she found that her freedom became more of a burden than imprisonment ever was. Even the sky seemed both leaden and beyond her, clogged with gauzy bleached clouds that arched high above, only to bend with the weight of the horizon to smother the far-flung hills.

On the sixth day of her incarceration in her human shape, she took quill and ink and a sheaf of papers out to the pavilion of seasons. She sat on the swept marble floor and attempted to compose a letter to her brother, her skirts massed about her in a bubble of silk and lace, the beds of her nails slowly staining India black.

The broken pillar had yet to be repaired. Whenever her gaze drifted to it, it seemed to grant a sideways grin back at her, as if a giant had come and taken from it a single bite.

Once, only once, she heard the thrush again. Her head lifted; she brought up a hand to ease the sudden crimp in her neck and her eyes now fell upon the manor, the line of glazed windows that led to the earl's balcony. The feathered gargoyle, sneering his limestone sneer.

Kimber was standing there on the balcony gazing back at her, his forearms braced against the railing, his weight on one leg. Ivory and tousled gold, a shirt that ruffled in an upsweep of breeze. He stood unmoving, watching her.

Like the little girl from the woods Mari had espied that bright afternoon not so long ago, she lifted a hand to him. But the earl only straightened and walked away.

Mari sighed and glanced around her at the crumpled balls of

paper she'd made from her seven botched attempts to explain to Sandu all that had happened. But she could not explain it; she hardly understood herself all the undercurrents tearing at her life, and the leader in her was loath to put too much into writing anyway.

There were a few things she did have a firm grasp upon, however.

One thing, at the very least.

She gathered her papers and quill once more. She went back inside the manor house.

She found him not in his chamber but hers, slouched in the chair someone had brought in to replace the broken Chippendale. This one was smaller, upholstered in blue and green and even more spindly delicate than the last. She doubted if one of its legs would even nick the door.

"Comfortable?" she asked him, as she leaned against the iron frame.

"Not very." He didn't look up from his contemplation of his shoes. "I can't imagine for whom they construct these things. I've seen kindling sturdier than these arms, and the cushion's so slick I can hardly stay in place."

"Tiny human ladies," Mari said. "Who take tea in sunny parlors, and nibble celery and twigs, and drink lemon water for dinner. They never fear sliding upon anything."

"Ah, that explains it. Perhaps all I need is a bit more lemon water in my diet."

"You'll be very hungry as you watch me dine on bread and wine. And I won't share, no matter how nicely you plead."

The corners of his lips lifted a little; his gaze remained lowered. Three of the seven candles in the candelabra were lit; they cast a false warmth across his cheeks. "I appreciate the warning. Although, 'tis a pity, since I've lately been thinking on how to polish up my pleading."

Mari entered the cell. She placed her belongings on the desk behind him, coming so close her pannier brushed his sleeve. He did not move.

It was not yet time to sleep, and not yet time to dine, not even tea and celery. She eyed the bed and then his back. The bandage wrapped around his chest shone a paler white beneath his ironed shirt.

She'd often touched it in the night. She would stroke her fingers across the linen wrappings, using all her tricks and senses to gauge his injury beneath, searching for fever, or infection, or even pain. But his heart always beat calm and constant against her hand. Nothing slowed it, not even slumber.

She sat upon the edge of the bed. She began to remove her pumps.

The earl said, "Why haven't you left yet, Maricara?"

She angled a glance up at him from beneath her lashes. His smile had become much more dry.

"You were so eager to do so before. I've the feeling twenty thousand dragons could not stop you if you really wished it."

"They tried very hard," she said, after a moment. "Two of them nearly caught up."

"Two! What stalwart fellows. I'll have medals struck for them."

"You're very harsh."

"No," he said. "Merely tired. And more than a bit at the last of my reserves." He rubbed a finger along the line of his nose, then raised his gaze to hers. "Why haven't you left for home yet, Princess Maricara of the Zaharen?"

She removed her second shoe, holding it in her hands. It was high-heeled and pink and the buckle was silver filigree, and her ink-stained nails looked very common against it.

"I did discover something more in London," she said to the pump. "More than Zane, or the *delis inimicus.*"

Kimber's voice sharpened. "What?"

"I discovered," she turned the pump slowly over and over in her hands, "that . . . I would surely die without you."

He paused. "How gratifying. I agree that I was somewhat useful in rescuing you, but I've no doubt you would have managed to determine a way out of it, Your Grace, had I not shown up."

"No." She looked up at him. "I mean, yes—probably. Eventually. But what I meant was, I love you. I discovered that I love you."

He stared at her, unreadable. He seemed very large and male in the satin-lined chair.

"You needn't gawk at me like that," she said, defensive. "It's true."

"Sorry. I find that I'm . . . I'm rather without words."

"Love," she enunciated, leaning forward from the bed. "I *love* you."

"Women in love typically don't flee the object of their affections. Not even *drákon* women."

Mari shrugged. "Well, I told you. It happened in London."

He began, softly, to laugh. He brought his hands to his face and drew his palms down his cheeks; she realized anew how pale he was, how handsome and haggard. His long hair captured the light in lion colors, gold and wheat and palest dun.

She set the pump aside and slid to her feet. She crossed to him and dropped to her knees, taking his hands in hers.

"I didn't want to be in love with you. I didn't want to believe in love at all. It's never happened to me before. And to be perfectly frank, I'm still not entirely happy about the whole thing. I think—it's going to be exhausting. You're domineering and devious and I've noticed that whenever we're not kissing, I wish we were." Her voice had grown nearly plaintive; she stopped and cleared her throat. "It's a damnable situation. I don't know what to do about it."

He eyed her from the chair. "I'm pigheaded, too. Pray don't forget that."

"Certainly not. It was the next thing I was going to mention."

"My sweet, your notion of love is unique, to say the least. I wonder that you haven't written me sonnets already. Something like 'Ode to the Blackguard.'"

"I don't know what a sonnet is. But I wouldn't use the word 'blackguard,' precisely."

"It's a poem. Nothing." He looked down at their hands, her fingers tight over his. His mouth took on a strange slant. "What word would you use, then?"

"To best describe you?"

"Yes."

"A single word. Let me think." She sat back on her heels, drawing her fingers slowly free; his feet were caught in her skirts, motionless between her knees. "I would say 'mine.' 'Ode to the One Who Is Mine.'"

He shifted. His feet pulled back and he bent closer, his eyes taking on a new cast, burning and intent beneath their brown lashes. "Are you thinking of kissing me now?"

"Well—since you mentioned it . . ."

Without taking his gaze from hers, he lifted her hand. His lips lowered, not touching her skin, just enough so she could feel the warmth of his breath across her knuckles.

"And now?"

"I had no idea you were such a flirt."

He brought her hand to his cheek, her fingers bent. He closed his eyes and released a shaky breath. "I think I have the remedy to your situation."

Mari rose up and pressed her lips to his.

"You were taking too long," she murmured, and that won a new smile from him, a taut curve against her mouth.

He buried his fingers in her hair. The kiss lengthened, deepened, until her chest went tight and her own breath was less than steady, and the dragon inside her that wanted to come was a jig and a fever beating quick through her veins. She pulled away, offered him her own dark smile, and at last—at last!—Turned to smoke.

The bed was only feet distant; even as smoke she could ruffle the blankets a little. She Turned to woman atop the mattress, gathering the crisp cool cotton in her hands, burrowing into the sheets. She tossed back the covers for him with a flourish as he stood by the chair, watching.

"My Lord Chasen. Would you mind very much just closing the door on your way over?" Maricara asked him.

He didn't mind at all.

The candles burned down to stubs. She was awake for that, although Kimber was not. He was stretched out on his good side, truly asleep, when the last flame smoldered into orange, and then black. For a few lazy minutes afterward the air carried a slight, acrid tinge that gradually dissipated back into more neutral stone and cloth and honey. And him.

She thought she'd never grow weary of that, his scent. Of how when she rubbed her face against his shoulder he was scented of her too, and that was a very fine thing.

"Lower," he said.

"What?"

"Try that a little lower." Kimber rolled to his back, reaching for her, his palms skimming up her arms. "Dear Princess. I'm putty in your most capable hands."

"Hmm," she said, exploring. "I hardly think so."

His laugh was a pleasing rumble. "Well . . . so to speak."

She found his bandage again, sobering, feeling the ridges of his rib cage, the heat that rose steadily from his smooth skin.

"I don't know how these matters are supposed to go," she said finally, in the dark. "I was raised amid mountains and the Milky Way. But it seems to me that if a lady tells a gentleman she is in love with him, even if she's actually just a serf, he ought to either reciprocate the emotion or else leave the room."

"Oh? Is there not a third option? Perhaps, say, a thorough ravishment instead?"

"That is hardly gentlemanly. And I don't think you should call me Princess any longer, either. I'll be a countess, I suppose."

"No, beloved. Remember? A king."

"I'll settle for queen."

"Queen Maricara. I like it."

She found his shoulder, muscle and solid shape, a feathery caress up to his jaw. He turned his head and kissed her fingers.

"I'm still waiting," Mari said.

"I beg your pardon. Ahem. My sweet lady of grace, I do most devoutly admire, cherish, and adore—"

She pushed away from him. "Never mind. If you can't take it seriously—"

He stopped her with one hand, pulling her back down to him. Both arms lifted to keep her there, sprawled half across him, the sheets a tangled mess at their hips.

"I love you," he said softly. "Black dragon, so much. I do love you. I..." She felt his fingers at the small of her back, restless, stroking up and down. "When you disappeared—when I thought they had taken you, and then when I found you there in that room, I..."

She said nothing, only laid her cheek to his chest, listening to his voice come from inside him, hushed and deep.

"I don't remember as much of it as I should. All I really recall is your face. The fire. Those men."

"You were very brave," she whispered.

He gave a short laugh. "Did you think it bravery? 'Twas only madness. The beast losing control."

"I think," she said, "we were all a little mad back there."

His hands fell still, warming her back. "Things are about to get worse. You know that, don't you?"

"Yes, Kimber. I do."

"Nothing can happen to you. Not ever again. When I saw you on that bed—the chains, and those bastards—"

He did not speak for a long while. She lay hushed now, her body rising and falling with the force of his respiration.

"Nothing must ever happen to you," was all he said at last.

"It will be difficult." She lifted her face to his neck. "The *delis* are sly, and widespread. But you were right before. We're stronger together than apart."

"I don't want this war," he said, rough. "I don't want to fight anyone, not the Zaharen, not the Others. I want to live in a world with you like the one I grew up in, one with families and laughter and the very best of secrets to bind our hearts together, but that's gone now. Rhys is gone, and more of our kind than I care to count."

"We *will* win."

"Do you think so?" She felt him shake his head. "It seems all I dream of is blood and death, my brother's face. That missing girl. And when that happens, I awake wanting only vengeance."

"Justice," she said.

"Death." He pulled a pillow from beneath him, tossing it hard aside.

Mari pressed her hand to his chest. "This is who we are. This is how we survive. They hunted us first; it's always been that they hunt us first. But we will be the ones to end this, my lord. I promise you that."

"I want to believe you. I wake, every goddamned day—"

"Yes," she interrupted, serene. "I know very well what it's like to wake from nightmares. It helps, very much, to have the one you love at your side when that happens."

His sigh lifted her high; as he exhaled his arms wrapped closer around her.

"Say it again."

"I promise we'll win."

"No." He rolled them back aside and raised to an elbow, his face touching hers, his hair draping soft and aromatic against her throat. "Tell me you love me."

"I love you, Kimber Langford, Alpha of the *drákon*. I love you."

"Then that's enough," he whispered, his lips to her cheek. "That will keep me believing."

Letter from Maricara, Countess of Chasen
to His Royal Grace the Prince Alexandru
Of the castle Zaharen Yce
Of the Zaharen
Of the Drákon

[*Translated from the Romanian*]

1 August 1782

Your Grace:

Others come. Prepare for Invasion.

—M.

EPILOGUE

S moke and war. Fire and betrayal. We've been rent into
tatters, so much less now than what we once were.

I suppose *you* might say this is only what we've earned. That if
we dissolve as a species into whirlwinds of dust, it is only what
the civilized world requires.

Yet we do not trouble your lives without provocation. We
dance at your edges, we drift and observe and lead our own
silent lives. What right had you to come and hunt us?

Brothers and sisters gone. Our children taken. You've pierced
our souls, and if we retaliate in kind, do not be so foolish as to
think we'll grant mercy.

We are dragons. If we eat you whole, that will be your mercy.

And when we cry diamond tears for our young ones, when we
weep for our broken hearts, you will never see.

Be ready. We're nearer than you imagine.

ABOUT THE AUTHOR

Shana Abé is the award-winning author of ten novels, including the bestselling Drákon series. She lives in Colorado with five rescued house rabbits and one big, happy dog. Please support your local animal shelter and spay or neuter your pets.

Visit her website at: www.shanaabe.com